To Suit a Suitor

To Suit a Suitor

PAULA KREMSER

SWEETWATER
BOOKS

An imprint of Cedar Fort, Inc.
Springville, Utah

This is a work of fiction. The characters, names, incidents, places, and dialogue are products of the author's imagination and are not to be construed as real. The views expressed within this work are the sole responsibility of the author and do not necessarily reflect the position of Cedar Fort, Inc., or any other entity.

ISBN 13: 978-1-4621-1933-2

Published by Sweetwater Books, an imprint of Cedar Fort, Inc.
2373 W. 700 S., Springville, UT 84663
Distributed by Cedar Fort, Inc., www.cedarfort.com

LIBRARY OF CONGRESS CATALOGING-IN-PUBLICATION DATA

Names: Kremser, Paula, 1978- author.
Title: To suit a suitor / Paula Kremser.
Description: Springville, Utah : Sweetwater Books, An imprint of Cedar Fort,
  Inc., [2016]
Identifiers: LCCN 2016030418 (print) | LCCN 2016032893 (ebook) | ISBN
  9781462119332 (perfect bound : alk. paper) | ISBN 9781462127115 (epub,
  pdf, mobi)
Subjects: LCSH: Man-woman relationships--Fiction. | GSAFD: Regency
  fiction. |
  LCGFT: Romance fiction. | Novels.
Classification: LCC PS3611.R467 T6 2016 (print) | LCC PS3611.R467
(ebook) |
  DDC 813/.6--dc23
LC record available at https://lccn.loc.gov/2016030418

Cover design by Rebecca J. Greenwood
Cover design © 2016 by Cedar Fort, Inc.
Edited and typeset by Jessica Romrell

Printed in the United States of America

10 9 8 7 6 5 4 3 2 1

Printed on acid-free paper

For my parents, Ron and Ria Hatch

Prologue

*L*ord Montague, the Earl of Halifax, had been debating for a month now what he should do. Today he had finally made his decision. He would propose marriage to Marianne North. As he had thought over the pros and cons of his decision, the pros had finally won out. She was a widow with a lively personality and endless connections. She was pretty, but more importantly, she agreed with almost everything he said. With so much in common, he felt she was a good choice. He himself was a widower twice over and he preferred being married. He had been without a countess by his side for the last several years and he sometimes found it difficult socially, not having a wife to act as hostess as he moved about politically. There were cons to marrying Marianne North as well, but with a little patience, he could maneuver his way out of those.

As he walked past the footman into the adequate drawing room, he noticed the broad smile on Mrs. North's face at his unexpected arrival. No doubt she had been hoping for his proposal for some time. She and her daughters received him with curtsies. They were about to retake their seats, so Lord Montague quickly spoke, "Mrs. North," he began, "may I have the honor of a private audience with you?"

Just as he predicted, Marianne urged her two daughters out of the room. They were of marriageable age, but as far as he knew they hadn't accepted any offers yet. He glanced at them as they departed and could tell from their expressions that they knew what to expect from his visit. They smiled at him—the younger girl's smile was especially broad—likely assuming that he would be their benefactor. They would be unpleasantly surprised.

Mrs. North invited him to sit. He declined and she remained standing as well. She cut a lovely figure in her gold gown, and he was pleased with his choice, but he did rather wish she would sit. Regardless, he would have the upper hand in this interview, and so he began in his usual direct manner. "Mrs. North, I have thought for some time that I would like to remarry. You and I get along quite well, and in fact I have admired you for some time now." The response from her was a modest smile, so he continued. "However, I decided—long before I met you—that were I to remarry, I would not let myself be exploited again." Her smile faded and a confused look replaced it. He would have to explain.

"When I married my first wife, she was the oldest of six children. As part of our marriage contract, I secured livings for her three younger brothers when they came of age as well as putting sizable dowries on the line for her two younger sisters. The expense would have been worth it if there had been an heir, but my wife died before recovering from our second daughter's birth."

He paused for a moment and Mrs. North took the opportunity to murmur, "How awful that must have been for you."

"Yes, it was a hard time. I remarried rather quickly so my two young daughters would have a mother. I found out after I had proposed to my second wife that her family had been hiding the fact that they had been on the brink of ruin for some time. As a result, that marriage also came with a lengthy marriage contract. I covered a large sum of debt for her father, and again I paid quite a large sum of money so my wife's sisters would have the opportunity to marry well." Lord Montague paused here, not wanting to sound like a skinflint. "She was a very good mother to my daughters and we had two sons and two more daughters before she died of fever, but I didn't ever quite get over the fact that I had been duped."

"I suppose I knew some of what you've told me," Mrs. North said, "but I had no idea of the circumstances of your second marriage. It was positively deceitful! *I* would never behave in such a way," she emphasized.

Ah, this was good; she understood the point he was making. It was time to strike a deal. "The reason for explaining all this to you is that I am keen to marry again and hope that you, Mrs. North—Marianne—will consider me for your husband." He didn't wait long enough for her to form an answer, but continued, "However, I don't want another marriage with strings attached."

"Sir, what do you suppose I would require of you if we were to marry? My only sibling is an older brother that lives in India, whom I haven't seen in years." Her voice was almost too innocent and Lord Montague narrowed his eyes.

"I think you would want me to provide your daughters with dowries, but after all I've been through, I am weary of being used." He watched her expression to see if this would be enough of a reason for her to walk away from the deal. She didn't look angry, but now her eyes narrowed and he wondered what she was scheming.

"You have a valid point, but my daughters have very little in the way of dowries. If I marry you and my daughters aren't provided for, it would look quite strange."

"That is true. You, your daughters, and even society would think terribly of me if we married and I didn't settle large sums on them." Mrs. North's smile was back as he agreed with her. Of course he had already thought of the pressure society would exert on him, which was why he had thought of the other part of his plan. "That is why I want us to come to an understanding today that we will only marry after both your daughters have married, and our entire agreement will have to be kept completely confidential. Our engagement will not be announced until they are both married."

It took a moment for her to really comprehend his meaning, but when she did, Mrs. North huffed out a breath of annoyed surprise. "Harriet isn't even out yet, and Julia's been out for two seasons, but hasn't even had a proposal!"

Lord Montague raised his eyebrows at this news. He thought that both the daughters were out. They were both pretty, sociable girls. He was sure it would merely be a matter of them accepting one of the many proposals they must often receive. He would have to be even more patient than he had thought. "I'm afraid that this condition is one I feel very strongly about. I don't want to wait too long to marry you though, so perhaps you can hurry them along a bit." It didn't seem unreasonable to him, and hopefully Marianne could see his perspective as well. In order to know for sure he asked, "Do we have an agreement, Marianne?"

She twirled a lock of her brown hair with a finger as she considered. He wondered if she was thinking of a way to argue the point, or get around it somehow, but she surprised him by saying, "Yes, I accept your proposal that we will wait to marry until my daughters have both married."

He felt a good deal of pride with how he had handled the situation and allowed himself the liberty of kissing his future bride. Lord Montague was sure that within six months, or a year at most, he would be married to Marianne North without any disadvantages to himself.

Chapter 1

*W*hy me? Why does this always happen to me?

The words ran through Julia's mind over and over again as she looked across the ballroom at Mr. Bedford. Another suitor had lost interest.

It had happened enough times that she shouldn't be surprised, yet she was. She had just seen Mr. Bedford yesterday and his regard for her had seemed steady. He had stopped to see her without a formal invitation, he had worn his usual pleased expression after she—with teeth gritted—had let him win at speculation, and they had walked through the garden with her sister nearby as chaperone. Yesterday had been just the same as the past few weeks of courting, which was more than enough time to raise her mother's hopes, but others had observed as well. He had given her too much marked attention for his desertion now to go unnoticed, especially as he was so obviously giving marked attention to another young lady. As Julia kept her fixed gaze on Mr. Bedford, she managed to catch his eye for a brief moment. He hastily looked away, but not fast enough for Julia to miss the guilt in his expression.

That guilty look confirmed it. He hadn't just missed seeing her; he was deliberately avoiding her. She couldn't believe she was being jilted, *again*. Mr. Bedford was her third suitor this year . . . and it was only April!

Julia glanced around the crowded room quickly to see where her mother was and if she had noticed yet. She spotted her as she was being led to the dance floor for the opening set by Lord Montague, the Earl of Halifax. Lord Montague asked her mother to dance exactly once at each ball they both happened to be at. Julia couldn't help but hate the man for the ridiculous conditions he insisted upon, but this evening his timing couldn't have been more perfect—at least her mother's attention was diverted for a moment. Julia returned her own attention to Mr. Bedford. It was interesting that before this evening, Julia had thought him moderately handsome, but as she watched him and Miss Tomlinson take their place in the set across the ballroom, she no longer thought so.

With a sigh of frustration, she thought about the problems Mr. Bedford was causing her. Her mother might not be paying attention to Mr. Bedford now, but she was sure to know before the evening ended. She would be furious when she found out; they would have to start all over again with a new suitor.

Julia didn't understand why Mother always made such a fuss about the effort of finding a new suitor. That was the easy part. It was keeping them that Julia couldn't seem to manage.

Julia had suspected for some time that there was something wrong with her, and watching Mr. Bedford from across the room, she knew it was true. But what *was* wrong with her? Of course, she knew she wasn't perfect, but she couldn't see that she was any more flawed than Miss Tomlinson, who now had Mr. Bedford's attention. Nor was she more flawed than other young ladies who seemed to regularly accept marriage proposals from suitors that were constant to them. Each new season, a fresh new batch of young ladies arrived in London ready to take the places of last season's successes. Julia was the exception. Here she was at the end of her third season without a suitable gentleman in sight to change her status.

No, the only man in sight was Mr. Bedford. As Julia watched him turn a circle with Miss Tomlinson's hand in his, she realized she was quickly beginning to despise him. She had been watching him since she arrived with her mother and younger sister, Harriet. They had gone their separate ways when they entered the ballroom, and Julia had waited, knowing Mr. Bedford was in the crush somewhere and would come find her for the first dance. Instead, only moments later, she had spotted him flirting with Miss Tomlinson. Then, as their host, Mr. Owen, had loudly instructed the musicians to open with a reel, Julia had watched Mr. Bedford lead Miss Tomlinson to the dance floor. It was the very sort of attention he had been giving Julia for the last month.

Julia's gaze remained unwavering as the music carried the dancers through the last few steps of the dance. Her self-pity was beginning to turn to anger as she watched Mr. Bedford. There must be something wrong with her to drive suitors away as she did, but Mr. Bedford's cowardly desertion earned her resentment. She wouldn't give him her attentions now even if he pleaded with her. But as she watched him escort Miss Tomlinson back to her mother, she had to admit it wasn't likely he would beg her for anything; their acquaintance was at an end.

Julia continued to glare at Mr. Bedford as she pondered her supremely bad fortune with men. He didn't look her way again, and it seemed intentional to her that he did not, but Julia's gaze remained fastened on him, hardly letting herself blink.

She felt someone come up beside her, but still she didn't turn and look. She could tell it was her sister,

Harriet, back from her first turn on the dance floor. She clutched Julia's arm in excitement. "Julia, I think I'm in love! I just danced with the most charming gentleman I've ever met!" That caught Julia's attention and she finally turned away from the traitorous Mr. Bedford.

"Harriet, your engagement to Lord Blakely is to be announced this evening. You can't be in love with another man!" Julia kept her voice low, but her tone was reprimanding. Harriet looked petulant but didn't reply. Julia took hold of her arm and backed her toward the wall. "You can't have forgotten such an important thing as an engagement from one turn on the dance floor, can you?"

Harriet sighed as she looked up and then off to the side. Julia was often told how much her sister resembled her, but their brown hair and lighter brown eyes seemed to be the only thing they had in common. Harriet wouldn't return her gaze, but replied, "Of course I didn't forget that I'm engaged, but the man I danced with just now was so charming that I wished I hadn't accepted Lord Blakely's proposal so hastily."

Harriet was right; it had been hasty. He had proposed a week before her mother had predicted as the earliest possible moment they could expect him to address her. But there was never any doubt what her answer would be. "Harriet," she waited until Harriet looked back at her before saying, "hasty or not, you agreed to marry Lord Blakely and you *can't* go back on that."

Julia considered the matter settled and turned back to stare at Mr. Bedford again. He was still with Miss Tomlinson and now her mother too . . . *Flirting more with the latter*, she thought.

But Harriet hadn't given up and she let out a little huff before saying, "I agreed to marry Lord Blakely, but lots of engagements get cancelled."

Without averting her gaze from Mr. Bedford, she replied, "You know Mother would never allow you to end your engagement. Besides, the only engagements that get cancelled are because of scandal. That is not something to hope for." Again Julia's tone was final. Harriet could be inconsistent at times, but even she must know that cancelling her engagement wasn't an option.

Harriet gave another little huff and then drew in a breath as if she were about to argue the point further, when she finally seemed to notice Julia's preoccupation. She followed Julia's gaze across the room and asked in confusion, "Why is your Mr. Bedford over there with Lizzy Tomlinson?"

"He is not *my* Mr. Bedford." Julia was quick to deny any possession of him.

"Oh Julia," she practically wailed, "not another one!"

"Hush, Harriet," Julia said in an angry whisper. "I don't want to make a scene."

"You should make a scene," she retorted, with a voice as stern as Julia's had been a few moments before. "He's embarrassing you. Why don't you do the same to him? Or better yet, go over there and fight for him. Tell Miss Tomlinson to find her own suitor and send her away."

Harriet's heart was in the right place. She wasn't trying to force Julia to marry; she just thought that falling in love was such a fun adventure and wanted Julia to experience it too. But Julia just shook her head at her sister's ridiculous suggestion. By confronting Mr. Bedford, she would only embarrass herself further. And fighting for him was out of the question; her interest in him was already gone. But again the question nagged at her: why had he lost interest in her? Harriet's suggestion of talking to him might not be such a bad idea after all. If Julia wanted to know why he had jilted her, she should ask him.

She blinked rapidly a few times as she turned the idea over. Perhaps Mr. Bedford would tell her his reason for deserting her. She wouldn't try to win back his affection, but maybe she would have more luck with the next suitor who came along if she could fix whatever it was that was wrong with her. She knew she was impulsive and sometimes a bit too competitive, but she never allowed herself to behave so in front of her suitors. Whatever was wrong with her was driving the men away. Her mother would insist she try harder to find, attract, and keep a new suitor once she knew that Mr. Bedford was no longer courting her. But Julia wasn't sure if she could possibly try harder to please her mother. However, if she could find out what was wrong with her, she could correct the flaw. Her mother reminded her often enough that marriage was the only option for her, and so if she was to have any hope of making a match, she had to uncover the truth.

"I am going to talk to him," Julia announced with determination.

Harriet gave a high squeal, "Oooh, this is going to be good! Do you want me to come with you?"

Julia just shook her head no and drew in a deep breath for courage; this would not be an easy conversation.

Chapter 2

*J*ulia walked straight toward Mr. Bedford. Couples were lining up for the dance that was about to begin, and she had to weave around them before reaching the opposite side of the room. Mr. Bedford was alone now and he watched warily as Julia approached him. But when she stopped directly in front of him, he gave her a chivalrous smile and said, "Miss North, what a lovely surprise to see you here this evening."

Julia gritted her teeth at his insincerity. He knew she would be there this evening; they had spoken of the ball only yesterday. And it wasn't lovely to see her either. His guilty face when he had caught her eye earlier by mistake showed that it was anything but lovely to see her.

Julia didn't bother with the same politeness. "Are you going to ask me to dance?" It was an incredibly improper thing for a young lady to do, but propriety was not her most pressing concern at the moment. His smile looked stiff, but he was too much of a gentleman to do anything else but agree. He offered his arm to Julia and she let him lead her to the dance floor.

Julia decided to broach the subject immediately. She had no interest in anything else he could possibly have to say and didn't want to waste time listening to his commentary on the weather, which was usually his first topic of choice. The musicians began playing and all the dancers down the line began moving in perfect rhythm as

Julia bluntly asked, "Mr. Bedford, why have you decided to no longer court me?"

Perhaps a little too blunt, she thought as he missed a step. An awkward hop brought him back to their correct place in the line and he cleared his throat before replying, "What makes you think I've made any such decision, Miss North?"

"Because you've been avoiding me since I walked in and you didn't ask me for the first dance, as you have done at every opportunity for the last month."

Julia could see a light sheen of perspiration forming at his hairline as she pointed out the obvious. He didn't miss any more steps in the dance, but he stretched his neck, as if his cravat was too tight, clearly uncomfortable with the subject. "Perhaps I've led you to believe I . . . felt more for you than is actually the case." He paused and cleared his throat before saying, "If you feel that there has been a breach of honor, then I will accept the blame for my actions and offer for you . . . of course."

Julia pulled her head back in mild alarm. No wonder he was looking like a caged animal; he thought she was forcing the issue so he would propose! Lucky her mother hadn't heard him. She didn't try to hide the aversion in her voice as she said, "No. That is the last thing I want." She could see how relieved he was at her words and felt a sudden surge of annoyance. But she couldn't forget why she was here: not to start an argument but to find out why he didn't want her. She drew in a deep breath and released it before she could politely speak again. "The only thing I want from you, Mr. Bedford, is the reason behind your actions." Her bravado failed her a bit as she admitted, "You are not the first suitor to give up on me and I want to know what it is about me that you don't like."

Mr. Bedford's expression turned curious. "You want me to tell you what I don't like about you?"

Her pride was not enjoying this exchange, so she just nodded her acquiescence. But he looked skeptical and said, "I don't think that would be a very gentlemanly thing to do, Miss North."

"Neither is jilting a young lady, Mr. Bedford," she retorted. He glanced around with a cautious look in his eyes and Julia realized she must have spoken a little too loudly. Luckily, the other dancers hadn't seemed to notice. Continuing the steps of the dance, and with her voice now lowered, Julia persisted, "Please just tell me what's wrong with me. What is my shortcoming that has made you decide I will not be a suitable wife?" Although she didn't want Mr. Bedford to see any weakness in her, she humbly muttered, "If you do not tell me, then I cannot fix it and I will continue to be abandoned by every suitor who comes along."

His wary look was gone now, replaced by pity. This was the most excruciating conversation Julia had ever initiated. If the answer hadn't been so important, she would have run from the room.

Finally, he reluctantly began. "I'm not sure if this will be helpful to you, but I decided after our conversation yesterday that we would not suit." Julia thought back to their conversation, but she couldn't remember anything of importance about it. He could see she didn't understand and continued, "I told you how I love walking on windy days and I even enjoy a light rain sometimes, and you teased me for it."

Julia's eyes grew wide in wonder at his ridiculous reason. Was he serious? It was the most flimsy excuse that she could have imagined. Her voice was low but incredulous as she asked, "Are you telling me that you have decided to no longer court me because I don't like walking in the wind and rain?"

She expected him to capitulate and tell her the real reason, but his answer wasn't what she expected. "When you put it like that I know it sounds unfair, but yes. I want a wife who shares my interests and likes the things I like, or who will at least love me enough to give them a try." Now he was the one who looked embarrassed to admit something so personal.

Julia looked away from him and let her gaze rest wherever it might as they continued the dance. *Good luck finding any young lady who wants to walk on windy, rainy days,* she thought bitterly. She was sure that Lizzy Tomlinson wouldn't. She was very particular about her appearance and would never want to arrive anywhere wet or mussed.

Julia was more annoyed by her lack of progress than by his actual reason for deciding not to pursue her anymore. This didn't help her at all. None of her other suitors had ever expressed a desire to spend time in foul weather, so Mr. Bedford's reason for deserting her must be a deviation from theirs.

She had secretly expected him to say that her fault was that she didn't ride. She had often been invited by gentlemen of her acquaintance to go riding. Perhaps once or twice she had noticed a disappointed look when she said she wouldn't. The truth was, she couldn't. Having grown up in London, Julia had never seen the need to learn. If she had really wanted to, she could have found a way, but she was somewhat afraid of horses. She had never asked her mother for riding lessons, and luckily her mother had never insisted. If her mother thought that it might help her catch a husband, she *would* insist.

Their dance was nearing its end, and Julia knew it would be the last time she ever danced with Mr. Bedford, so despite the fact that he hadn't helped her in the least, she gave him a polite smile that was so often necessary in society and said, "Thank you for answering my question, Mr. Bedford. Please accept my best wishes for your future happiness."

The words were more polite than her tone, but Mr. Bedford bowed deeply and as conversations around them surged and the final notes of music died he replied, "You're welcome, Miss North. I hope I have helped you in some small way."

He hadn't, so she just mustered one more polite smile and turned away. She made her way back across the room and found her sister just returning from dancing again, this time with Lord Blakely.

Julia wasn't in the best mood after speaking with Mr. Bedford, so her tone was a bit sarcastic as she asked, "Is the engagement back on?"

Harriet answered the question with a seriousness it didn't deserve. "I was wavering again while we danced as to what I should do . . . but then he looked into my eyes so deeply and told me he thinks I'm perfect." She sighed with a far-off look in her eyes and said, "Lord Blakely is the man for me."

Their mother was approaching her daughters and heard the end of what Harriet was saying. "Of course he's the man for you. You're engaged. In fact, now might be the perfect time to announce the engagement."

Julia had known the engagement would be announced at the ball, but she hadn't worried about it. She wasn't engaged of course, but Mr. Bedford's attentions had at least helped her feel secure enough to weather her younger sister's engagement. But now, this was awful! Mother was counting down the days until Mr. Bedford would propose. She'd be furious when she learned he was no longer an option. Julia was wishing for at least the thousandth time that she didn't have to bother with such things. She was more than halfway through her third season and she didn't have a single suitor, but her younger sister, in just her first season, was engaged. And if it hadn't been Lord Blakely who offered for her, there were several other gentlemen eagerly waiting in the wings to pay their addresses.

As Mr. Owen, their host for the evening, quieted all the guests for the announcement, Julia slipped away from her mother and Harriet. Lord Blakely took her place as Julia retreated to a corner of the room. When he had the attention of the room, Mr. Owen began, "I have sad news to announce to you all this evening." But he couldn't keep the smile out of his voice and Julia glanced around at all the guests gathered in the Owens' ballroom and saw smiles of anticipation on their faces, awaiting the joke. "Another of our esteemed members of the House of Lords has been captured by a most devious foe." Shaking his head as if with regret, he went on, "Without ever suspecting a thing, our dear friend Lord Blakely has been lured into a perilous trap. I suppose we can only be grateful that he thinks he has chosen this fate himself, never knowing that once Miss Harriet North set her sights on him, he never had a chance." Everyone laughed at that just as they should and Mr. Owen turned to shake hands with Lord Blakely as Harriet blushed prettily next to him. "So instead of condolences, we will offer congratulations, and Lord Blakely will never know that he didn't go willingly to his doom."

Julia was feeling quite low as she listened to the polite laughter at Mr. Owen's clever quips. She didn't wish for the same silly announcement for herself. If she had her choice, she wouldn't worry about catching a husband at all, but their relative poverty and her mother's situation meant that she didn't have a choice. So she tried. Over and over she tried, with every new suitor, season after season. But her character was flawed in some way that made all her efforts worthless. This flaw, this unknown failing in her, was the cause of the repeated rejections she had endured. Her confidence fell a little each time a suitor chose to walk away. Her conversation with Mr. Bedford was still fresh in her mind; his expression full of pity, a memory she wished she didn't have.

In this mood of self-doubt, Julia wished more than anything to leave the ball and seek the solitude of her room. But, of course, their carriage was the last one ordered. Her mother and Harriet were enjoying all the success of the evening and didn't want to miss even one guest who would offer congratulations. For every happy wish for her future happiness that Harriet received, Julia had to listen to either a consoling, "Surely your turn will come soon, dear." Or a jovial, "You'll have to be quick now; with a younger sister soon married, you'll be left on the shelf!"

Chapter 3

The next morning, Julia's outlook was somewhat better when she realized Harriet's newly announced engagement could work in her favor. Mr. Bedford's desertion would hopefully go unnoticed by her mother for a few more days. She had entertained high hopes for Mr. Bedford as a son-in-law. He had certainly been Julia's most promising suitor this season, but perhaps the hectic wedding preparations would prevent at least some of her mother's annoyance. Typically, after Julia lost a suitor, Mother would increase their social engagements, saying that Julia needed to "cast a wider net" by being seen more. Julia would have to dance every dance and sit by a new gentleman every time they were invited to dine out, and her mother would always insist that Julia perform on the pianoforte at any opportunity to show off her talent. She really hated that. She loved playing; she just hated being compared to other young ladies whose talent was superior to her own. She knew she shouldn't feel like it was a competition, but she wasn't the best and she hated the feeling. But perhaps with Harriet's wedding to plan, she wouldn't have to do all those things.

Julia knew she was arriving late to breakfast this morning, and was still dragging her feet as she went downstairs. Their London town home had been just the thing when the North family had begun ownership two generations ago, but now it was in desperate need of repair and refurbishing. Her mother had complained about it for as long as Julia could remember. She had the servants move furniture around often, hoping that some new arrangement would hide the shabbiest sofas. Mother would sometimes buy new screens or vases or statuettes and they would always be put in the sitting room or dining room, the only rooms where they received guests. But Julia felt more at ease in the rest of the house. The room her mother referred to as the breakfast parlor was next to the kitchen and just off the servants' wing. The wood table had scratches that they never bothered to hide with a tablecloth, the sideboard was lighter on one side from too many years of sunlight, and none of the serving dishes matched anymore.

When Julia walked into the breakfast parlor ready to cheerfully discuss the wedding arrangements, she instead found her mother and Harriet in conversation over the post. Mother seemed to be groaning in annoyance.

"What's the matter, Mother?" she asked.

"I've just received a letter from your father's cousin, Martha Abbot," Mother complained.

Harriet looked up as she said, "I didn't even know Father had a cousin."

Julia had a flash of memory though. She was only ten when she last saw her, but she vaguely remembered 'Cousin Martha.' "Is she the one who came to stay with us after Father died?" she asked.

Her mother didn't look pleased by the reminder. "Yes, that's her. She came to comfort me, but she was so upset herself that it wasn't all that comforting." Her tone was exasperated. "She stayed for half a year to help."

Julia nodded as memories came to her recollection. "Cousin Martha . . . I think I can remember sitting in the nursery with her as she read me stories. She was so kind."

Her mother looked like she had a dilemma on her hands. Guilt and annoyance were both evident in her features as she reluctantly admitted, "Yes, she was very kind." Mother drummed her fingers on the table for a moment. "She asks in her letter if I can come to her for two months. She has had a paid companion for many years who has just left to tend to her sick mother. While she has hired a new girl to take her place, the girl's father won't let her go until she is fifteen, in two months." Mother got up from the table, saying, "I'd better respond immediately so she can make other arrangements. I feel indebted to her, but I'll have to repay her kindness to us some other time. I can't leave London while we are planning Harriet's wedding. I'm sure Martha will understand."

It was a shame that her mother couldn't help her, but Julia agreed that there was no way Mother could leave London now.

Harriet waited until Mother had left the room and said, "I'd better get dressed; I'm going for a carriage ride in the park this morning."

Julia just nodded her head as she left the room, distracted by her last thought. Mother couldn't leave London now, but there was no reason Julia couldn't. As soon as the thought occurred to her, she knew it was exactly what she wanted. Leaving London wouldn't fix her problems, but all she wanted right now was a reprieve from them.

Suddenly feeling very excited, Julia abandoned her breakfast and rushed upstairs to her mother's room where she was sitting at her desk composing a letter. "Mother, I could take your place!" she exclaimed.

Her mother looked up at her with a confused expression. "What was that, Julia?"

"I could go to stay with Father's cousin. Harriet can't possibly plan her wedding without you, but I'm not necessary, am I?" She didn't wait for an answer; she was too enthusiastic about her new plan. "I will just be in the way on all your shopping expeditions, and taking up room in the carriage when it will already be too full from your many purchases." This had happened before, so it wasn't just a petty argument.

"Julia!" she exclaimed in censored surprise. "You can't possibly leave London now! Why, what would Mr. Bedford think? He will surely be offering for you soon. And considering your luck with suitors, I wouldn't expect him to wait around for you for two months while you run off to Somerset. He'll think you don't care for him and begin courting someone else."

Julia didn't reply right away and she dropped her gaze to her feet, not wanting to see her mother's annoyance at her latest failure. She wasn't surprised to hear the reprimanding tone already in her mother's voice as she asked, "Has something happened between you and Mr. Bedford?"

Still looking down, Julia quietly replied, "He already began courting someone else."

Her mother let out a frustrated sigh before echoing Harriet's words from the night before. "Not another one!"

Julia finally looked up and let out her own frustrated sigh, but kept silent.

"Why does this keep happening to you? This is more than just bad luck." Mother glanced at the door and lowered her voice a bit. "Harriet's not even as pretty as you are and she has multiple suitors who want to marry her. You haven't had a single proposal. What is it that you are doing wrong?"

Julia was all too familiar with this lecture and the disapproving look that went with it. She didn't understand why her mother's suitors and her sister's suitors never lost interest the way hers did. Her mother, in fact, was always the one to discard suitors, not the other way around. Since her father's death, Julia had seen her mother accept attention from many men, and none of them ever seemed to find fault with her, but never until she received a proposal from an earl had she remained constant.

Julia didn't want to disappoint her mother, but she honestly didn't know how to solve her dilemma. She agreed with her mother that there was something wrong with her, she just didn't know what, and Mr. Bedford hadn't even provided a clue. Julia waited quietly through the oft-repeated scolding. She could tell her mother was winding down when she said, "I know of at least three balls in the next two weeks; I'll make sure we have invitations to all of them. No breaks now, Julia. We have to try harder than ever."

Julia was feeling more desperate than ever. How could she convince her mother to let her leave London and all its potential husbands behind? She thought of one argument that had occurred to her before and decided it was worth a try. "Mother, perhaps we're trying too hard." She was already shaking her head in disagreement, but Julia lifted her hands in supplication. "Just hear me out. Maybe that is the thing that is wrong with me. We can't be sure, but perhaps there are gentlemen who have noticed me, but I'm *too* obtainable. If I leave London for a time . . . when I return they will be more pleased to see me." Mother looked as though she was seriously contemplating her words. Julia didn't really believe it herself, but if she could only convince one of them, she hoped it was her mother. "There might even be a gentleman or two interested in me now, but they aren't courting me because they know they can find me everywhere they go.

But if I was absent for a time, perhaps even until Harriet's wedding, then they might be more compelled to seriously court me."

Julia could tell that Mother was willing to consider this new idea, but she was skeptical enough to ask, "But what if that doesn't happen? What if while you aren't here you are completely forgotten instead?"

"Perhaps that would be for the best as well. It's likely that I'm beginning to get a reputation."

Her mother's look made Julia wonder if she already knew of gossip circulating about her. It hurt her pride a bit, but her mother looked convinced. "You may have a point there. And I won't be able to focus on helping you find new suitors with Harriet's wedding to plan."

Julia didn't actually want the help that her mother always insisted on giving, but she was ready to agree with anything if it meant she could leave London. "Of course, Mother. You'll be so busy, I'm sure it will be a relief not to have to worry about me for the next few months. Besides that, I'll be able to repay Martha's kindness for coming to us when Father died."

Playing on her guilt seemed to, almost, finally convince her, but she still made a last feeble resistance by saying, "Julia, it won't be an easy task. Martha lives in a tiny village that is near nothing in Somerset. I can't ask you to do it." She seemed to be changing her mind back as she spoke. "In fact, I'm sure it is too small to have any eligible gentlemen. I don't want you to waste two months when I've already been waiting almost a year for you to find a husband. Harriet's wedding is a good excuse and Martha will understand, I'm sure, that none of us can be spared just now."

The more her mother tried to talk her out of it, the more she wanted to go. Julia sounded a bit desperate as she said, "But, Mother, we're indebted to her! I remember her kindness and I feel I owe her for coming to our aid." Mother wasn't going to let her go. Julia could see that she had convinced herself with the thought of no eligible gentlemen in Somerset. But even though the idea had just been introduced to her a quarter of an hour before, she knew she would be severely disappointed if she couldn't go.

In her desperation she said, "If you let me go, I promise that when I return, I'll let you choose whose attentions I allow, and I'll accept the first proposal I receive."

There was a gleam in Mother's eyes now. That was too good a deal to pass up. Julia had never received a proposal, but it was because she was selective of the gentlemen who courted her. Mother had tried to convince her to permit attentions from older widowers, gentlemen with a bit of a reputation, and even some wealthy merchants with rather crude manners, but Julia wouldn't consider them. Julia already regretted making such a promise until her mother said, "Very well then, you may go."

Julia felt a rush of excitement and pushed the rash promise out of her mind. A two-month break from husband hunting, which for her was often a humiliating experience, sounded like heaven.

Her mother immediately began a new letter to Martha telling her that Julia would be coming in her place. Julia read over the letter when it was finished, and when she watched the footman carry the letter away to be posted, her heart raced with anticipation. She knew she had only gotten her way because of her hasty promise, but she was too excited to care.

When Harriet returned from her outing, Julia gave her the happy news that she was leaving London for two months. Harriet looked offended at this news, however.

"You can't go, I need you." It was with infinite patience that Julia used most of the same arguments with her sister that she had used to finally convince their mother. The extra room in the carriage for shopping was an argument that carried weight; Lord Blakely would be paying for Harriet's new wardrobe for the wedding. With Harriet appeased, Julia only had to wait a week to be on her way.

Chapter 4

*T*he journey began as others before it. Julia helped her maid pack a trunk, and rose early on the morning of their departure.

Julia's mother had rarely taken them outside of London. So many families left town when the season ended, but the three North ladies stayed. Their father's family had invited them to their estates in the country, but Mrs. North had not stayed close to her husband's family after his death. Julia used to wonder why her mother had allowed an estrangement there. The Norths were an old and well-connected family. But Julia had come to realize that her mother only gave something up when she hoped to get more in return. Her mother must have chosen to ignore the Norths in favor of courting again soon after her husband died.

Several times she, her sister, and her mother had been invited to house parties in the country, and once in a while, when London was particularly slow, her mother would accept. Julia's favorite had been a trip to Hertfordshire for a whole month when she was twelve. Her mother had turned her and Harriet over to the children of the house and their governess, who allowed them to run free.

This journey into Somerset would take quite a bit longer than their long-ago visit to Hertfordshire. One night would have to be spent at an inn. Julia enjoyed the quiet in the carriage at first, but before long, the novelty of traveling on her own wore off and she found it difficult to sit in the confined carriage hour after hour. She tried several times to start up conversations with her maid. The girl had come to their family only a three or four months before and Julia had never gotten more than a few words from her. Unfortunately, the long journey together didn't change that. Perhaps their age difference was too great, or she had been trained too well not to talk, or she really was just incredibly shy; whatever the reason, Julia eventually gave up trying to overcome it.

At the end of the first day of travelling, the carriage stopped for the night and the coachman informed Julia that they had passed the halfway point of their journey.

The next day was quite a bit like the first—a long day inside the carriage. Julia was able to drift to sleep for a bit of the journey. Stretching herself awake again and wondering when they would stop to eat, she pulled off her gloves and pushed back her bonnet. Across from her, her maid slept and Julia was left with nothing to do but think. Despite her happiness at leaving London, her mind still went back to her conversation with Mr. Bedford. Really, her situation seemed almost hopeless. After three London seasons, there still wasn't a single gentleman who wanted to marry her.

Julia worried a bit about the promise she had made to her mother that had finally convinced her to let her go. Her mother had often suggested she flirt with gentlemen that Julia had been repulsed by. She would probably have to think of a plan before she returned to London to delay her mother's matchmaking efforts at least a little. If she just knew why her suitors had lost interest, then she could correct the problem and make a match of her own choosing. It was more imperative than ever to do just that or her mother would have her married off to a man she couldn't stand as soon as she returned.

It was such a shame Mr. Bedford hadn't been more helpful. Recalling his ridiculous reason for ending their courtship was amusing in a way, but it just left Julia all the more curious as to what truly drove her suitors away. She realized she was biting her nails as her thoughts turned it over and she quickly pulled her fingers away from her mouth. Could that be it? Not likely, she didn't do it that often, and she almost always wore gloves when she was out, but better to stop completely. She shook her head in amusement at herself now; surely such a simple habit couldn't be what was keeping her from catching a husband.

Julia felt a little guilty at the thought of "catching" a husband. She didn't want to think of it that way, but it was so often spoken of in such terms. Young ladies and their mothers were always discussing who would catch whom by the end of the season. Julia tried to avoid that sort of gossip, but among the London socialites, little else was spoken of.

Julia had never wanted to catch a husband; she wanted to fall in love. But perhaps that luxury was beyond her now. If she couldn't even catch Mr. Bedford, she certainly wouldn't be able to catch someone better, whom she actually loved.

The coachman stopped in a village called Wincanton in the late afternoon, and Julia asked him how much farther. It had to be the tenth time at least that she had asked and she could see he was weary of the journey and the question, but he answered politely, "Another two hours, miss, and we should arrive in Barrington." That was encouraging. At least this would be their last stop.

Julia's maid and coachman went inside the inn to arrange a meal, but she didn't follow them in right away. The inn had a small garden to the side and Julia decided to wait there for their meal rather than going straight from the confines of the carriage to the musty inn.

She realized she'd left her bonnet and gloves in the carriage, but decided to fetch them later; standing in the afternoon sun felt wonderful. Without the rumbling of the carriage, her thoughts seemed louder now. When it came to marriage, Julia didn't have a choice in the matter; she had to marry. Because she knew this was her fate, she had tried to pick suitors that she thought wouldn't be difficult husbands, men that were definitely gentlemen, but who wouldn't need much of her attention. At her mother's urging, she tried harder than most young ladies to be noticed, but she was never too demanding of her suitors. How was it then that she had such a horrible lack of success at catching a husband? Not a single gentleman had ever fallen in love with her. Not once had she been able to capture a heart. What a failure she was.

That summer she had spent in Hertfordshire when she was twelve, she and Harriet had loved to catch frogs. Her mother would never have allowed it, but the governess hardly paid them any mind and they caught ever so many. Harriet had been better at it than Julia, which had been frustrating. She hated having her younger sister pass her up at anything. Julia had applied herself to the task and had improved greatly before they had had to return to London. The thought occurred to her that she had probably lost her ability to catch a frog, much less a handsome gentleman.

Julia was leaning against the fence, out of sight of the front entrance of the inn and because her mind had suggested it, she looked around the garden near her feet for any sign of a frog. There wasn't one, of course, just grass growing too tall right through the wooden slats. But her eyes followed a fly as it landed on the fence nearby. *Well, perhaps I could catch that*, she thought. She concentrated on it as she moved slowly forward. The fly was large and its shiny green back looked like a dark sparkling emerald in the sunlight. She moved closer, holding her breath. She could see the small creature rubbing its front legs together, oblivious to her approach. She desperately wanted to prove to herself that she could catch *something*. A slight noise behind her didn't deter her, any sudden movement now and it would be lost. She was so close, her open hand moving so slowly through the air, and then when she was sure she had it, she brought her hand down fast and scooped it up.

Julia was so surprised by her success that she joyfully exclaimed out loud, "I caught it!"

An equally surprised voice behind her echoed incredulously, "You caught it?"

She turned quickly around in triumphant surprise to show her audience her victory. "I finally caught something!" She was quite pleased with herself, but looking at the man standing in the garden with her, Julia quickly realized his expression was not admiration, but rather disbelief. In fact he looked as if he thought she was insane. That quick glance was enough to discern that the man was tall and well-dressed; he held himself like a gentleman. But the feeling of a fly flapping inside her hand distracted her from everything else and just as she opened her hand to release it, she felt a sharp pain on her palm. With a very startled movement, she jumped back and exclaimed, "Ahhh, ouch!" She jumped in place as she shook her hand, trying to rid herself of the sensation, and then wiped it on her dress several times in the same attempt. "It bit me!" she said in disbelief.

She was only speaking to herself again, but the man watching still seemed surprised but also immensely amused as he answered, "What did you expect would happen when you caught a horsefly?"

Julia turned away from him as she lifted her hand to examine the wound. "I didn't expect to catch it," she replied with some asperity. She heard him laugh from behind her and her annoyance grew. "A gentleman would offer assistance rather than laugh at me," she reproved him. Her palm was red now with a small, swollen bite at the center, which was quickly swelling more. It hurt terribly, and she was in no mood to have a stranger laugh at her.

He came up behind her and looked over her shoulder as she held her injured right hand in her left one. "Let me see," he commanded as he reached a hand over her shoulder and opened her hand wider to look at the wound. Julia's breath left her in a surprised exhale. She was not used to having a stranger so close to her. She was so shocked that she just stood there, frozen to the spot. She was frightened for just a moment and then she felt his breath on her neck as his thumb gently rubbed her palm. She began to feel light-headed before she finally remembered to breathe in again. His voice was too close when he spoke again. "You know, if you cut open an onion and rub it on the bite, it helps."

Julia hadn't quite recovered the ability to move her limbs and pull away from him, but her mind wasn't similarly affected. "Helps me smell like an onion," she muttered under her breath.

He was standing so close that he heard her, though, and he chuckled a little before saying, "Yes, you won't be able to catch anything for a while; the flies will smell you coming."

Julia turned to look at him then, so he would see her glare; after all, it was meant for him. It was unlikely he had a chance to register her glare though, because her response to really looking at this man for the first time was amazed surprise.

She had never seen a more handsome man in her life.

He still stood quite close to Julia, making every perfect feature seem magnified. He had thick, dark blond hair, so thick that it would break a comb that wasn't sturdy enough. He had a perfectly formed masculine face. His jawline was strong and square, but the angles weren't sharp. His eyes were a brilliant green that was far more mesmerizing than the emerald fly had been. Julia felt herself lean slightly toward him as she stared. His eyes were made more outstanding by beautiful, dark eyelashes and eyebrows that almost verged on too thick, but managed instead to fit his face perfectly. He was tall; she had to look up to see him and his wide shoulders cast a shadow over her. She felt like her eyes were darting from one feature to another in near astonishment at so many perfect features united in one person.

Julia returned her gaze to his mesmerizing green eyes and that was when she noticed that her obvious admiration didn't seem to surprise him one bit. His expression was a supremely confident one. Julia regained her senses enough to take a step back. The gentleman gave her a half-mocking smile that seemed to indicate he knew just what she was thinking. "I was just leaving, but I would be happy to offer you my 'gentlemanly assistance' in procuring an onion for you," he offered.

He waited for a moment, probably waiting for her to make some polite reply, but she wasn't about to.

No matter how good-looking he was, he had still witnessed her humiliate herself, and her throbbing hand was making her mood steadily worse. Instead, hoping to undo the impression of her admiring gaze from before, she narrowed her eyes and pursed her lips, giving her best stern look. Contrarily, his smile grew and he said, "But I'm sure you don't need my help anyway. If you can catch a fly, I'm sure you could convince the cook to part with an onion."

Julia made sure there wasn't any trace of admiration in her expression anymore. Her competitive nature wouldn't let him have the last word. He had already turned to leave when she replied, "You're right. I don't need your help." For a parting retort, it was weak and Julia knew it. The man turned back and gave her another knowing smile. He knew it too.

Julia stayed in the garden and watched just long enough to see the man take his reins from the stable hand and mount his tall horse. Then she purposely looked away. She didn't want to be caught staring. She had never felt such a strong immediate attraction to anyone before. She had met many handsome gentlemen, but none had ever had this same effect on her. She didn't want to ever see him again, purely for the sake of her pride, but she looked up at him once more, just to see if he was traveling the same direction she was. If she hadn't completely humiliated herself, she may have felt disappointed that he rode off in the opposite direction. But as it was, she was not sorry to see him go. She had never behaved so stupidly before. She couldn't believe she had tried to catch a fly, just to prove she could! Catching a fly was *nothing* like catching a husband. Julia let that thought settle for a bit before asking herself if maybe it wasn't similar after all. She thought about how she had crept so slowly toward the fly that it hadn't noticed her coming. *Maybe that approach would work on a man*, she thought with her first amused smile since receiving the bite on her hand. She was certain Mother would approve of any method that produced results.

Julia's maid stepped out to find her a moment later when their meal was ready. A half hour later they were ready to set off again. Before they left, however, Julia took a moment to ask for a wedge of raw onion and was obliged by the proprietor returning from the kitchen with one. She rubbed it over the red and swollen palm of her hand, and there was a sharp sting, but then it began to feel better. So resigning herself to the strong smell of onion for the rest of the journey, she made her way back to the waiting carriage.

As he prepared to mount his horse, Henry Chamberlain glanced several times at the young lady he had just left standing in the side yard of the inn, but as far as he could tell, she didn't look his way again. He rode away reluctantly. If he were on his own business today, he might have turned back and tried for an introduction. A strange idea for him; that was the kind of impulse he hadn't acted on in over three years. It was, in fact, the first time he had even felt such an impulse in that time. Three years and he hadn't felt so much as a flicker of attraction to any young lady his mother insisted on introducing him to, and suddenly today he did. He thought it odd that he should feel so at such a strange moment.

She was a beautiful young woman; there was no denying that. Her chestnut brown hair had glinted in the afternoon sun, coming slightly loose from its knot and free of any bonnet. Her face, too, was beautiful, with defined cheekbones, although that could have been because of her blush. But these traits weren't any more fantastic than those he often saw in other young ladies. But for some reason he couldn't name, the girl he had just met had attracted him. So much so that when there had been an opportunity to touch her, he didn't even think of resisting. There was a quick rush of guilt, but he talked himself out of it. He couldn't help the feeling of attraction he felt for the young lady, but he didn't go back, so there was no reason to feel uncomfortable.

With such logic, he allowed himself to dwell on their brief exchange. It had been amusing and refreshing to watch her enthusiasm over catching—of all things—a horsefly. He had noticed her as he left the inn and it was her intense concentration that had caught his attention. He had watched her slowly move toward the fly sitting on the fence and her features had been so expressive. First, there was her absorption as she crept forward with wide, unblinking eyes, then the thrill of success, which was more surprise than anything, as she lifted her hand, followed by shocked disbelief upon receiving a bite. Most amusing of all had been the flush that stole upon her face in her embarrassment as realization dawned. It was all so humorous that Henry found himself smiling as he rode.

When he had approached her to get a better look at the bite on her hand, he had caught her scent, like lilacs, and leaned in closer. But the moment that had truly caught him off guard was when she turned and looked into his eyes. An awareness that he had never felt before overtook him for a moment. Her eyes had widened once more in startled surprise. His own surprise kept him perfectly still while she took in his features. He was used to the reaction. It was typically followed by a look of calculated scheming, but not this time. She had stayed mesmerized a few moments longer than most, and then her expression had returned to defensive embarrassment. He had smiled at that.

Perhaps it had been her expressive eyes that had caused him that unusual feeling of attraction. He had seen her single-minded expression only in profile as she had crept toward the fly, but when she had turned around the triumph in her light brown eyes had been vivid. The dismay when she felt the sting of the bite on her hand had also been reflected clearly in her eyes. Then there had been the wide-eyed surprise he had seen when she finally looked closely at him. There had been an extended moment of what he was sure was attraction on her part too.

As he left the outskirts of Wincanton, he continued to try to pinpoint a reason why his reaction to her was so strong. He was too used to admiring looks to expect anything else. He had always been admired, and didn't know any other reaction. But the young lady who could catch a fly had taken in his features with the usual admiration, then surprisingly had gotten over it and glared at him for teasing her. That was unusual.

Henry had hated his appearance in his youth. His mother, so proud of his looks, would always introduce him as her "handsome boy." It was so detestable that he had actually asked his younger brother, Charles, to hit him hard enough to break his nose. He hadn't had to ask twice, and the memory of the crack he heard as his brother's fist connected with the bridge of his nose still made him shudder. His mother had been devastated, but Henry was hopeful that he wouldn't be teased for being handsome anymore. With double black eyes and a swollen nose, it had worked, but only for a week. His nose had healed perfectly straight. As he grew older, his eyes had turned more often to girls than to anything else, and he was glad he hadn't succeeded.

But three years ago, his life had tragically changed and he knew he would never again need his good looks. He didn't consider trying for a broken nose again; there was no use. Young ladies often looked for handsome gentlemen, but more often they looked for fortune, titles, and land. Since he had all of them, he would be pursued even if he had a crooked nose.

Thinking back to the young lady at the inn, he felt for the first time in three years that being pursued wouldn't be completely awful. Which was why it was a good thing he would never see her again.

Instead, Henry turned his mind back to where it should be: his business today with Mr. Dunn. For the last few years, no one had demanded anything of Henry. His parents had left him without responsibilities so he could wallow in peace, but before his father left for Parliament, he had mentioned his disappointment in himself at his failure to negotiate a land deal with Mr. Dunn. His father hadn't suggested that Henry give it a try while he was away, but Henry had seized the opportunity anyway. It felt wonderful to have a project to work on, and even though working with Mr. Dunn was nearly impossible at times with all his conditions and lengthy negotiations, even down to the detail of when his daughter would be allowed to accept her new position as Miss Abbot's companion, Henry felt sure they had just about reached a solution. He could hardly wait for his father to return home in a couple months to show him all he had accomplished. Perhaps even better than showing his father was showing himself that even if his heart was broken beyond repair, at least he could still be useful to his family and community.

Chapter 5

$\mathcal{W}$ ithin a few days of arriving in Barrington, Julia had a new routine that she loved. After breakfast, Julia would go for a long walk. So far, she had found Barrington and its surroundings both beautiful and peaceful. There were fields and pastures lined by hedgerows along gently rolling hills, as well as wooded forests where the trees were so thick that the cold wind could hardly get through them. After her walk, Julia played Martha's lovely pianoforte for hours in the afternoon, and took tea with Martha, who was very regular about teatime, and then Julia would read or do needlework until dinner. Her cousin had several social engagements, and Julia was easily included in the visits with neighbors. The family at Barrington Court were particular friends of Martha's, and she informed Julia that they would dine there regularly through the course of her visit, which Julia happily anticipated. But getting to know Martha again was the highlight of all of it. Julia's only family had been her mother and sister for so long, but with Martha, she finally had a family member she could relate to.

When she had first arrived, her carriage had rolled through Barrington, the town passing in a blink. Julia had worried that her mother had been right; she would hate it here. It was so small she thought she might be willing to walk just to get herself back to London.

Becoming reacquainted with Martha had reassured her. She was a slightly stout lady of about fifty with nearly black hair except for the strands of white dispersed throughout. Her features denoted sternness, but for Julia she had a kind smile. She had greeted Julia with an embrace and exclaimed, "Julia, welcome. It's so lovely to have you here. You probably don't remember me. It's been so long since we've seen each other." She wasn't overly enthusiastic or warm at Julia's arrival, but her words seemed sincere.

"I do remember you," Julia had replied, "although it's just vague memories of dear 'Cousin Martha' from when you stayed with us."

"I am surprised that you can remember me at all. You were so young and we've not had any contact since then." She shrugged and resolved it by saying, "I did spend much of my time with you when I was there." Her voice turned tender as she said, "You seemed to feel the loss of your father most keenly. Perhaps because it was such a difficult time for you, your deep feelings created deep memories."

Julia felt on the verge of tears at her simple statement. She hadn't thought about her father too much in recent years; he had been gone so long. How strange it was for her to be so moved by her cousin's sympathy. Julia had been reacquainted with her for no more than half a minute and she felt that she had uncovered something hidden inside her. Martha had given her a kind smile and embraced her again. Julia swallowed the lump in her throat with some effort and pulled back, returning the smile.

From that moment, they had been quite comfortable with each other. They had had several long conversations coming to know each other, and now their discussions were even more interesting as they came to understand each other. But most of the days weren't spent relying on each other's company. Martha wasn't demanding of her time, and Julia loved her solitary morning walks. It was ridiculous now to remember how she thought she would be bored here. She loved walking through Barrington and had soon seen the whole town, but walking out in the countryside was even better.

Today's walk had been the best one yet. It was still cold, but Julia had had a brilliant idea while out on her morning walk and it brought her back to Martha's home with a smile on her face. Perhaps she could stay in Barrington permanently. She didn't want to return to London and she didn't want to marry, especially someone her mother chose for her after making that rash promise. Perhaps Martha could be the answer to her problems. Mother couldn't marry the earl until her daughters were married because he didn't want to provide for them. But if Julia could secure a home with her cousin, she wouldn't have to marry!

She had thought the solution to her problem was to marry someone she chose, rather than to have her mother choose for her. Falling in love was a dream she had given up long ago. But she never thought she could avoid marriage altogether, at least not until meeting her cousin again. Martha had never married, but had the means to have an independent life. Julia and her sister had both inherited a very small annual sum at their father's passing. While she could never be independent, if Julia could stay with Martha, she could at least contribute a little to the household. Julia had seven more weeks before she was supposed to return to London. Perhaps she could convince Martha before then to let her stay.

With these hopeful thoughts, Julia entered the hall, untied her bonnet strings, and hung her cloak and bonnet up on the pegs by the door. She made her way to the sitting room where she knew she would find Martha. Even with the cool weather, Martha had told Julia that she refused to light every fire in the house in May, especially during daylight hours. So it was that the sitting room—the only room with a daytime fire lit, as well as being a south-facing room—was where her cousin could be found with the door firmly shut to keep in the heat.

As Julia came down the hall, she was surprised to see the sitting room door open, but then she heard Martha's voice and realized she must have company. It was confirmed a moment later when she heard a man's voice say, "How can you say everything has worked out for the best? It's been less than a week; you cannot know so quickly if she will be a problem. I still think you should not have sent for her."

It couldn't be more obvious that whoever he was, he was referring to Julia. She was surprised to hear herself spoken of at all, but the negative comments were quite unexpected. Julia always made a good first impression; it was only after courting her for some time that a gentleman became disenchanted with her. She was immensely curious which of her cousin's neighbors had already taken a disliking to her and why.

Always, she wanted to know why.

So she stood outside the door to listen further. Martha didn't respond right away, and Julia could just picture her sitting on the other side of the wall, silently counting as she looped the thread around the needle as she embroidered. Julia briefly wondered what her cousin's response would be, and she hoped it would be positive. Julia already had her heart set on staying in Barrington permanently and it would all depend on Martha's judgment of her. She felt that they were getting along very well, but what was Martha's opinion?

Finally she heard her say, "I didn't send for her; I sent for her mother."

"Which makes it even worse," came the reply. "She passed off her duty to her daughter, who surely must be angry at being banished from London, and you are the one who will suffer for it with a reluctant and sullen companion for the next two months."

"Julia hasn't shown any reluctance about being stuck here with me. I am lucky Marianne sent Julia in her place. As my cousin's widow, Marianne would always be welcome here, but our characters are so different . . . It would have been a trying two months."

"That is another reason you should not have sent for her at all. If you had told me or my parents that Miss Fie was leaving you early to tend to her mother, we wouldn't have let you stay alone for two months. We would have invited you to Barrington Court to stay. You needn't have called on any distant family relations who have never given a thought for you." Ah, now his identity was revealed. He must be a son of Lord and Lady Chamberlain. Julia had yet to meet any members of the great family of the neighborhood. But Martha had assured her that she would meet them soon; she had a standing invitation for a weekly dinner at Barrington Court and any other social outings usually involved the Chamberlain family as well.

"Perhaps that is why I didn't tell you," came Martha's voice. "Being away from my home for any length of time has always been a great sacrifice for me. I've grown too independent —or perhaps I should say stubborn—to ever enjoy being a long-term visitor."

"It is likely you won't enjoy having a long-term visitor in your own home any more than being one yourself. Surely your cousin's daughter will prove to have a character just like her mother." Julia clenched her teeth at his persistence, wishing she could defend her character right then, but vowing to herself to make sure this man would never have the chance to say such things once he knew her. What an annoying person he must be! Why did he continue to try to convince Martha that she wasn't happy with the situation when she so obviously was?

"No, Henry, it's just as I've been telling you. Everything has turned out better than I expected. Julia and I are getting along fine."

It wasn't the highest praise she'd ever heard, but Julia was content to know Martha was pleased with her. Although if she knew Julia was standing outside the door, she might change her mind. Of course, listening to their private conversation was inappropriate. Julia knew the gentleman's opinion of her couldn't matter at all as they had never even met, but she didn't want anyone trying to present her in a poor light to Martha. She decided it was time to make her entrance.

Chapter 6

$\mathcal{J}$ulia pushed open the door wider to the sitting room, saying as she entered, "Hello, Martha, I'm back from my walk. The sunshine is misleading; it is still so cold today! Thank you for letting me take your cloak. You were right; it's much thicker than mine."

Julia purposefully didn't cast her eyes about, knowing that she shouldn't be expecting anyone else in the room with her cousin. She was feeling defensive over the words she had just heard this stranger speak and she was prepared give a formal curtsy and then to be cold and distant when Martha introduced her to Mr. Chamberlain. Her resolve was immediately thwarted when she heard him speak, "It's you!" and a bark of laughter followed his pronunciation. Julia's eyes shot over to where Mr. Chamberlain stood and her jaw fell open as she recoiled in horror.

It was him: the man who had seen her most foolish act since childhood. He had witnessed her first and last attempt at catching a fly. The very man she was *sure* she would never see again. He was every bit as handsome in her cousin's sitting room as he had been in the side yard of the inn, but Julia wasn't overwhelmed by him now. Her embarrassment at seeing him again was too great for that.

Her reaction seemed to amuse him even more than just her presence and she could see a gleam in his eye as he surely was anticipating humiliating her with the story of their first encounter.

Before he could speak, Martha voiced her curiosity, "Henry, have you already met my cousin? You must know her from town, but why did you not say you were already acquainted?"

"We are not acquainted actually; we've merely crossed paths. But it was quite a memorable experience."

His perfect mouth was curved up in a wicked smile, which helped Julia recover from the shock of seeing him again. She quickly blurted to her cousin, "Yes, isn't it strange that I saw him as we traveled here? We stopped at an inn for a late meal, and he was just leaving." Julia emphasized the last few words, hoping he would take a hint and leave now.

His grin grew broader, but he remained standing where he was.

Martha remained sitting and by now she had set her embroidery down. Julia thought that her cousin had probably discerned that there was something unspoken going on as her eyes darted between Mr. Chamberlain and Julia several times, but she chose not to address it, saying, "Well, that is quite a coincidence. Since you aren't yet acquainted, Henry, this is my cousin's daughter, Miss Julia North, and Julia, this is Mr. Henry Chamberlain, the Baron of Eldridge."

Mr. Chamberlain bowed and said, "Miss North," but she could see the amusement on his face at the irony of the formal introduction.

Julia curtsied and muttered reluctantly, "Lord Chamberlain."

"Henry just goes by Mr. Chamberlain," said Martha.

Julia looked from her cousin to Mr. Chamberlain with curiosity and Martha explained. "He has the lesser title now, but one day he'll inherit his father's title. And in the meantime, it's just too confusing to have two Lord Chamberlains in the neighborhood. Now sit and tell me what happened when you met at the inn." Julia didn't want to admire him, but it seemed his character must at least have a small streak of humility to forego being addressed with his title.

Julia replied to Martha's request, anxious to speak before Mr. Chamberlain could, "Nothing happened, Martha . . . Well, it was so insignificant. He was kind enough to educate me about horseflies after I received a bite from one." Julia should have left it at that, but she was feeling defensive about the whole situation, besides what she had overheard, so with an arch look for Mr. Chamberlain she added, "It would have been more fortunate if he had told me *before* I received the bite."

Julia knew it was a mistake as soon as she said it. It was as though she had given him permission to tease her about it, and he proceeded by saying, "Ahh, but I saw the look of the hunter in your eyes. I've seen that look too many times on young ladies' faces; it's clear that you would let nothing stop you from catching your prey." It annoyed her completely that he had made the connection between catching a fly and catching a man, but she would never admit it. With real incredulity in his voice he added, "I must admit, I never dreamed you would succeed. It's the first time I've ever underestimated a lady."

Martha seemed thoroughly confused by his response and asked, "I feel I've missed something. What was she hunting?"

Again Julia answered before he could. "Not hunting, really, it was just that . . . all my attention was on one thing," she began. She was looking at Mr. Chamberlain as she spoke and his green eyes stole her attention now.

They were just as mesmerizing in the dim sitting room as they had been at their first encounter. She struggled to recall what she was saying. ". . . and I was so focused that I, um, disregarded everything else and was therefore, inadvertently, bitten by a horsefly."

Mr. Chamberlain was smiling now as if remembering a fond memory. Martha noticed his look and then turned to Julia and asked a bit skeptically, "All your attention on one thing, was it?" Julia had no clue what her cousin was implying, but she just nodded and hoped fervently they could stop talking about it.

Martha seemed to finally understand that Julia wasn't keen to discuss it and her deliberate change of subject was anything but subtle. "The weather has been awfully cold this spring, don't you think, Henry? I hope it won't affect the harvest."

Mr. Chamberlain responded appropriately and Julia felt her solid footing return, although she couldn't really feel comfortable again in his presence. He was on his way soon after and Julia walked into the hall with him to see him out. His arm brushed hers in the narrow hallway, and when they reached the door he casually sniffed as he passed by her and asked, "Do I smell onions?" Julia's heart was already beating faster at his nearness, but she managed to give him the glare he must be expecting. She was relieved that Martha was out of their hearing.

"I hope you're finished now. Surely you've squeezed all the entertainment you possibly can out of one trivial little thing."

"On the contrary, Miss North, I was just getting started."

She narrowed her eyes at the threat, hoping it was a joke, but his close proximity distracted her from any retort she had ready. Of all the handsome men she had ever met—and London had quite a few to offer—this one was by far the most perfect of his kind. Julia could see the flecks of gold in his green eyes, which must surely be the reason his eyes seemed to have a knowing gleam in them. His smile and the quirk of his eyebrow told her he knew quite well the effect he had on her.

Julia wanted to find her earlier defiance and remove that look from his face, but she didn't get a chance. He bid her farewell and pulled his hat on as he stooped under the doorframe and began walking away. Julia again wanted to have the last word, but restrained herself from saying something to his departing back, remembering that last time it had just made her feel foolish. Unfortunately, he turned back and caught her staring after him from the doorway and she felt foolish anyway.

She shut the door harder than it needed and returned to the sitting room, hoping to distract her cousin with talk of anything besides her earlier encounter with Mr. Chamberlain. Martha, however, had other plans.

"What did you think of Henry?" she asked without preamble.

Julia had sensed while eavesdropping that Martha had a high regard for Mr. Chamberlain, but she thought that it was very unlikely that her cousin would want her to make a match with him. Martha had barely mentioned that the Chamberlains had two sons, while she had described most of her neighbors and friends to Julia in detail. These clues led her to think that her cousin didn't want Julia chasing after her neighbor. Besides the humiliation she experienced every time she even thought about him, this made her answer easy to give. "I think his good looks have given him too much confidence, bordering on conceit." She sounded a bit haughty, she knew, but Martha just shook her head.

"Don't set your sights on him, Julia. It will only lead to heartache."

Feeling slightly offended, she replied, "I've just told you, I think he's arrogant and being too handsome hasn't done him any good. Why would you think I need to be warned away from him?"

"Because I saw you looking at him, and I can see that look in your eyes even now. Henry would be quite a prize for any young lady, but he has a very good reason for not being interested in love or marriage, and there have been many young ladies with broken hearts to prove it."

Julia probably should have guessed as much herself. He was far too *everything* to be a bachelor still, unless it was by design. She wished she didn't care, but her curiosity got the better of her and ignoring Martha's comment about how she had looked at him, she asked, "Why doesn't he want to marry? What is the reason?"

Martha heaved a big sigh before saying, "It was about three and a half years ago that he met a young woman named Miss Corey when he was in Bath. She and her mother were invited to stay at Barrington Court for a house party that summer, so I had the opportunity to meet her and it looked to be an ideal match. Every young lady was in love with Henry, and Miss Corey was no different. The remarkable thing was that Henry was in love with her too. I've known him all his life and I've seen the admiring girls come and go without ever holding his attention for any length of time. Miss Corey was the one who finally touched his heart. Before the end of Miss Corey's stay, Henry had proposed and she had accepted.

"Lord and Lady Chamberlain were pleased with the match. She had a large dowry, but her lineage was nothing to speak of. I don't think Henry gave a single thought to dowries or lineages. He had fallen in love and would have pursued Miss Corey no matter what. Luckily for them, both families were pleased and nothing stood in their way.

"Miss Corey and her mother were shopping for wedding clothes in Bath several weeks before the wedding. The consensus later was that their coachman was probably drinking while he waited for them to finish shopping. When they set off for home, their coachman let the horses travel too fast down a hill. He lost control at a corner and that was that. A farmer heard the crash and came running, but the coachman, Miss Corey, and Mrs. Corey had all been killed.

"Henry found out the next day. He only stayed in England long enough for her burial. He was so heartbroken that he left for the continent immediately after and stayed away for months. It was understandable that he needed time and distance for his broken heart to heal. Upon his return, everyone thought he must be ready to proceed on with his life. He is Lord Chamberlain's heir and the neighborhood talked it over and decided he would marry another. But it's been three years now since he returned and Henry feels no obligation to please the neighborhood, or his parents. He attends all the balls and parties, where he socializes with all the young ladies who bat their eyes at him, but he is very careful to never give too much attention to any one of them. He was a catch before with his looks, and his title, but now he is the ultimate prize. Every young lady imagines herself as the one who will heal his poor heart, but I'm telling you now, Julia, don't let yourself get involved. If you fall in love with Henry Chamberlain, you will leave Barrington broken-hearted."

As she finished speaking, she looked directly into Julia's eyes with a stern look to add conviction to her words. Julia hadn't realized that she was leaning forward and biting her nails as the story unfolded. At her cousin's stern look, she quickly lowered her hands and smoothed them down her skirts. She couldn't help but be fascinated by Mr. Chamberlain's story.

"Of course I won't fall in love with him. As I said, he seems quite arrogant to me, probably the effect of all the attention he receives. But I'm glad you told me his history. It will be quite interesting to be an outside observer of it all during my stay here."

Martha looked at her through narrowed eyes, surely wondering if she should believe her, so Julia added, "Really, Cousin, if I can make it through three London seasons without ever falling in love once, I'm sure I can handle a couple of months in Barrington with ease." Julia was as confident as her words. And when the two months passed without incident, perhaps Martha would let her stay.

It seemed as though Julia had finally convinced her, for she replied, "I'm pleased that you can be so level-headed about it all. Truly, it's for the best."

Julia smiled and let the subject drop there. If Martha thought she should stay away from Henry Chamberlain, then she would. Whatever it took to earn an opportunity to stay with Martha permanently, she would do it. Picking up a book that she had begun earlier, it took some time for her to focus on the words. She had a hard time turning her thoughts away from Mr. Chamberlain and the tragedy that had ruined his perfect existence.

Chapter 7

*J*ulia's first ball after arriving in Barrington took her by surprise before it even began. It was to begin with the primary families in the neighborhood dining together at the Martock priory and then continue through the evening. The greater part of the day would be spent in company. Julia hadn't anticipated being invited out during her stay in Barrington at all, but to be spending practically an entire day in society was quite unexpected.

When she had so readily agreed to take her mother's place by staying with Martha, she felt sure that it would be a two-month break from the incessant social activities of the last three years. But apparently even in the country they seized every opportunity to have a party.

Julia left London wanting that break, but now, knowing Mr. Chamberlain's history as she did, and despite her embarrassment in his presence, she was curious to see him again. It would be interesting to watch how he interacted with all the women vying for his attention as Martha had claimed was the case. His tragic loss along with his physical perfection and aristocratic status was such an intriguing combination. She knew her cousin's advice was sound—falling in love with him would be a mistake—but she wasn't worried. One very compelling reason to avoid him was that she wanted to stay with Martha forever, so she would stay away from him to please her cousin. Only slightly less compelling was the fact that he had seen her humiliate herself and seemed to enjoy reminding her of it. But being intrigued because of his circumstances was certainly not love, so Julia looked forward to the evening more than she thought she would.

As she arrived at Martock priory, Julia noticed that it was an ancient building, but once inside it was less obvious. Most of the walls were covered with tapestries and the floors with rugs wherever one would fit, effectively protecting the occupants from the cold stone walls and floors. But more than the furnishings, Mr. and Mrs. Stephens made it feel warm. They were gracious hosts and behaved toward Julia as though she was an old family friend rather than a new acquaintance.

Julia looked for Mr. Chamberlain as soon as she arrived, but couldn't see him anywhere. Her anticipation for the outing had been because of Mr. Chamberlain, and without him it was all for nothing. She wanted to observe how he interacted with an adoring crowd. When the large group all made their way to the dining room and found their seats, she could see that he really wasn't present and couldn't quell her disappointment.

She wasn't seated next to her cousin or she might have asked where he was, but then even if she could she shouldn't. She didn't want to betray her interest and ask Martha where he was, so she resolved to endure not having her curiosity satisfied.

After dining in their great hall, Mrs. Stephens took Julia under her wing for a bit. She pointed out several people, but the crowd was too large to make introductions. She particularly caught Julia's attention when she pointed out Lady Chamberlain. Julia had assumed that because her son, Mr. Chamberlain, wasn't present that the whole family must be absent.

Mrs. Stephens led Julia through the large room and introduced her to several other young ladies. Then, leaving Julia to these new acquaintances, Mrs. Stephens moved on to ensure the comfort of her other guests.

Julia applied her attention to her peers and she was surprised how much some of them reminded her of acquaintances from town. One young lady was overconfident but tried to disguise it by acting demure; another girl was too solicitous, and another was acting bored. Julia wondered if these roles were almost requisite for their society to function or if rather society was what created these roles for them to fill. Julia's role was the one she should have been most interested in, but she found she didn't want to fit into place. Even after they moved into the great hall where they could converse more easily, she found herself necessarily with the group of young ladies, and though she felt herself above it, she couldn't help but listen with interest when their conversation quickly turned to Mr. Chamberlain.

There were four young ladies but Julia could only remember one of their names. Miss Dripple, with her constant dull expression, just seemed to fit her name so well, and so it had stuck with her. But the lady who seemed to know the most about Mr. Chamberlain's every move Julia just referred to in her head as "Miss Pathetic." It was she who spoke with authority about why Mr. Chamberlain wasn't here yet this evening. "He left for Devon last week and Papa says he must have been meeting with Mr. Dunn, who has stubbornly held onto the land that borders Lord Chamberlain's to the west," Miss Pathetic rolled her eyes at the stubborn Mr. Dunn. "No one knows if he's returned yet and I'm sure Mama will be so angry if he doesn't turn up tonight because I've skipped all my lessons for the last week so that I could finish my gown for this evening especially so he could see it." She smoothed the folds of her burgundy gown as she spoke and the other young ladies began complimenting her on the fine stitching and lace overlay, as the girl had probably intended them to do.

Just hearing that Mr. Chamberlain might still turn up returned Julia's previous anticipation and her thoughts went not to Miss Pathetic's dress, but to her own. She couldn't deny that she wondered for a very brief moment what Mr. Chamberlain would think of her own gown. It was one of her newest dresses, a white gown with a delicate pattern in blue across the bodice and the hem and a matching blue sash at her waist. She was pleased that the style was simpler this season with fewer frills and ruffles on the gowns; it suited her better.

Banishing that thought, she informed her new acquaintances about Mr. Chamberlain's return. "Actually he is back from Devon. He called on my cousin yesterday." Innocent as the remark was, Julia immediately regretted volunteering even that much information as four pairs of very suspicious eyes turned on her.

Miss Dripple quickly demanded, "When did you see him?"

Julia pulled back slightly in surprise at the intense question that seemed out of character for her new acquaintance. Miss Dripple seemed to realize her rudeness and took a step back as she looked down, probably in order to recover her listless expression. The others still looked at her with expectant glares.

"It was yesterday morning . . . He was there when I returned from a walk," Julia hesitantly replied.

Miss Pathetic, whose possessiveness of Mr. Chamberlain seemed the strongest, was condescending as she said, "Are you sure it was Mr. Chamberlain?" She turned an amused smile to her companions, and then looked back at Julia, "You wouldn't really know, would you? Seeing as you are so new to the neighborhood, you probably wouldn't even recognize the Chamberlain crest if you saw it."

Julia was torn between wanting desperately to give Miss Pathetic a set down and not making enemies in such a small town as this. Luckily her more rational self prevailed and she merely responded, "My cousin introduced him as Mr. Henry Chamberlain, the Baron of Eldridge." She kept her smile complacent, not wanting their ire for merely knowing Mr. Chamberlain's name, and asked, "Is he who you were referring to?"

They did not look pleased, and Julia began to turn away, hoping that she could escape. But Miss Pathetic stopped her with a hand on her arm and asked, "What did you think of our Mr. Chamberlain?" The possessiveness of her tone and her hand still on Julia's arm made her realize just how serious Miss Pathetic's pursuit of Mr. Chamberlain was. She was intense and obviously saw Julia as a threat. If only she knew that Julia had the ability to scare away suitors without even trying, she would know how little of a threat Julia truly was.

Miss Pathetic was undoubtedly in love with Mr. Chamberlain and she seemed to search Julia for any hint that she felt the same. Julia could see the other three young ladies eyeing her suspiciously as well. She could tell that although they let Miss Pathetic have her say, they all were possessive of Mr. Chamberlain and secretly in love with him too. As a newcomer, Julia was clearly not allowed the privilege of being in love with him. The ridiculousness of the situation struck her and a disbelieving chuckle escaped before she could cover it up and quickly reassure them, "I didn't think much of him at all . . . He's nothing like the men in London I'm so used to."

Julia could see them visibly relax as they met each other's eyes. Miss Pathetic even smiled at her, but without letting the subject drop she asked Julia, "So you didn't think him handsome, witty . . . charming?"

He was undeniably handsome. That was a ridiculous understatement. He had been quite witty too—although Julia hadn't enjoyed it as his wit had been directed at her. But charming? "Not at all," she replied, happy with her success in diffusing their ire. "His manners were not at all the thing, and I have to say I was quite unimpressed."

"So if perhaps . . . he were to ask you to dance this evening, you wouldn't oblige?"

Julia was on a roll now and responded with conviction, "No, trust me; I have no desire to dance with Mr. Chamberlain." This was an easy promise to make. Julia wanted to prove to Martha that she wasn't chasing after Mr. Chamberlain, and besides, she had seen already that there were more women in the room than men. She was sure that she wouldn't be asked for any dance, but especially not by Mr. Chamberlain. Besides, after conversing with Miss Pathetic and her friends, Julia was fairly certain they wouldn't let her near him anyway.

Miss Pathetic seemed to finally be satisfied that Julia wasn't a threat to her, and she removed her hand from her arm, only to now link their arms together in the friendliest way. A positive sign surely, but it left Julia with no means of escape until a few minutes later when the gentlemen rejoined them and she was able to re-station herself by her cousin after the interruption.

There was a flurry of activity near a window not long after that as one young lady saw a carriage pull up and many of the younger guests crowded around to get a look and see if it was one of the Chamberlain carriages arriving. They were all fairly certain that it was and soon an exclamation was heard, "That's him!" and, "He did make it back, then." Julia thought that the excitement of his impending arrival was contagious because she couldn't help but feel a flutter of excitement herself. It was his tragic story that drew her to him, and despite what she had said to Miss Pathetic and especially emphasized to Martha, she couldn't help but wish she could be the one to reach his heart. It must be her competitive nature, because considering her history, she knew she was the least likely girl to accomplish such a thing, but as she told herself, she couldn't help it.

Mr. Chamberlain entered the room with an air of assurance that showed he knew the reception he would receive. The young ladies didn't disappoint. Miss Pathetic was the first to claim his attention, with an over-bright smile and a hand on his arm, but she wasn't given any opportunity to monopolize him. Several other young ladies were there too, exclaiming over him.

Julia couldn't help but feel that they were all making fools of themselves, drooling over him so. Just watching such a spectacle made her glad she had resolved to avoid him. He seemed to enjoy the attention, which made her earlier words to Miss Pathetic even more true: she was quite unimpressed. Her pledge to the girl that she wouldn't dance with Mr. Chamberlain would be an easy one to keep.

Julia joined a table of whist players and tried very hard to concentrate on the game. She was usually an exceptional card player. She loved the thrill of an excellent hand and the strategy involved in playing a poor hand. But this evening her attention was diverted as Mr. Chamberlain made his way around the room. Even she had to admit that he managed all the admiring youth with impressive skill. They looked at him adoringly with their upturned faces and he gave them several minutes of attention and politely moved on. Julia's play was poor and her elderly partner, Mrs. Thurston, complained that young people weren't taught to play cards properly. She just sighed in resignation; she couldn't contradict her after the hand she had just played.

Chapter 8

$\mathcal{H}$enry made his way around the room in his usual manner. He greeted his mother first; then he exchanged a few sentences with everyone and stopped to speak a little longer with closer friends. He eventually made his way to Mrs. Stephens, who was appreciative of him coming. "We weren't certain you would be back in time for our party this evening. I'm so relieved your business didn't keep you."

"Yes, I was relieved to make it back in time too. I didn't want to miss your famous hospitality," Henry had responded with a smile. But it had never been a concern. His arrival had been timed perfectly. By arriving late, he wouldn't have to spend the entire day in company. He had arrived after the card tables were arranged, so he didn't have to join in. Next there would be dancing, and then it would be time to go. He had told his mother he might not be back in time so she wouldn't plan any surprises for him this evening. Sometimes she invited young ladies—acquaintances of acquaintances—to come stay so they could be introduced at events just such as this. It was the very reason he had moved to the empty Dower house rather than deal with flirtatious young women at breakfast every morning.

And his plan had worked; there were no surprises waiting for him this evening. He was only surprised at himself. After another amusing encounter yesterday with Miss Julia North, he had told himself to ignore her from then on. There was an inexplicable appeal that went hand-in-hand with a guilty conscience whenever he saw her. The surprising thing was that even though he had been quite firm with himself, he had been aware of her since he walked into the room.

As he moved about, he looked up every few moments to gauge her distance and note whom she was speaking with. He didn't even have to look directly at her. Sometimes he just let his eyes wander far enough to catch a glimpse of her at the edge of his vision. Her white gown with touches of blue was easy to spot. And her brown hair, which had been loose and windblown the first two times he had seen her, was pulled away from her face in perfectly smooth waves and curls that shone in the light and continually drew his attention. With each glance, he was hoping to see her expressive eyes, but she was never looking at him. Hopefully he was discreet enough that no one noticed, but his wandering glances were frequent enough that he could see she wasn't much of a card player as she and Mrs. Thurston lost every hand. When the dancing began, he approached their hostess, Mrs. Stephens, this time for a dance. But still he knew the precise moment Miss North joined the dancing when Miss Abbot introduced her to Alec Hibbert. And when the dance ended, he noticed she didn't return to her cousin, but moved across the room to a less crowded corner and observed the dance from there.

That was when her eyes met his and his only thought was *"Finally."* Despite a residual feeling of guilt that Henry knew he didn't need to feel, he decided he wanted to see if the same attraction he'd felt the last time they were together was still there. He excused himself from Mrs. Stephens and made his way to Miss North.

As he approached her, he began smiling in anticipation. He certainly enjoyed reminding her of their first encounter. "Do you not think I'm brave?" he asked by way of greeting.

She looked confused at his question, then mistrustful, probably aware of what he was leading up to. "I don't know you well enough to judge, sir," came her proper reply.

Her effort to be proper and distant made it almost too easy. "It's how well I know you that makes me brave. I've seen you catch your prey, and yet I've just taken my life in my own hands and approached you."

Her annoyance was evident, but Henry was happy to observe that she was trying to hide her amusement. He could see her smile in her profile as she turned away from him. He wanted to recapture her attention.

"I hope you will reward me for my bravery by dancing the next set with me, Miss North." He waited for her to say yes so he could take her hand and lead her to the floor.

She didn't answer right away, and he looked down at her in surprise as her eyes darted about the room. With indecision in her countenance she said, "No, thank you, Mr. Chamberlain, I . . . I umm . . ."

Was she trying to think of an excuse for refusing him? "You . . . what?" He waited expectantly. It was an extremely uncommon thing for him to be turned down—so uncommon that he couldn't remember a single instance when it had ever happened.

She finally just shrugged one shoulder and said, "I won't be dancing with you."

His eyes narrowed just a bit as he scrutinized her. "I saw you dance with Alec Hibbert, your first catch of the evening. I assume he didn't bite?" She gave him a withering look for that comment, which caused him to smile broadly. "So surely it's safe to dance with me too."

He held out his hand to her, feeling quite sure that her unusual reluctance would give way. Instead, she obviously contrived a casual manner and said airily, "No, thank you."

He pulled his hand back and lifted it to his face to rub his jaw. Henry couldn't think of a reason why she would decline. He had teased her a bit, but while it brought color to her cheeks each time, he could tell she wasn't offended. He was very curious to know what her reason might be. "So it must be me that you take exception to," he said with mock humility, hoping it would prompt her to reveal her true reason for refusing him.

She narrowed her eyes, not falling for his trick, but luckily she still answered him. "I don't take exception to you, sir. I refused to dance with you because I told some of the other young ladies earlier that I wouldn't dance with you."

Henry glanced around with a puzzled look and then looked back at Miss North and voiced the obvious question. "Why would you tell them that?"

She looked as if she was trying to decide whether to tell him or not. Finally she said, "It was the only way to avoid hostilities. They seemed to view me as a threat. I felt that the best way to avoid an angry mob was by saying I wouldn't dance with you."

Henry tried to grasp her meaning. Would the young ladies of the neighborhood really intimidate or threaten someone? He had to admit that he didn't know them well enough to guess. To talk too long to any of them would just be asking for trouble, but they all seemed like sweet enough girls. "An angry mob?" he asked skeptically. "Surely you're overstating things."

"No," she shook her head. "They definitely think of you as their possession and they are not willing to share." Her voice hinted at doubt, which made Henry smile. Of course it wasn't true. He never gave any young lady more attention than any other to avoid that exact scenario. Somehow, she had misunderstood something they had said to her.

With a disbelieving grin, he asked, "So you are saying that you promised not to dance with me to appease some of the other young ladies who perhaps think of you as an outsider and therefore not *worthy* of dancing with me?"

She looked torn between feeling ridiculous for thinking such a thing and annoyance that he didn't believe her. She folded her arms and gave him a defiant look. "Yes, that is precisely what I'm saying."

For a brief moment, Henry felt his confidence slip. She was refusing to dance with him. He shook his head. No, someone had said something to her that had confused her somehow. She wasn't saying no to him, just to dancing with him because of some ridiculous promise. She looked away, as though she thought their conversation over. Henry wanted to keep talking with her; he wanted to surprise her the way she always surprised him. Maybe she would find him just as interesting. "I can see dancing together is out of the question, Miss North. But would you instead do me the honor of not dancing with me?"

She slowly turned her gaze away from the dance floor. She looked so confused as to what he was asking that Henry thought he might laugh out loud. "I beg your pardon?" she asked.

"Since you have so imprudently promised not to dance with me, I thought that perhaps you and I could sit this dance out together."

"So . . . we'll spend the set together . . . not dancing?"

"Precisely. I think, under the circumstances, it is the only option." Henry saw her tentative smile and his confidence was completely restored.

Miss North might be different from the young ladies he was used to, but he could still treat her the same. He would flirt and enjoy her smiles and compliments, and even every unexpected thing she said, and then he would move on, like he always did. He moved closer to her and stood with his back to the wall just as she was. He leaned closer to her as if they shared a secret and said, "I never liked this dance anyway."

"How flattering. You sought me out for the dance you don't enjoy," she retorted.

That was unexpected. Usually when he flirted with a young lady, she would flutter her hands, or pull out a fan or something as she smiled and tried to think of a reply. But despite her quick response, Henry was too practiced in the art of flirting to let it discompose him. In fact, it would be more entertaining by far to accept it as a challenge. With a sly grin he said, "I was certain if I danced the quadrille with you, it would be my favorite from this night."

She turned to face him as she said, "And I would doubt the intellect of anyone who told me the quadrille was his favorite dance, no matter the reason."

"We have that in common then, Miss North. Neither of us enjoys the quadrille," he replied, happy that he was able to turn her words in his favor again.

"Mr. Chamberlain, I'm surprised that you are interested in finding common ground with me. From what you were saying to my cousin the other day, I rather assumed you were disinclined to have me here at all."

That discomposed him, at least a little. He felt slightly unsure as he asked, "What is it that you're referring to?"

"You told Martha that she shouldn't have sent for me. You said she should have stayed at Barrington Court rather than have an unknown relation here to help."

"Did you overhear our conversation, then?"

Miss North looked uncomfortable but admitted, "Yes, just those few words as I hung my cloak up in the hall."

He arched an eyebrow at that, wondering if that was really all she had heard. "Miss Abbot has lived in Barrington her entire life. She has served so many in our community and I just felt that now that she needs help, she should have turned to us rather than some cousins who have never visited before."

She didn't respond, but just looked at him with a penitent expression. He felt remorseful himself for making her feel guilty and said, "You are doing her a great favor by coming now. Miss Abbot seems to appreciate it very much."

"You've got it backward, sir. She is the one helping me. I wanted to leave London."

A mysterious remark, but she didn't expound on it. They should have been having merely a light, flirtatious conversation, but instead she stood there with a sad, far-away look and he wanted to know why. He shouldn't want to delve deeper into her past and find out what made her so unique. Trying to keep their conversation light, he said, "I would have invited you to Barrington myself if I had known your skill as a hunter. We have rather good sport around here, although typically with foxes, not flies."

A startled chuckle escaped her and she just shook her head and with a reluctant smile muttered, "Will it never end?"

Henry knew she wasn't really asking him, but he responded anyway with a smirk, "Not ever. I love to talk about hunting, especially strategy. Just ask my brother. Now that I know we have this in common, you are my new favorite person." He was surprised to realize she really was his new favorite person, although not for the reason he gave.

"I'm sure our similarities end there," she replied.

Henry didn't know why, but her sad expression returned with those words. Again, Henry waited intently for her to say more, but she stayed silent. He could feel himself slipping under her spell. He wanted to pursue her with every resource he had and at the same time he wished they'd never met because of the inner turmoil he felt.

He had probably leaned in too close, because Julia startled him out of that thought by taking a small step away from him and asking, "Where is your brother? Is he here this evening?" The change of subject felt deliberate to Henry and he felt it would be safer to go along with it, rather than ask what troubled her.

"No. He finished school last year and is on a tour of the continent. He'll likely come home this summer and you can ask him then."

Henry felt a tap on his arm from behind and turned his head to see Miss Clifton pulling gently on his arm. Her voice was sweet as she entreated him, "Mr. Chamberlain, I hate to be so forward as this, but I need your help fixing the tie on my slipper. I'm sure no one could fix it as quickly as you could. In fact, I'm sure you could have it done in time for us to dance the next set."

He felt as if he were being pulled back into safer territory. Miss Clifton he knew how to deal with. She would flirt and agree with everything he said and never say anything unexpected. "Of course, Miss Clifton, I am at your service." He turned back to Miss North and said, "If you'll excuse me, Miss North?" She nodded her head with a resigned smile, but her eyes barely met his for an instant. Instead her gaze lingered on Miss Clifton, whose hand was pulling gently on his elbow, urging him away. Feeling strange, like he was leaving their conversation unfinished, he followed Miss Clifton to a bench in the hall, but it was some time before he could put Miss North from his mind. If a simple conversation—not even a dance—had left his thoughts so preoccupied, he might be in real danger of succumbing to his attraction to Miss North.

Chapter 9

Julia watched Mr. Chamberlain walk away. He didn't have any choice of course. Miss Pathetic, or rather Miss Clifton, actually, had left him with no option but to gallantly help her with her slipper and then stand up with her for the next dance. He didn't seem to mind, but Julia wanted to feel outraged on his behalf at her forwardness. But she shouldn't feel possessive of him. He wasn't hers and he never would be. Despite the fact that he had tried to find similarities between them, there was sure to be something dissimilar. They both hated the quadrille, and enjoyed hunting apparently, but what if he enjoyed walking aimlessly in horrible weather, or some other trivial thing? Every other gentleman of her acquaintance had found her lacking; surely he would too.

Julia felt unsettled as she watched him lead Miss Clifton back into the room for the next set. If *not* dancing with him left her this flustered, how much more would actually dancing with him affect her? Part of her hoped to never find out and part of her wanted to chase after him and demand a dance this instant, regardless of the possessive Miss Clifton.

Her confidence had deserted her, but she knew it didn't matter. If this had been her first season, she would never have resisted her attraction to him. She would have pursued him with all the fervor of the other girls. She wouldn't have heeded her cousin's warning that he would leave her broken-hearted. She would have thought she had a chance. But three London seasons had taught her there was something about her that drove men away. The best she could do for herself now was please Martha so that she wouldn't have to return to London and marry someone her mother chose.

Disheartened by the thought, Julia left her spot on the wall and found Martha and asked, "May we leave for home now? I'm awfully tired. I suppose I'm not used to such long parties as this." Before her non-dance with Mr. Chamberlain, anticipation had made her feel she was on the verge of something exciting. But now that the anticipation was gone, she just wanted the evening to be over.

Martha probably didn't want to leave so soon, but she said, "I had forgotten that London parties are more frequent but not as long. We can leave if you like. I haven't had a chance to speak to Lady Chamberlain yet. Just let me bid her and Mrs. Stephens farewell and we can be on our way."

Julia accompanied Martha as she made her way to where Mrs. Stephens and Lady Chamberlain were talking. Julia moved to the background while Martha visited with them, hoping to avoid the introduction for now. But Lady Chamberlain almost immediately addressed her as though they were already acquainted, "Miss North, I very much want you to meet my son. Now where has Henry got to?"

Another interview with Mr. Chamberlain was exactly what she was trying to avoid, so she quickly said, "I've already met him." It sounded rude and abrupt, so she added, "Thank you, though, Lady Chamberlain."

She didn't seem to notice the rudeness. She just asked, "I didn't see you dance with him. Surely if you were introduced he asked you to dance?"

Julia very much did not want to explain to his mother that he had asked her to dance, that she had said no, and why she had said no. Martha answered before she had to, "I'm sure they can arrange things without our help, Lady Chamberlain." An ironic statement from her cousin, who had told Mr. Hibbert to ask her to dance. "If Henry had wanted to ask her to dance, I'm sure he would have."

Julia was anxious not to be asked a direct question again and so she said, "We spoke for several minutes, but he left to dance with Miss Clifton. They seemed almost inseparable."

Lady Chamberlain's brows went up at this information and she seemed quite interested. "Miss Clifton, you say?"

Julia nodded and Lady Chamberlain looked as though she had more questions to ask, but Martha spoke first, saying, "We'll have to call on you tomorrow to talk over the whole evening. I'm sure our carriage is waiting for us by now. Goodbye, Lady Chamberlain. Thank you for a delightful evening, Mrs. Stephens."

On their journey home, Martha asked Julia what she had thought about Martock Priory, the fine dinner they had enjoyed, and her dance with Mr. Hibbert. It seemed quite intentional that she never mentioned Mr. Chamberlain once.

Chapter 10

It was late the next morning when Julia and Martha made their promised visit to Barrington Court. She had seen Barrington Court from a distance several times. And twice on her morning walks, she had been close enough to really gauge its size. But still, walking up to the front door with her cousin and knocking felt more intimidating than she imagined it would. The house was a grand structure and just going from one end to the other of the long building would be considered a significant walk. It had been built from golden stone, like so many of the buildings in this part of England, but it was more impressive than most in that it stood alone and was much larger than the many smaller buildings built of the same golden stone in a place like Bath, for instance.

A long, straight path led from the gate to the front door, providing plenty of time for butterflies to take up residence inside her. She recognized that it was not just intimidation of the place affecting her, but of its owners. Mr. Chamberlain probably wasn't even home; in her experience men weren't usually home for morning visits, but she couldn't help but wonder if being in his home would reveal more about him. She had also spent a few moments prior to the visit contemplating how she would avoid revealing to Lady Chamberlain that she had refused to dance with her son last evening. She thought she would probably manage as long as Lady Chamberlain didn't ask her directly again if he had asked her to dance.

It was such a trivial thing to worry about and completely unlikely that the subject would come up, so Julia had brushed aside her concerns.

Lady Chamberlain received them in an elegant drawing room that befitted the Barrington Court estate. The fine furnishings could have caused her visitors to feel more acutely the difference in their stations, but Lady Chamberlain's informality prevented it. She welcomed them with real gratitude for their visit and asked a servant to bring in refreshments. She made sure that Julia and Martha were comfortable before she sat down herself. It was only then that Julia realized how eager their hostess was to discuss last night's party. She began by asking, "Miss North, you mentioned that you saw Henry dancing with Miss Clifton last evening, didn't you?"

The abruptness of the question caught her off guard and she wasn't sure what reply to give. She hesitantly answered, "Yes, I saw them dance together. I believe it was shortly before Martha and I left."

"Were they together most of the evening?"

"I'm not sure. It did seem to me as though wherever Mr. Chamberlain went, Miss Clifton was nearby."

Lady Chamberlain seemed disappointed by her answer. "You don't think he showed a marked preference for her?"

"I'm not . . . um . . . I don't know your son well enough to say." Julia's words were true. She wished she could tell just from observing him what his thoughts and feelings were. But all she had noticed was that he didn't mind the admiration he was surrounded by. It didn't seem that he showed a preference for Miss Clifton's admiration more than the other young ladies, but he hadn't been annoyed by it either.

Lady Chamberlain turned her attention to Martha, "Did you notice if Henry was particularly attentive to Miss Clifton during the dancing last night?" She clarified her question by stating, "I was visiting with Mrs. Stephens and didn't pay attention like I should have."

Martha smiled politely and said, "No I didn't notice any behavior out of the ordinary. Henry danced with her I believe, but I don't think he gave her any more of his attention than he usually does."

"I asked Mrs. Thurston after you left if she had noticed anything between them and she told me that Henry had stepped out into the hall for several minutes with Miss Clifton before coming back in and dancing with her."

"I'm sure Henry was merely being helpful as Miss Clifton often has something or other that she needs help with. Did you ask Henry about it?" There was something in Martha's voice that made Julia think she already knew the answer to that question.

"Yes, Henry was disinclined to tell me much of anything, though. You know how everyone knows every detail of his life before he ever thinks to tell his own mother."

Julia had been with Martha for a little over a week now and even in that short time she had gained a few insights into her character. As her cousin patiently answered Lady Chamberlain's questions, Julia could hear the underlying amusement she felt at her friend's obsession with her son. It became clear to Julia that Martha was very used to having these conversations with Lady Chamberlain and that she was quite capable of calming her down.

"I don't think Henry has the kind of character that shares his deepest feelings openly with anyone, Lady Chamberlain. So I'm sure there is no need to think anyone will know his heart before you do."

Lady Chamberlain looked skeptical at this observation, but finally admitted, "That could be true. I will definitely pay better attention next time. I have been asking Henry about it since last night and he has denied that he has any special feeling for her, but it could possibly be that he just isn't ready to admit it yet."

With a consoling voice Martha replied, "It's much more likely that he isn't ready to fall in love again."

Lady Chamberlain looked grieved. "I just want him to be happy. I wish there was some way I could give him the happiness he deserves."

"You are a good and kind mother to him; right now I'm sure that's all he needs."

Again, Julia had the distinct impression that this was a regular exchange between these two women.

After a somber moment or two, Lady Chamberlain looked over at Julia again and said, "I had hoped my son might be interested in you, Miss North."

Julia's eyebrows went up in surprise and her eyes darted involuntarily to Martha, who she knew had the opposite hope. She couldn't think of an appropriate response to such a statement, but Lady Chamberlain made one unnecessary by continuing, "We meet with all the same families so often that I had hoped a new young lady in our midst would be the one to finally catch his interest. If only he would agree to spend the season in London, I'm sure he would fall in love, but he refuses to go. I stay here with him now, while his father attends Parliament alone every year. I just can't leave the poor boy on his own."

It was quite an uncomfortable position to be in, listening to his mother talk about his private matters so openly. Julia knew that if she expressed an opinion that Lady Chamberlain would read far too much into it.

Knowing the consequences of her offhanded comment last night, Julia was quite nervous to say anything. She felt she needed to think over each word before she said it to be sure it couldn't be misinterpreted in some way. Any opinion on the subject would only continue the discussion and Julia was ready for a change of topic at the very least. Hoping to achieve that, she said, "London does have plenty of variety, but I don't think it can compare to the beauty of Somerset. I have so enjoyed exploring Barrington."

"Henry isn't interested in the variety of London either; he prefers to be at Barrington Court above anything else." Her change of topic hadn't worked and now they were apparently going to discuss Mr. Chamberlain's likes and dislikes.

"Did you not think him handsome?" Lady Chamberlain asked. Julia was slightly incredulous she was being asked this again. No one could deny that Henry Chamberlain was handsome, but a discussion of it would only make her sound hopelessly smitten, which she was very conscientiously trying not to be, so she just smiled slightly and nodded.

Her less than rapturous response wasn't satisfying to Lady Chamberlain and she said, "He was just as handsome as a boy too. The truly remarkable thing about Henry is that it hasn't spoiled his character. He is always a perfect gentleman. Did you not think so, Miss North?"

Julia was almost surprised at herself for not hesitating with her answer. "Yes." Reflecting on it, she realized it was true. He had teased her, and he seemed arrogant with all the attention he received, but despite that, his manners were disarming. Then, because Lady Chamberlain was still looking at her expectantly she added, "Quite gentlemanly."

Julia could tell it wasn't as much praise as Lady Chamberlain had been hoping for, but Julia wasn't about to say more. Lady Chamberlain asked several more questions, trying to prompt Julia into admitting admiration for her son. She was grateful when her diplomatic answers led Lady Chamberlain to take up his praises herself.

A sigh escaped her when Lady Chamberlain finally paused for breath, prompting Martha to say, "Julia, why don't you go for your walk and I'll meet you at home later?"

"Do you really not mind?" she asked, already beginning to rise. Martha reassured her it was fine, and after bidding Lady Chamberlain goodbye, Julia gratefully let herself out. Lady Chamberlain's questions had kept her tense through the whole visit and she felt her escape keenly. Once she reached the main gate, she felt the freedom to take a deep breath and she turned away from the village, hoping for a silent walk in the countryside after the interview with Lady Chamberlain.

The day hadn't passed over to afternoon yet, but Henry felt as though he had already had a long day. Last evening, his mother had insisted on riding home in his carriage and had asked him subtly at first, but gradually more directly, if he was thinking of courting again. He had insisted he wasn't. Then this morning, she had sent for him to come up to the main house for breakfast and repeated her questions about whether he was forming serious intentions for any young lady. Miss North had immediately come to mind. He was starting to think he might want to court her. But it was the last thing he would ever admit to his mother.

Henry hadn't been able to guess what had caused his mother's sudden suspicions, but something had set her off. He had given vague answers to her subtle questions and waited for her to give specific reasons for her suspicions so Henry could refute them. Finally, his mother had said, "Miss North mentioned that you and Miss Clifton were inseparable last evening. Are you sure you aren't thinking of courting Miss Clifton? Because you can tell me, you know."

He had been startled for a moment when his mother had said Miss North's name, and he could only be relieved when his mother named Miss Clifton as the one she thought he was interested in. He didn't even want to admit to himself, much less his mother, what his real feelings were for Miss North. It was strange that the blame for his interrogation was because of something Miss North had said. Why would she say such a thing to his mother, of all people?

Henry reassured his mother more times than he could count that he wasn't at all interested in Miss Clifton. His reassurance left his mother looking disappointed and, knowing he couldn't change that, he escaped to the stables and off on a ride. It had been refreshing and helped restore his optimism that his mother would let the subject drop . . . eventually.

He was just returning from his ride and as he made his way to the stable, he saw Miss North walking down the west lane. Her back was to him, but he could tell that it was her by the way she held herself. Changing his course, he rode toward her. He dismounted and called out, "Miss North!"

She stopped and turned back and he could see her reluctant expression right away, but he didn't let that deter him. "May I accompany you on your walk?"

"Er, yes, of course."

Henry knew that it was his abrupt appearance and direct question that had caused her to say yes. She looked as though she would rather not have his company, an unusual reaction in his experience, but he chose to ignore that and accompany her anyway. If she was going to be in Barrington for two months, she would need to understand a few things about his mother. His horse drifted to the side of the lane as they walked, keeping Henry between his horse and Miss North.

"You spoke with my mother last night." It was a statement, but he waited for her to confirm it.

She closed her eyes briefly before answering, "Yes, before we left."

Making sure there was no accusation in his voice, Henry said, "I'm sure you didn't mean to, but a comment of yours has inadvertently made quite a bit of trouble for me."

Miss North winced at his statement and he realized that she had likely just come from speaking with his mother. He gave a rueful smile and said, "I don't blame you, Miss North. You didn't know of course, but my mother is like a tenacious bloodhound. You have to be so careful around her. I'm sure you only made some small comment as an observation, but she has hounded me ceaselessly since last night, trying to get me to admit I'm in love with Miss Clifton."

She held up her hands as if to hold off any accusations, "Yes, I don't doubt it. I have just spent the last hour being questioned by her myself," she confirmed. She looked slightly overwhelmed by remembering the conversation with his mother. With wide eyes she gently shook her head. "Why is she so overly concerned about you?"

Mr. Chamberlain looked at her with some surprise, "Surely you've heard my history by now, that I was engaged a few years ago but my fiancée . . ." He paused momentarily. Even after all this time it was difficult for him to speak of it. ". . . She died, tragically, a few weeks before the wedding."

She cleared her throat uncomfortably but met his eyes as she kindly responded, "I did hear about that; Martha told me what happened."

"Yes, well, my mother is convinced that I won't be happy again until I . . . find another young lady I want to marry." He had been about to say "fall in love again," but stopped himself, not wanting to sound emotional about it anymore.

Miss North looked thoughtful for a moment and then said, "I wonder if your mother thinks her interference is helpful."

"I doubt she has considered the fact that her extreme interest is actually hurting her cause. I do try to be quite careful about whom I speak with and for how long when I know she is watching." After a moment he added with candor, "It's actually exhausting. Every time I have to be in company with her is such an unpleasant task."

Miss North smiled, obviously thinking he was exaggerating. "Have you ever considered just picking one of the many young ladies you frequently encounter, and courting her to appease your mother? At least then she wouldn't worry over you anymore."

He looked at her with raised eyebrows. With a gentle shake of his head he explained, "You really don't know my mother if you think that. If I were to give any young lady even a hint that I intended to court her, my mother would start planning the wedding. The pressure would not abate; it would increase tenfold."

Henry was watching her in profile as she laughed at that. And he could see that from her point of view his predicament must seem a little ridiculous. Reluctantly he smiled too. "It is quite a farce, isn't it?"

"It's obvious to even an outsider like me that your mother loves you very much," she replied. "If your biggest misfortune in life is too much love, you are fortunate indeed." As soon as the words were said, she suddenly turned toward him with a horrified look that at first quite startled Henry. "I don't mean you, but rather one . . . one whose misfortune is too much love. I, I wasn't . . . or rather I didn't mean to imply that you have not had much worse misfortune . . ."

Interestingly, Henry had been feeling today like his mother really was his greatest trial in life. He hated to admit it, but Miss Corey was fading from his memory. He noticed that Miss North was looking extremely embarrassed. Trying to reassure her, he said, "I understood your meaning. Do not trouble yourself about it. You are right. Compared to others, I have very little to complain of." But still she kept her gaze averted.

After a moment of uncomfortable silence passed, his horse suddenly nudged its head between them. An involuntary squeal emerged from Miss North and she jumped to the edge of the path. His horse was startled by her reaction, causing it to prance quickly back from them and shake its mane as it huffed out a startled noise too.

Miss North regained her composure quickly, or at least tried to. Henry could hear a tremor in her voice as she let out a nervous giggle and said, "Oh, that startled me. I'm sorry to have distressed your horse like that. He just took me by surprise is all."

Henry gave her a questioning look. She was obviously very frightened by his horse, but was not about to admit it. "What were you saying before?" she asked.

She so obviously didn't want to discuss the fact that she was terrified of a horse. Henry gave her one more long look before replying, "As I was saying, I have much to be grateful for." He thought about all the blessings in his, despite losing Miss Corey. Keeping it light, he said, "My health . . . my horse . . ." After a longer pause he added, "My horse's health."

She laughed at his quip, which is exactly what he had hoped for. "And a wonderful mother," she said decisively, seeming to regain her confidence. His humor had erased her embarrassment so much more effectively than his reassurance.

"And a wonderful mother," he conceded. "Thank you for reminding me. Perhaps as a repayment I could teach you how to ride."

Her smile instantly disappeared. A flush crept up her cheeks and she turned away from him. Henry couldn't help but notice, even looking at just her profile, how the pink in her cheeks made her cheekbones more prominent and she looked even more beautiful. By her embarrassed reaction, it was obvious that she hated to be so transparent. She didn't answer right away, and he could tell she was trying to think of a polite way to say no or, more likely, an excuse. She finally looked back at him and shook her head, "I'd rather not."

Henry had learned how to be persistent from the many young ladies he had known and he used that skill now by not letting her turn him down. He just acted as though she had said yes. "We can start tomorrow if you would like. I can meet you after breakfast. But we should meet in one of the back pastures so my mother doesn't find out. She would think a simple horse riding lesson was reason to plan a wedding." Then remembering that Miss North had just convinced him to be grateful for his mother, he tacked on, "It's really to spare her feelings that we should meet in private."

There was no hesitation this time as she replied, "I don't particularly want to learn how to ride a horse. But thank you for offering."

Henry stopped on the path, and his horse took several steps closer before stopping too and bending down to graze. Miss North had stopped when he had, but took a telling extra step away as his horse approached them.

"This is Felix," Henry said, reaching his hand out to pat his horse on the neck. "He's a very athletic horse, but he is very calm around people." He paused, wondering if that reassurance would be enough for her to approach. It wasn't. "I have several gentle horses that you could take your pick from. Why don't you try it just once?"

Miss North looked a bit desperate as she responded, "I just don't think it's necessary. Why should I learn to ride when I can always walk or go by carriage?"

"There are plenty of reasons," he responded. Miss North looked up suddenly, as if she feared what the reasons might be. Henry felt curious about her response, but continued, "As much as we rely on horses, it doesn't seem wise to fear them. In many ways, riding is safer. At least the rider is in control. In a carriage, you are completely at the mercy of the driver." Perhaps he shouldn't have given that reason, but it was the one that carried the most weight with him.

Miss North visibly swallowed and nodded. "I understand why you would think so, but it seems to me that when you are riding, you would be at the mercy of the horse." As if to further emphasize, she gestured toward

Felix and said, "He could decide to run away with you any time and you'd be stuck up there on his back."

The thought had never crossed Henry's mind. "That would never happen with my horses," he reassured. "They are too well trained to even consider it. They are so calm, in fact, that you might find you actually like it." Then thinking of one more reason, he added, "Besides, I can't stand the thought of a friend of mine being terrified of horses when I could help it."

Miss North scrunched her eyes shut for a moment, as if gaining courage, and said, "Very well. I'll try, at least once, to learn to ride."

Henry didn't realize how much he really wanted her to agree until she said yes. He was pleased with the small victory. And wanting to build on that, he asked, "Will you come with me now to return Felix to the stable?"

She hesitated again before saying, "I don't think I should. You wouldn't want anyone to see us together and jump to a false conclusion after all. I'll just finish my walk."

Henry was surprised by her again. He wasn't used to being told no even once, but Miss North did it repeatedly. Every young lady he knew wanted to be seen with him. He was intrigued by her and began to wonder if spending more time with her would lead to something more. He had avoided anything of the sort for so long, but now the thought of moving on only caused a brief feeling of guilt, quickly replaced by anticipation as he thought of spending more time with Miss North.

Henry wouldn't let her walk away until she had arranged to meet him during her morning walk in three day's time in a pasture out of sight of Barrington Court. He would have liked to start sooner, but he had remembered that Mr. Dunn would be arriving sometime today and would stay for at least one night, possibly two if he could convince him. Hopefully they could finally conclude their business. Henry was certain that he had finally convinced Mr. Dunn that their agreement would be to everyone's benefit and Henry anticipated the pride he would feel at finally accomplishing something on his own.

He let Felix graze a few more moments as he watched Miss North walk down the path until a bend took her from his view. She didn't look back once. It made him want to pursue her even more. Henry pulled Felix reluctantly away from his patch of grass to return to the stable.

Miss Abbot had told him once that his heart would heal when he wasn't noticing. He hadn't believed her then; it hadn't seemed possible. But perhaps she had been right after all, and perhaps it was her own cousin, Miss North, who had helped him realize it.

Miss Abbot had always lived in Barrington and had always been a good friend of his mother. But it was after Miss Corey's death that the older lady became his friend as well. After the funeral, she had been the first person whose words had actually been comforting. He had never known her history but she had told him how she had also lost the only one she had ever loved before their wedding. Just knowing he wasn't the only one to ever feel that overwhelming pain helped enough that when Miss Abbot suggested he leave for a time while he grieved, he had been able to make that decision. She had given a compelling reason. "You will be allowed to grieve for a short time, but your friends and your family will want to see you happy again. Every young lady who was filled with disappointment when you announced your engagement is now filled with false sorrow and hope." Henry couldn't have put it into words as she had, but he had already sensed the same thing. He had received too many looks of pity while his hands were squeezed for uncomfortably long moments not to notice. Miss Abbot's advice had been so true. She had said, "It's going to be miserable for a time. Just let yourself be miserable. Keep taking care of yourself, don't stay in one place too long, send plenty of letters home to your parents, and just be as sad as you want through it all."

Incapable of even making a decision, he had asked, "How long should I be gone for? Until I'm ready for my mother to find me a new bride? I'll never return."

"You *may* never be ready for a new bride, but you should still come home. Come back when you feel like you can cope with your mother." She had smiled because she knew how his mother was, but they were still dear friends. "Time will be the best thing for you, Henry. Even though you can't imagine it now, someday while you aren't paying attention, your heart will heal and you'll be ready to fall in love again."

Henry had hated it when every other person had said something similar, but Miss Abbot's words had been comforting. Knowing she had had the same experience made all the difference. He hadn't truly believed her words for himself. But now, that long ago sadness had been so muted that he hardly felt it. Time and the arrival of Miss North may have been just what his heart had needed.

Chapter 11

On the morning of her riding lesson, Julia's maid helped her dress in her simplest gown with sturdy fabric. Her maid's quiet, "Are you sure you want this 'un, miss?" as she pulled the buttons together let her know the gown wasn't flattering, but she didn't have a riding habit, so this would have to do. She made the same kind of choices with her gloves and bonnet, choosing the ones she cared about least for this unknown adventure.

Julia hoped Martha wouldn't notice her nervousness. She had never wanted to learn to ride and had admitted to herself that the reason was that she was a bit afraid of horses. When Mr. Chamberlain's horse had surprised her the other day, it had been an intense panic that made her jump away in fright. But still, she had thought her fear was because it had been so unexpected. Now that she had agreed to a lesson with Mr. Chamberlain, she realized she was more afraid than she even knew. Her stomach swirled and her breakfast stayed on her plate. Julia wanted to spend the rest of her life in Barrington, enjoying quiet breakfasts and peaceful walks, so it was imperative that Martha not find out she was meeting Mr. Chamberlain. Her cousin would never want a companion who went directly against her wishes. Julia's first goal was to get an invitation to return permanently after Harriet's wedding; learning to ride was part of her back-up plan if she still had to return to London and try to find a husband. At least it would be one flaw out of the way.

She was overly cheerful when she announced her intention to go walking. But she had done the same thing every morning of her visit and her cousin was so used to her habit that she didn't seem to notice.

Julia had to walk about a mile before arriving at the pasture Mr. Chamberlain had designated for their lesson. As she walked, she tried again to talk herself out of being fascinated by him. But the more she knew of him, the more he consumed her thoughts. She was beginning to realize that it was more than his circumstances as a tragic hero that she found so interesting. When she was with him, their conversation consumed all her attention, a trick he had obviously perfected. Yet even though she knew he had no interest in her beyond friendship, she had to reluctantly admit that he was often on her mind.

She saw Mr. Chamberlain waiting for her with two horses, saddled and grazing. She glanced around, wondering whom the second horse was for. She saw at the far side of the pasture that there was a man who must be a groom leaning against a tree, but it was quite obvious that their distant chaperone wouldn't be joining in the lesson. Her nervous gaze returned to Mr. Chamberlain. He watched her approach and Julia briefly wondered if he thought her dress was hideous, but there was a much more pressing issue. "Why do I need two horses to learn to ride?"

He glanced at the horses and back at her, "One is for you and I've brought Felix for me."

"We're both riding?" she asked with alarm in her voice.

He looked concerned, like he didn't know what she expected, or what he should say. Julia had thought she would sit on a horse for a few minutes while Mr. Chamberlain led it around in circles. Harriet had taken a few lessons years ago, and that was all Julia had observed from a safe distance.

She raised her hands to her cheeks and looked at the horses again. She recognized Felix; he was brown. The new horse was honey-colored and must be for her. She realized her hands had drifted to her mouth and she was biting at a nail through her glove. She pulled her hands back quickly and turned to Mr. Chamberlain, who was watching her with a concerned look. "Miss North, we'll start very slow, and I won't make you do anything that's too difficult." He finished with an encouraging smile that felt completely patronizing to Julia.

That patronizing smile was all too familiar. It was the exact expression that he used for Miss Clifton. He was looking at her in just the same way and she felt pathetic. Another reminder that she shouldn't be fascinated by him. For her, every conversation with Mr. Chamberlain drew her to him more. But he saw her just the same as he saw all the other infatuated young ladies who threw themselves at him.

His condescending smile was the challenge she needed. She wasn't any less afraid, but she could face it. "I am frightened of horses, which means this will be difficult no matter what, but I'll manage." She said it with a determined nod of her head and took a few steps closer to the horses. She couldn't quite touch them, but she reached a hand toward the honey-colored horse and asked, "What's this one's name?"

When Mr. Chamberlain didn't answer after a moment she looked up to find him regarding her thoughtfully. She thought that his slight smile looked to be admiring now. Ridiculous. Her words had showed her determined nature. Her mother had insisted she always act demurely with all the gentlemen of her acquaintance because her spirited behavior would be found objectionable to any man.

He finally replied, "Pegasus. Your horse's name is Pegasus." Julia was alarmed again, but before she could protest riding a horse with that name, he said, "Relax, he doesn't fly. It's hard to get Pegasus to move above a trot. I named him as a pony and he just never lived up to his name."

"Pegasus." Julia slowly nodded her head, looking at Mr. Chamberlain; then she turned to look at the horse she would ride. "Thank you for not living up to your name."

Her acceptance signaled the beginning of the lesson and Mr. Chamberlain was very calm and confident as he named and described everything. He patted her horse down his neck as he spoke and encouraged her to come closer and do the same. Knowing Pegasus was such a lazy horse really helped her confidence, and for the first time ever, Julia touched a horse voluntarily.

With a big grin at her progress, Mr. Chamberlain said, "The last thing is mounting, but I didn't want to haul a mounting block all the way out here, so I will help you onto your horse. And of course your sidesaddle is facing left, but you always mount from the left anyway."

He closed the distance between them and Julia drew in a quick breath and froze. Her body must have visibly stiffened because Mr. Chamberlain paused with his hands reaching for her waist.

"Don't be frightened. I promise Pegasus won't run off with you."

He thought it was her fear of horses that had caused her reaction. She hadn't been thinking that Pegasus would run off with her, but now that he had reminded her of the idea, it was as alarming as his nearness. He was waiting for her response.

"Are you certain?" she asked nervously.

"Yes."

"What would you do if he did? You can't ever really be in control of an animal that has a mind of its own."

He was standing quite close and Julia was entranced at the amusement in his eyes and the quirk of his mouth as he said, "Trust me, I know this horse and he tries to *never* run, but if he did today for any reason, then you could pull hard on the reins to stop him, and if that didn't work then Felix and I would run after you and save you."

Julia turned to stare at the saddle on Pegasus's back so Mr. Chamberlain wouldn't see her smile at that. Turning back, she said, "I trust you. I'm ready."

His eyes looked like he was admiring her again, but Julia didn't focus on that. She was looking down as his hands wrapped around her waist. She quickly placed her hands on his forearms to keep her balance as he lifted her into the saddle. Even through her gloves she could feel his muscles tighten as he lifted her.

Mr. Chamberlain picked up the reins, handed them to her, and walked over to Felix. He pulled himself up in a fluid movement and turned to her, smiling. "Shall we have a race, Miss North?"

Julia glanced down at the beast she was riding and had no control over, and then met Mr. Chamberlain's eyes with false pity. "I'll spare you the embarrassment of losing to a novice like me. No race today."

"Which implies that another day you'll say yes. I'd better teach you to gallop so you have a chance."

Julia clenched the reins in her hand at the thought of galloping. But she pasted a bright smile on her face when she looked up. "As long as you teach me to stop first."

Mr. Chamberlain chuckled and then nudged his horse forward. "Let's try a walk around the field. Pegasus will probably just follow Felix, so you can just give him a nudge and try to hold his head up so he doesn't stop to graze." Felix began to walk, although she couldn't see what Henry had done to make him move—some nudge she hadn't seen—but Pegasus began a slow walk after them and Julia felt her whole body tense as she tried to hold on tight to both the reins and the saddle.

Mr. Chamberlain looked back at her and in an assuring voice said, "That's fine, just try to relax a little. If you are too stiff, riding will feel jarring."

Julia forced her muscles to loosen and felt herself sliding in the saddle as Pegasus followed Felix without any urging from her. In her sidesaddle position, she began to slide toward the ground. She scooted backward in the saddle too far to keep from falling and her behind went over the edge of the back of the saddle. She held on tightly to the reins but couldn't right herself.

"Henryyy!" she screamed. She'd never called him anything but Mr. Chamberlain; she didn't even think of him as Henry in her mind, but as she slid toward the ground his name came out at a high squeal.

She descended to the ground backside first with her legs above her, sliding down the horse's side. Pegasus stopped walking and her hold on the reins meant it was a slow slide, but she still landed on her backside with her feet in the air resting against Pegasus. Her long skirts stayed pinned between her feet and the horse. It didn't hurt at all, but it was surely the most ridiculous fall off a horse that had ever occurred. All Julia could do was lean back on one elbow before Mr. Chamberlain had dismounted and was there, trying for a sober expression and failing miserably. He had been ahead of her, not looking back, and she wished more than anything that she hadn't called out his name. Then, perhaps, he wouldn't have witnessed the most embarrassing moment of her life.

Again.

She let go of the reins and used her free hand to cover her eyes, wishing to be unseen as easily. With the reins loose, her legs finally landed on the ground as Pegasus stepped away.

There was a long pause and Julia wondered how hard he must have been struggling not to laugh. "Let me teach you how to dismount," she finally heard Henry say. There was a tremor in his voice, and Julia moved her hand away from her eyes to look at him and see that his eyes were shining with what could only be amusement.

Julia rolled away from him and stood up. "I've already dismounted for the last time ever!" she declared as she moved a few steps away from him and both horses.

"But Miss North, we've barely begun," he cajoled. "Your, er, . . . fall was just a little setback."

"No, it was a sign that I should never ride a horse. I can't believe I even thought to try." Julia was ready to bid him goodbye and flee from his presence.

His expression was thoughtful again and he said, "Interesting. When I decided to bring Pegasus for you today, I really thought yours was the stronger character." Julia looked up in hurt surprise at the insult. But Mr. Chamberlain continued, "I've seen you hunt and catch your prey; I've seen you defy even the politest request for a dance," he smiled in a self-deprecating way, "and you've even been interrogated by my mother and lived to tell about it. Surely you aren't going to let Pegasus get the better of you?"

Julia took in a deep breath and released it slowly. It wasn't an insult; it was a compliment, sort of. And it was definitely a challenge. And with it, she knew she had to try again. She could surely do better.

She cleared her throat. "Fine. But perhaps you could tell me *before* I climb in the saddle how to relax without sliding off the horse?"

A huge answering grin overtook his whole face, making his eyes crinkle up. He had never looked so attractive. *This man should be happy all the time,* she thought as he explained to her how to let her body move with the horse and keep a good posture.

Julia gathered her determination to once again face her foe. As Mr. Chamberlain pulled on the reins he spoke to the horse, "Pegasus, be a gentleman and try not to buck the lady off this time."

"A gentleman horse?" Julia asked. She thought of the horses she had seen pulling carriages around London. They all seemed so big and full of energy. Even when the carriages were standing still, the prancing steps of the horses caused the carriages to rock and sway. "Surely such a breed doesn't exist."

Mr. Chamberlain moved close to her again and set his hands on her waist, but paused with his hands there and said, "Well, perhaps not, but Pegasus is as close as they come. He'd never mistreat a lady."

After he lifted her up, Julia waited for her heart to slow down before concentrating on her posture. As Pegasus began to follow after Felix once again, she tried to move with the horse. It didn't feel natural and the jarring sensation was still there, but when she finally dared lift her eyes, she watched how Mr. Chamberlain moved and tried to mimic his posture. As they went around the pasture again, she felt a measure of success, and when he complimented her progress, she even smiled.

After leaving the pasture and walking home, Julia couldn't believe how happy she felt after riding a horse, and she had to give all the credit to Mr. Chamberlain. Despite Martha's warning that he had a permanently broken heart, it was getting harder and harder to resist the pull she felt each time she was with him. For a brief moment, she stopped resisting and daydreamed about being the one who earned his regard. If they courted, she would call him Henry always and he would challenge her, but help her succeed, too. If he courted her, they would dance together and walk together and he would be the best suitor she'd ever had. In fact, if he courted her and her mother insisted she marry Henry Chamberlain, Julia wouldn't feel as though she were being forced to marry at all. A strange thought for her, as the idea of marriage to any of her other suitors had left her feeling extremely reluctant. But if she could have her choice, he would be it.

Her daydreams carried along until she realized the inevitable: she couldn't have her choice. He would lose interest in her just as her other suitors had. He wasn't even a suitor and that thought caused a pang in her chest that made her catch her breath. In fact, they were meeting in private for riding lessons so that no one would think he was her suitor. Could it be any clearer that he didn't want to court her? The connection she felt to him must just be in her mind. She took a few deep breaths to stop tears from forming, which was ridiculous; she had never cried over any man.

Why was Henry different from them? Well, obviously he wasn't actually her suitor. But besides that, she realized that when those other gentlemen had decided they didn't want to marry her, she had known that they didn't really know her. They knew the girl that her mother insisted she be when being courted. She was proper. She put on an air of humility when she announced her accomplishments. She never tried to prove herself when challenged. And she *never* embarrassed herself. But Henry did know her. If she let herself be fascinated by him and let her daydreams take flight, it would be devastating when he rejected her. He didn't want a wife, but even if Julia somehow convinced him to court her, he would eventually reject her, not just the version of her that her mother insisted on in front of suitors. In fact, Julia had to admit, Henry had already seen far more of her faults than she had allowed suitors to see before. His first impression of her to his last must be of a girl with no poise at all.

When Julia thought about staring into his eyes when he had paused before helping her on the horse, she was sure her heart missed a beat. But it must just be the effect he had on all young ladies. Perhaps that was why so many had their hopes set on him. He gave them hope without even realizing it. His condescending smiles earlier had certainly put her in her place. She would just have to remember that he was treating her the same way he treated all the young ladies he knew, giving her a careful amount of attention, but never enough to actually be mistaken for courting.

Chapter 12

$\mathcal{H}$enry truly thought he had convinced his mother that he wasn't forming an attachment to Miss Clifton. But when he arrived at Barrington Court for Saturday dinner as he always did, he found Miss Clifton alone in the drawing room.

He paused a moment, finding himself caught off guard, but then addressed his mother's guest. "Miss Clifton, good afternoon."

"Hello, Mr. Chamberlain." She stood up quickly and approached him. Henry backed away a little.

"I expected to find my mother here with her guests. Where is she, do you know?"

She smiled brightly and inclined her head toward him, as though she was telling him a secret. "She is showing my parents and Mrs. Thurston the new layout she has planned for her rose garden."

Ah yes, his mother's rose garden. "You did not join them?" It was a stupid question, of course.

"I'm not so interested in roses, so your mother suggested I wait here."

Of course she did. Henry was surprised with himself for not expecting this. It wasn't like him to be caught off guard by his mother's schemes. He had been looking forward to joining his mother and her guests today, and his anticipation had made him forgetful.

He had expected Miss North to be one of the guests.

He glanced at the door to make sure he had left it open. Relieved that he had, he resigned himself to a few minutes of conversation with Miss Clifton. She wasn't an unattractive girl, with blue eyes and blonde hair. Henry was certain he had heard her mother describe on more than one occasion how sought after her daughter was by other gentlemen. But Henry had always thought her eyes a little too close together and her nose a little too long. Really though, nothing she said ever held his attention.

To give himself space, Henry walked over to the window where he would have a view of any other guests as they arrived. "Do you know who else my mother is expecting for dinner today?" Miss Abbot usually joined them and if she was coming, Miss North would be too.

Miss Clifton crossed the room and joined him at the window before responding. "You are the last to arrive, I believe. Your mother said we wouldn't dine without you and suggested I wait here in case you came while they were out in the garden." While he was adjusting to the disappointment, he felt her hand touch his shoulder and trail to his elbow. "Large gatherings are preferable most of the time, but don't you think an intimate family dinner is more enjoyable occasionally?"

Henry warily glanced down and saw her looking up at him with a doting look in her eyes. He was intelligent enough to know what his mother had in mind. She would want to walk in the room and catch him in a moment just like this. Despite all his denials—or perhaps because of them—his mother hoped he had feelings for Miss Clifton. The trap was far too obviously laid for him not to see it. She must think that if Henry were left alone in a room with Miss Clifton that he wouldn't be able to deny his feelings any longer. It was ridiculous the lengths his mother would go to, but it was more ridiculous that her plan had almost worked. Not that he had feelings for Miss Clifton, but if anyone saw them in this moment, it would be difficult to deny. Henry took a large step back and gestured to the room with an arm out. "Shall we sit while we wait for the others, Miss Clifton?" he asked as formally as possible.

She gave him another smile—far too bright for a response to his inane suggestion—and sat to one side of the sofa, patting the space next to her gently. Henry almost smiled at that. Not for the wide world would he sit next to her. Ignoring her gesture, he took a chair as far across the room as he could get. "How is Anthony doing?" he asked, knowing Miss Clifton couldn't be flirtatious during a conversation about her brother in the army. And his strategy worked. A few minutes more passed before his mother, along with Mr. and Mrs. Clifton and Mrs. Thurston, entered the drawing room. Henry made sure the look on his face was bored; he even went so far as to yawn. It was a fine line he walked: making sure his indifferent feelings were understood without offending Miss Clifton's sensibilities. "I'm starving, Mother. Let's eat."

His mother looked at him, then across the room at Miss Clifton. She looked disappointed, for which Henry could only be grateful. "Where are your manners, Henry? We can't begin until all our guests have arrived."

Henry looked up eagerly as the sound of more people entering the hall reached his ears. "So sorry, Mother," he said. "I was under the impression that this was everyone."

With huge relief and the knowledge that his entire evening had just been salvaged, he watched Miss Abbot and Miss North enter the room. Henry took in Miss North's beautiful features as if checking them off a list: her brown hair, which looked darker as she stood in his mother's drawing room than it had out in the sunshine of the pasture; her brown eyes, which were a lighter brown than any he had seen before; her cheekbones, which always became more defined when she blushed but always gave her face elegance. But today he was distracted by a feature of hers that he shouldn't be. His gaze dropped to the hem of Miss North's light green gown, where he saw her slippered feet emerge and withdraw with each step as she crossed the room to greet his mother.

That very limited peek of her feet had him reliving the moment from the day before when he had caught a glimpse of her ankles. Immediately after beginning their riding lesson, he had heard a squeal of alarm, which made his heart race with fear, and he quickly glanced over his shoulder to see Miss North in a slow descent off her horse. He had never seen anything quite like it and his only reaction at first had been surprise. He had turned Felix around and dismounted in no time at all, worried that she might be hurt. But he could quickly see that although she was falling off Pegasus, it was a slow, backward descent.

The very nature of her backward slide had pulled her skirt down around her feet. Henry had stood over her as she lay on the ground with her legs leaning against the horse. Part of him was annoyed with himself for letting this happen; he knew how frightened Miss North was of horses and he should have started slower. But a larger part of him—knowing she wasn't hurt in the least—wanted to laugh out loud. It had been the most completely ungraceful thing a young lady had ever done in his presence. But then, her legs had landed on the ground as Pegasus stepped away. That was the moment the hem of her gown had flipped up, revealing her ankle boots and a good portion of both her legs. He had been on the verge of laughing, but the view of her slim ankles had chased the humor from him. All rational thought had left him, except perhaps the thought that remaining a bachelor for the rest of his days was unreasonable. His mouth had gone instantly dry and his voice wasn't completely steady when he had asked her if he could teach her to dismount. The moment of exposure had been brief and he was certain that Miss North had been too embarrassed over her fall to even notice. She had jumped up, ignoring the hand he had offered in assistance, and stomped away from Pegasus, but the memory of it was recurring. In her presence once again, his thoughts could hardly focus and he found himself staring at her feet.

"Henry what's the matter with you today?" he heard Miss Abbot ask. He was aware that conversation was going on around him; he just hadn't been paying attention. "I've greeted you twice and you haven't even looked up."

Henry lifted his gaze up directly into Miss North's golden brown eyes and saw the curious expression there before he turned to Miss Abbot to respond. But his mother spoke before he could, saying, "Ah, don't mind Henry. He's tired today. I keep catching him yawning, and now he can't do more than stare at the ground. Perhaps some food will revive him."

Henry placed a hand over his mouth to hide a guilty smile and let his mother lead them to the dining room.

The dinner was uneventful. Henry's thoughts hadn't completely settled, and as he wasn't seated near Miss North, he didn't make much effort to talk. After dinner, cards were suggested and no one objected, so the tables were soon arranged.

Henry waited for Miss North to state her preference before voicing his own so he could be sure to be at a table with her. Miss Clifton and her mother made up the rest of their quartet, and after agreeing to a game of whist, they cut the deck to decide partners. Henry was disappointed when he was partnered with Mrs. Clifton and her daughter partnered with Miss North.

Henry dealt the first round of cards, turned to Miss North on his left, and said, "You play first."

She gave him a questioning look and replied, "I already have." Henry glanced at the table in front of him and realized she had already begun.

It was soon evident that Miss North had a skill for strategy. Mrs. Clifton tried to support his play, but had no ideas or strategy of her own. Miss Clifton was another story altogether. Although partnered with Miss North, she kept laying down cards that helped him.

Despite her partner's traitorous play, Miss North still won more rounds than she lost. When he was dealt exceptional cards, he and Mrs. Clifton would win a few rounds, but it wasn't enough, and Miss North and Miss Clifton led the game. Henry found it fascinating to watch her expressive face as she played. She concentrated so much on the cards that she didn't contribute much to the conversation. He soon abandoned the conversation as well—Miss Clifton hardly needed single-word responses to keep talking—in favor of observing Miss North. He could almost read her cards on her face. She tried so hard to hold back a smile by twisting her mouth to one side when she was about to make a brilliant play, and when her cards were poor, she pulled both her lips between her teeth and pursed them. The second time he saw this reaction as she looked at her cards, he grinned in anticipation of finally scoring some easy points. Miss North still played her poor cards so strategically that he was impressed. He won the round, but it wasn't as easy as he had anticipated, even with both his partner and hers helping him.

After the final round was played they tallied the points. Miss North said, "Five points for us, which means we win." And she set down the slate and chalk in front of her with a look of satisfaction on her face.

Henry couldn't help but compliment her. "Miss North, it seems you are quite skilled at whist. Even with that terrible hand you still managed to win a point."

The grin that she had been holding back was bright now as she replied, "You're thinking of when I trumped your ace, aren't you Mr. Chamberlain?"

He couldn't help but smile back. "That's precisely what I'm referring to. I thought I would have a point that round for sure, but I can see now that when I play against you, I can never be sure of anything, even an ace."

"We were lucky, weren't we Miss North?" asked Miss Clifton, sounding annoyed at their good luck. "Mr. Chamberlain is the best card player; I don't think I've ever won a round against him."

Henry glanced at Miss Clifton as she spoke, then over at Miss North, wondering what her reaction would be. He was quite familiar with Miss Clifton deferring to him constantly. She was certainly not the only young lady to do so. He was resigned, when in the company of young ladies, to playing games of cards stacked in his favor. It seemed a trick that young ladies learned before they left the schoolroom to help them secure a husband. Henry was certain that all young ladies behaved that way with gentlemen. But Miss North had beaten him soundly and practically single-handedly. She even looked quite smug about it. The game was getting interesting.

Miss North finally responded to Miss Clifton, saying, "Perhaps his luck changed when I arrived." Henry wasn't sure if it was his luck that had changed with Miss North's arrival, but something was certainly different.

"Then it's a good thing you're just visiting, Miss North," Miss Clifton responded acerbically.

Henry saw Mrs. Clifton give a gentle shake of her head in reprimand to her daughter then jerk her head toward Henry while giving her daughter a meaningful glare. Did they honestly think he didn't see or notice all the silly posturing? He decided perhaps an end to card games was in order.

"I'll hope for better luck the next time I challenge Miss North to cards. Or rather, perhaps I'll study up on strategy, as I think luck had very little to do with it. Miss North and Miss Clifton, it was a well-deserved win. You are quite skilled." Henry said, including both young ladies in the compliment, although it was Miss North's skill alone that had impressed him. "Speaking of skill, I would love to hear some music this evening. Would you ladies be willing to entertain us?" Henry asked, again, including Miss Clifton when he would rather not.

When Henry asked if she would be willing to entertain their party by playing music, Julia very much wanted to answer "No." She loved playing cards; she was usually quite good at cards, but on the pianoforte, she was only just average. An answer from her was unnecessary, as Miss Clifton—her good nature instantly returning—readily agreed to Mr. Chamberlain's suggestion for both of them.

Despite Miss Clifton's presence, Julia had been having a wonderful evening up to this point. This was exactly what she had been hoping for when she first thought about leaving London. She didn't have to throw a card game to impress a suitor here.

Julia had reminded herself before she entered Barrington Court that Henry Chamberlain was not her suitor, and never would be. In London, with her mother looking on, she would play poorly when up against a gentleman that needed to be impressed. She didn't have to throw every hand, but just enough that she didn't quite win. For the most part, she enjoyed the strategy of it as well, to get as close as she could to victory without succeeding. Miss Clifton could take lessons from her on how to throw a game. It had been too obvious that she played her cards to help Mr. Chamberlain. But Julia had played to win, and it was the first time she had ever won a game against a single gentleman. The thought of playing the pianoforte for their small crowd tonight was quickly diminishing the thrill of her victory.

Miss Clifton sat at the instrument to play first. After selecting a piece that even from a distance Julia could tell was a difficult one, she began to play with admirable skill. Mr. Chamberlain approached Julia as she looked through a stack of Lady Chamberlain's music. "What are you going to favor us with, Miss North?"

"I haven't decided yet," she said as she flipped through the stack. Several were beyond her capabilities, and a few that she could play included lyrics, and she didn't want to sing. "It will be difficult to follow Miss Clifton's performance." She glanced over to the instrument where Miss Clifton's fingers flew up and down as she sang. Her voice wasn't exceptional, but her talented fingers made up for it.

She looked intentionally away from the superior performer and into Mr. Chamberlain's eyes instead to find he was giving her a knowing look. "Every young lady demures just as you are doing now, then sits down to play and astonishes the room with her talent."

"What if I'm the exception?" she couldn't help but ask.

There was a small *V* where his eyebrows met as he drew them together skeptically. Why did she find him even more handsome with such an expression? "Let me ask you a question," he said. "For how many years have you played the pianoforte?"

"I began lessons when I was ten, and learned until I was fourteen," she told him matter-of-factly. "Since then, I've practiced on my own. So I suppose that is eleven years that I have played."

"Do you not think that eleven years of experience will serve you well?"

"But only four years of lessons," she protested.

"Why did you stop taking lessons if you wanted to learn more?" he asked, and because his curiosity seemed genuine, she told him.

"It was my mother's decision to make, not mine. After four years, my governess had taught me all she knew. I wanted to take lessons from a London master, but my mother thought my skill was sufficient." Julia still regretted that she hadn't been able to learn more. Her mother's sentiment had been, "You have learned enough to impress any gentleman. All of them will want to have a talented wife, but none are too particular. They won't know the difference between something composed by Mozart or his worst student, so you don't need to either." Julia had wanted to be the very best, but all the practice in the world couldn't make up for deficiencies in knowledge. Just as with all else in her life, everything she said or did had to further her mother's purpose for her: securing a good match.

"Should we judge your performance this evening to see if she was right?" Mr. Chamberlain asked. Julia could see he was teasing by his raised brow and his mouth curving up on one side. He continued, "After you play, we can have each person rate how well you played. If you play very well, you will get a rating of 'exceptional,' if we can't even discern the tune, the rating will be 'poor,' and somewhere in the middle could be 'sufficient.'"

Julia rolled her eyes good-naturedly at his absurd suggestion. She understood that he thought she was far too concerned about public opinion. But men weren't subjected to the same standard of performance. "It won't be necessary; I can already predict what my rating would be. You, Lady Chamberlain, and my cousin would say I was 'exceptional' regardless of my performance. And the others, who would feel no obligation to be polite, would decline rating my performance at all." She paused a moment as she could picture the scene so easily. Her eyes darted toward Miss Clifton as she played, and she added without trying to disguise her sarcasm, "Perhaps Miss Clifton would even be so kind as to suggest I practice more."

Mr. Chamberlain was looking at her with a thoughtful expression. Julia worried that her response had revealed more of her insecurity than she had wanted to; he confirmed she had when he said, "It's a shame that you can't display some of your other talents in a drawing room."

Her "other talents," according to him would likely include hunting for flies and falling off horses. The real shame was that she had ever displayed them at all. Julia looked at the teasing glint in his emerald eyes and forgot what she had been about to say. She wanted to gather her wits to respond, but he shifted closer to her and held her gaze, and she couldn't bring herself to care that he would tease her. She felt on the verge of being mesmerized by his beautiful eyes.

Julia finally broke their gaze, swallowed once, and tried to resume breathing without him noticing that she had stopped. She knew this was his way and yet she almost fell for it.

In or out of a drawing room, this was his talent. Mesmerizing young ladies. She could tell that it wasn't even intentional. Henry Chamberlain didn't mean to make young ladies fall in love with him, it just happened. He probably didn't even know that his eyes were sending false messages that he would cherish her forever. Julia knew her response was too long in coming for him not to notice the pause, but still she forced herself to lean away. She crossed her arms as she did so and said with a challenge in her voice, "I was able to 'display' my talent for whist to my satisfaction."

An admirable recovery for her.

"True. I shouldn't have neglected mentioning your talent there." Julia had leaned away, but now, Mr. Chamberlain leaned closer than before to say, "In fact, your talent for strategy could be used outside of a drawing room as well. Wellington could surely use your skill to help plan his battles."

Julia moved her gaze to his left ear so she wouldn't get caught in his gaze once more. "If I was so good at strategizing, I would find a way out of displaying my poor skills at the pianoforte in front of everyone."

"Ah, too easy for a skilled strategist such as yourself." His response surprised her a little and she made the mistake of looking into his eyes again. "You could easily claim some headache and no one would press you to perform. But, if you could come up with a strategy that didn't include any little falsehood, I'd be truly in awe of your talent."

Julia shook her head at the impossibility of the challenge, but her eyes were still on his. Suddenly she had an idea and narrowed her eyes in thought. "Do you play, Mr. Chamberlain?"

He shook his head. "Thankfully I do not." He was smiling, probably thinking his lack of ability had foiled her plan.

"Perfect," she responded. "I think it would be quite gallant of you to play next, a very poor performance so that mine will sound better in comparison." Julia raised her eyebrows at Mr. Chamberlain, pushing her challenge.

His smile turned to a look of surprise, and perhaps even a hint of awe at her strategy. He looked like he was about to admit just as much, but then something over her shoulder caught his attention and he just said, "A commendable strategy indeed, Miss North." With a nod of his head he moved away and Julia wondered for a moment about his abrupt departure. Turning to look over her shoulder, she saw Lady Chamberlain and realized why he had left. Just when she was on the verge of forgetting herself, she realized his attention was carefully rationed and she had had her share.

She watched Mr. Chamberlain move across the room and begin speaking with her cousin and Mrs. Thurston instead. Resigned, Julia turned her attention back to the pages of music in front of her and tried to concentrate, finally finding one with a pretty tune but no words. It was a piece she had played in public before, and she knew it would please her audience. Miss Clifton was playing her third piece and before she finished, Mr. Chamberlain had left Martha and Mrs. Thurston and was standing by the instrument, giving her his attention. Julia felt a bit deflated. She knew already that Mr. Chamberlain had no intentions toward Miss Clifton, but watching him treat Miss Clifton with the same careful attention he treated her reminded her that he had no intentions toward her either. Julia shouldn't have been, but she was a tiny bit pleased when Mr. Chamberlain's full attention caused Miss Clifton to make a mistake as she played.

After escorting Miss Clifton to the sofa, Mr. Chamberlain returned directly to the instrument and sat down. Julia just stared in surprise. Was he really going to do it? He looked her direction and smiled, probably at the look of astonishment that must be evident on her face, and announced, "I have decided to favor you all with a short performance of my own this evening."

Julia heard Lady Chamberlain ask, "Henry, what are you about?" but he didn't pause to answer. With dramatic flair he played "The Grand Old Duke of York" for his mother's surprised guests, one finger at a time. Julia tried her best not to laugh out loud, but when he sped up then slowed down dramatically for a grand finish, a small "pbfft" escaped her lips.

After Mr. Chamberlain finished, he stood up and made a deep bow as everyone applauded but shook their heads in confusion. He looked up and met her eye and Julia felt as though they were coconspirators. He might not want to court her, but he was quickly becoming a good friend. She had never had anyone embarrass himself for her before.

Mr. Chamberlain came toward her and offered his arm. Julia took it and let him lead her to the pianoforte. Before she sat down he quietly asked, "Was that what you had in mind, Miss North?"

She looked at him to share a private smile and said, "Just so, Mr. Chamberlain."

His performance served its purpose. Julia played her piece perfectly and the break between Miss Clifton's performance and her own prevented the comparisons she had dreaded.

Chapter 13

*R*iding lessons had become the highlight of Henry's week. Really they had become the highlight of his life, but they had only been at it a few weeks. Three lessons so far, and today would be the fourth.

Henry couldn't believe how thoroughly thoughts of Julia North had taken over his mind. He had called on Miss Abbot this week too. His given reason was to return a book, but really he was there to spend a few more minutes with Miss North.

When Miss Corey had died, so had his heart. She was his only love, and he knew—he just *knew*—he would never love again. His heart had died the day he lost her; he hadn't ever dreamed it could be resurrected. Every family member and every friend who had expressed the sentiment that time would heal his wounds hadn't known what they were talking about. But as much as he hated to admit it, all those well-wishers might have been right. He was beginning to think Julia North was a miracle worker. His feelings for her had been almost unrecognizable at first, but he could see now that he was infatuated. All the signs and symptoms were there and he couldn't deny it any longer. In fact, it wouldn't take much for him to admit his feelings and commit to a real and earnest courtship.

Henry didn't think he was arrogant, merely aware of the way he was viewed by young ladies. They were all quite taken with him. Julia seemed to be as well, but she was the only young lady (Miss Corey included) who had ever resisted a connection with him. Henry had found pursuing her to be a welcome change to being pursued. She hadn't fallen at his feet or used artifice to get his attention. In fact, he'd wager that she would have wished his attention anywhere but on her several times. That was one of those things that made her so irresistible. All he had to do was remember that moment of surprise when she caught a fly and he found himself smiling.

Henry waited in the pasture with the two saddled horses, thinking of all of the other ways he found her so charming. When he saw her enter the pasture, she smiled as her eyes met his and he mentally added her beautiful smile to his list.

When she came a little closer and said "good morning," he thought that her smile didn't quite reach her eyes today.

He helped her on her horse and, just like each time he came near her, he felt his heart pound nearly out of his chest. He savored the feeling as he reached for her and lifted her up on Pegasus. She adjusted in her seat and waited silently as he mounted Felix and they began their usual circuit of the field.

After a few minutes of silence, Henry decided to ask, "Miss North, you seem out of sorts today; is there something the matter?"

Julia looked a little surprised, but after only a slight hesitation, she didn't deny it. "Yes, I'm sorry, I am a little out of sorts today," she admitted. "I'd better put everything else from my mind and concentrate on riding. I'd hate for Pegasus to toss me off again," she said with a smile.

Henry loved that she was able to tease herself. It was amusing for him to tease her over her embarrassing moments, but that she could laugh at herself impressed him immensely. Despite her words, they rode in silence for almost a quarter of an hour. Felix and Pegasus walked side by side now, rather than Julia lagging behind, so Henry could look over and see her expression. She was looking at Pegasus's ears and it seemed her thoughts were far away.

He didn't want to be rude by prying, but he was curious to know why she was so distracted today. He began, "Miss North, I feel quite proud of my skills as a riding instructor; your progress has been exceptional."

She looked up and sat a little straighter in the saddle. "Do you really think I'm doing well?"

"Most definitely; so well in fact, that you don't have to think about it. Why, just a fortnight ago you would hardly touch Pegasus and now you ride with such ease that you can be miles away in thought as you do so." It wasn't a subtle hint, and Henry hoped that he could get her to reveal what was distressing her without asking directly.

She seemed to be searching for the answer she wanted to give him. "I'm just thinking today how sad I'll be to leave Barrington. I feel so at home here."

Henry again thought how different Julia was from the scheming young ladies he knew. It wasn't uncommon for those other girls to befriend his mother and obtain extended invitations at Barrington Court just to be near him. Julia, however, was already thinking about leaving. At least she wasn't cheerful about it. "You don't need to think about that for some time. Miss Abbot said you would be here for two months."

"It's already been more than three weeks; my stay will soon be half over." She sighed, and then added, "I had a letter from my mother this morning, reminding me of my return to London, and I'm afraid the very idea of it has brought me down."

Henry hadn't precisely forgotten that she was to return to London, but he hadn't bothered considering it. The idea brought him down as well. "What don't you like about London? Most young people are clamoring to go."

"Most young people don't have my mother," was her quick reply.

After a pause, he tactfully said, "Miss Abbot has hinted that she might be a difficult woman. But won't you be happy to return for your sister's wedding?" Henry had been hesitant to pry, but now that she was opening up, he felt it wouldn't be rude to ask such a question.

Henry watched her shift the reins so she could hold them in one hand and tuck a stray lock of hair away from her face, and he wondered if she even noticed how relaxed she had become on Pegasus's back. "I'm afraid it won't be a very happy occasion for me," she replied. "I'm losing my sister to marriage and my mother desperately wants me to share the same fate."

He took a moment to think about her reply and realized he didn't like it. "Is your sister's fate lamentable then? You don't want to marry?" Henry almost held his breath waiting for her answer.

"Whether I want to marry or not doesn't matter. My mother is insistent that I marry as soon as possible." She looked up to the sky for a moment and contemplated the clouds, then turned back to him and said, "You see, my mother is a bit like yours. She desperately wants me to marry." With a sad smile she added, "The difference is your mother wants your happiness; my mother wants her own. She wants to have me and my sister out of her way."

"Are you sure?" Henry asked skeptically. "Perhaps you got that impression from her, but she actually feels differently."

"I'm extremely sure," she defended herself. "My mother has informed me in no uncertain terms that I must get married quickly."

"Did she send you here to find a husband, then?" Henry asked. He didn't like to think that Julia was trying to ensnare him as all the rest, but here they were having a secret riding lesson. Had this been her plan all along?

"Oh no," she answered with surprise. "Mother expects me to find a husband in London. She didn't even want me to come to Barrington." Henry was relieved at her answer, but his curiosity was growing by the minute.

"Then why did she allow you to come, if she wants to marry you off so quickly?"

Julia bit her lip with a worried expression before replying, "I made a rash promise before I left London. When I offered to come to Barrington to help Martha, my mother wasn't going to let me come, so I told her that if she would allow me this reprieve in Barrington, I would marry whomever she chose when I return."

Henry couldn't form a reply to that and his surprise must have been evident on his face. He hadn't imagined there was so much going on that he had been unaware of. Julia continued in a subdued voice, "She felt I was being too particular before about whose attentions I would allow."

"You are going to let her choose whom you marry?" he asked incredulously.

Julia let out a deep sigh. "Unless I can find a way out of returning to London, I'll have to keep my promise. My mother informed me in her letter today that she has someone in mind for me. A man twice my age that has recently come into some money and joined society. The news has obviously left me unable to concentrate on riding."

"Undoubtedly," Henry muttered as he was having a difficult time concentrating as well. The very thought of this vivacious girl with an inappropriate old man left him distracted in disgust for several minutes. In fact, as he now looked around, he realized that Felix was leading them back to the stable. They were halfway there already and he didn't bother turning them back to the pasture.

It seemed that Julia was scheming after all, trying to find a way to stay in Barrington. Not so she could trap him into marriage, but so that she could avoid marriage altogether. He couldn't fathom why a mother would want to help her daughter to a disastrous marriage and said, "It was an unfortunate promise to make, but do you think your mother will really hold you to it?"

"Yes," she replied without hesitation. "She wants me out of her way."

Henry became lost in thought again. He still wasn't completely sure how he wanted to proceed with Julia. He liked her quite well and thought he would like to court her, but now there was the pressure of time that made him feel uneasy.

"Mr. Chamberlain," Julia began, pulling him out of his thoughts, "our horses are taking us back to Barrington Court. We're nearly there, I think."

"Right, we'll just lead them to the stables then, shall we?" he replied.

"But what about your groom? Won't he be waiting in the pasture to ride Pegasus back?"

Henry shook his head and asked, "Did you not notice? He wasn't there today. He told me this morning that his wife wasn't feeling well and he wanted to stay close to home." Henry hadn't thought much of it. No one ever interrupted their lessons, so there would be no one to disapprove of their meeting in private. It seemed harmless enough to carry on without a chaperone.

Glancing over at Julia, he realized she was nervous. Her eyes were darting around and he could tell she didn't want anyone to see them. In fact, he watched as she pulled Pegasus's reins gently to the side, making a larger gap between them as they rode. It was the strangest thing that she didn't want to be seen with him. Keeping his mother in the dark had been his only reason for them to not be seen together. But obviously Julia had a reason of her own for not wanting to be seen in his presence, or at least caught alone with him.

His arrogance suddenly hit him. He had been assuming all along that Julia wanted his attentions and that he was withholding them, but what if she wasn't interested in him at all? Thinking back on her words, a niggling doubt entered his mind. Julia was upset that her mother wanted to choose her husband, but what if Julia was already in love with someone else and her mother didn't think him rich enough and had refused her permission?

Barrington Court came into view and Henry hoped his mother wasn't looking out the window. But he realized that mattered less now than the worrisome thought he'd just had. He urged Felix around to the stables and was surprised when Julia and Pegasus passed him at a trot. Was she hurrying so that no one would see them together? For perhaps the first time in his twenty-eight years, Henry felt unsure of himself. If he asked to court her, would she reject him?

His groom would hear their return and probably come soon to care for the horses. Henry dismounted and walked over to help Julia, who had dismounted, for the first time (except for her accidental dismount during their first lesson), without his help. Henry could tell she was in a hurry to depart.

She began her farewell, "Thank you for the lesson, Mr. Chamberlain—"

But Henry interrupted, "The lesson isn't over, Miss North."

"It's not?"

"No," he replied. Then, finding inspiration from somewhere, he said, "The rest of your lesson is taking care of the horse after riding."

"Oh, I didn't realize I was supposed to do that," she glanced around, seeming to look for someone to take away the responsibility.

"Well, sometimes a groom isn't available," he paused to gesture at their empty surroundings, "but your horse still needs to be tended to."

She swallowed and stepped back toward him as he held out Pegasus's reins. "What am I to do?" she asked.

Henry led her through the process of removing the saddle and bridle. He put them back where they belonged and put Felix in his stall, then brought a brush for Julia and instructed her in brushing the horse down. She brushed him quickly, walking around him as she went, and then held out the brush to him and asked, "Which stall is Pegasus's?"

He couldn't take it anymore. He had to know. He ignored her question and gathered his courage. Prepared to throw his pride away, he asked, "Are your affections engaged to someone else in London? Is that why you are so unhappy about your mother's plan for you?"

Henry watched her contemplate his question. First she seemed surprised to be returning to their earlier topic; then her face contorted in a look of distaste and she replied, "No. I'm unhappy about my mother's plan because it's very unlikely that Mr. Jenks and I will suit one another. I'd rather go for a leisurely stroll in a thunderstorm than let my mother choose whom I marry."

That seemed a strange comparison to Henry, but now his pride had truly taken a hit. If she didn't care for anyone in London, then why didn't she care for him? Julia glanced over her shoulder toward the door, as if checking that no one was coming. What could she be thinking? Henry had to know.

"Miss North, why don't you want to be seen here with me?" Henry questioned her.

Her eyes rounded in surprise again, and she looked around as if even at that moment someone had caught them alone together. Then she looked back at him and said, "I just . . . Um, because of your mother." She paused to clear her throat and then continued, "Your mother will get the wrong impression if she hears about our riding lessons."

"But why does it matter so to you? It would be difficult for me because I would have to answer hundreds of questions from her, but there isn't a negative consequence for you."

"Well . . .," she hesitated again. "We're friends, so I thought I was helping you by avoiding detection."

"Friends," Henry murmured, trying to think quickly. There wasn't more than friendship between them, but he felt disappointed that she had used that term. Saying they were friends was safe. She wasn't giving anything away. How could he know how she felt? The uncertainty of not knowing was unbearable.

He looked down and Julia was still holding the brush out toward him. He reached both hands forward and took the brush with one hand and her wrist with the other. He gently pulled her toward him until they were just a foot apart; she didn't resist, but her eyes widened as she moved toward him, possibly wondering what he would do next. He gazed down into her eyes, trying to see if he could tell just by looking whether she could feel more than friendship for him. He let go of her wrist and slowly brushed a few loose strands of hair from her face. By the end of their lessons, her hair was always coming loose. He watched her with a nervousness he had never felt before. He wished she would just confess her feelings, but her light brown eyes continued to hold his gaze with wide uncertainty and he had to ask, "Julia, could we be more than friends?"

"But your mother . . . ?" she asked as her brow creased in worry.

Henry wasn't thinking about his mother; he just wanted to erase the look of worry from her face. He lifted his other hand and let his fingers trail gently from her cheekbone to her chin, amazed to be feeling her smooth skin and more amazed that she was letting him.

She searched his gaze for a long moment. Henry didn't know what she was looking for or what she saw, but he leaned closer and she didn't pull away. It was all the permission Henry needed. He closed the distance between them and lowered his lips until they touched hers. It was as if he had been resisting a magnetic pull since the moment he met her and he finally let his attraction to her have its way. It was a relief to stop fighting the attraction, but he could hardly believe how much more he wanted to kiss her once it was already happening. How could you want something you were already experiencing? He could feel her gently returning his kiss when her lips moved against his own, and his confidence soared. He felt her move even closer as her hands slid up his arms to his shoulders. He dropped the brush as he wrapped both arms around her, pulling her into an embrace and pressing more deeply into the kiss.

After a few moments of bliss, Henry pulled back and looked into Julia's eyes, wanting to see her reaction for proof that her feelings were real. She smiled tentatively up at him.

Along with the relief Henry felt, there was a strange feeling of surprise. Even though he had kissed her, he was almost surprised with himself for actually doing it, for finally allowing himself to feel again. While he had been slowly realizing his feelings, he certainly hadn't planned on acting on them today. But Julia was smiling up at him and he was sure she cared for him, which was all that mattered.

She pulled back and said shyly, "I should probably go, before Martha wonders where I am."

At the mention of her cousin, Henry felt an uneasy feeling at the thought of everyone finding out his intentions toward Julia. If Julia told Miss Abbot and Miss Abbot told his mother, their courtship would be out of his control. It was all too new and he needed time to understand himself better before others questioned him about it. "Please don't mention what's happened to your cousin. She can be discreet, I'm sure, but if my mother found out I have feelings for you, we'll never have any peace." He smiled in conspiracy; it might even be enjoyable to have a slow courtship without anyone else knowing.

Julia's gaze looked a little confused, "You think it should be a secret?"

Before Henry could respond, he heard voices and quickly realized they were coming toward the stable. He only had time to nod and say, "Yes, I think it would be best," then quickly put some distance between Julia and himself. He hurried over to Pegasus, who was still not in his stall, and proceeded to put him there. Henry could see his groom, who had finally come to care for the horses, and another servant from the main house just outside. His groom knew, of course, what Henry had been up to the last fortnight, but the servant from the main house caused him a moment of worry. If the tale of his court-ing again made its way to the servants at the main house, his mother would know by the end of the day. Henry's panic caused him to move quickly toward the entrance. The groom continued past him while the servant waited as he approached.

"Mr. Chamberlain, you've a visitor arrived just now. Waiting for you in the upstairs parlour, sir."

"Thank you, I'll be there directly." Henry's words were meant to dismiss, and the servant turned and left.

With a sigh of relief, Henry retreated back into the stable and saw that his groom was attending to Felix and Julia was saying goodbye to Pegasus. Henry again felt that relief that his feelings for her were reciprocated, but also that underlying nervousness of how to proceed from here. "It seems I have a visitor, and you need to return to your cousin." He stopped and turned to face her. "I very much enjoyed our lesson today, Miss North."

"As did I, Mr. Chamberlain."

Realizing his next chance alone with her would be their next lesson, he said, "I can't wait another week for your next riding lesson. Will you meet me again tomorrow?"

She smiled, not tentatively this time, but a broad grin, and said, "I'll be there."

She turned and they both left the stable, a discreet distance between them. He bid her a more formal fare-well and watched as she walked toward the main gate.

She looked back twice to grin at him, which brought Henry happiness he hadn't meant to feel.

With a light step he walked toward Barrington Court, but he didn't care a whit who his visitor was or what business he would have to attend to. He would deal with this and perhaps go for a long, fast ride on Felix. He had the desire to really move.

Henry had a whistle on his lips that instantly died when he entered the upstairs parlour at Barrington Court and saw his visitor. It was Jonathan. He had a short beard now, probably grown to try to make his boyish features look older, but other than that he was just the same.

He stood up and greeted Henry with a vigorous handshake and his old carefree enthusiasm that Henry remembered from their short acquaintance several years ago. "Hello there, Henry, been forever since I've seen you. Thought I'd drop in for a visit." But Henry's mind was slow to hear it as he wondered what Miss Corey's brother was doing here.

"Jonathan. You're here for a visit," he repeated, feeling almost dazed as the sadness that accompanied the memories from Miss Corey's death came flooding back in an instant. He was overwhelmed once more by the guilt that he felt for living. "That's . . . Well, that's wonderful. How good to see you."

Henry's tone didn't match his words and he couldn't force his tone any lighter. Miss Corey's brother was here. This man should have been his brother, but for the death of the woman he loved.

"I have a few spare weeks before my father expects me home, and I thought how good it would be to visit here and reminisce about old times."

"Old times" for them was just that one summer that his family had come to Barrington Court. Henry avoided those memories; they made him feel like doing nothing. He didn't want the return of the ache he already felt in his chest.

How could he have thought he could court Miss North? He couldn't. He certainly cared for her. Too much, in fact, as he pictured her in an overturned carriage. Her life lost. He couldn't go through that again; it was too much. He felt like kicking himself for letting his guard down.

"Old times," Henry repeated. "It might be good to think about old times . . . before the accident." Henry couldn't separate the good from the bad in his heart though. Those wonderful good times had led to the worst suffering he had known and they were irrevocably connected for him. "Has the housekeeper shown you to your room?"

She hadn't, so they rang the bell and Jonathan Corey was established once again as a guest at Barrington Court. When Jonathan left the parlour, Henry drew the curtains and poured himself a drink.

Chapter 14

Julia had worked so hard to not allow herself to hope, and it had mostly worked. She had still enjoyed Henry's company more and more each time she was with him, but she had convinced herself to appreciate his attention as friendship. When she arrived for a riding lesson with Henry yesterday, she had not thought about how she wished he would like her—at least not much. Her thoughts had been so distracted after her mother's letter had arrived yesterday that she had been worrying more than ever about returning to London.

She could still hardly believe he had kissed her.

Martha had warned her there would be no point in hoping for Henry's affections. The local young ladies she had met at Martock Priory had shown her there was too much competition for her to even be a contender. And her own self-doubt had robbed her of her confidence. But despite it all, Henry wanted her.

Yesterday, after he had kissed her, she wanted to run home and could barely restrain herself to walk. But she made herself slow down so she would have time to stop smiling before Martha saw her.

During their few riding lessons, Julia had repeated Martha's warning over and over to herself. She had concentrated so hard on believing that Henry saw her the same as every other girl that she had been taken completely by surprise when he asked her if they could be more than friends. The sweetest question had caused an almost violent reaction in her heart; it had wanted to jump out of her chest. But the thing that stood out the most—the part she would never forget—was the look of uncertainty on Henry's face. She had never seen him anything but completely confident. She hadn't been able to speak but had held her ground when he leaned in and kissed her. Another surprise, but a most welcome one. She had wondered before what she would do when she was kissed. She smiled at the thought. In the moment Henry's lips had met hers, there was nothing to think about. She had returned the kiss without a conscious thought. It was a perfect moment that she felt she belonged in, or perhaps it was Henry that she belonged with. Either way, she felt at home with his lips on hers. And she felt a happiness beyond any she had thought was possible for her.

She had convinced herself that Henry was keeping their lessons a secret because he didn't want to court her, or be pressured into feelings he didn't feel. But his kiss had given her confidence. It was a little odd that Henry wanted their courtship to be a secret. She'd never thought to court in secret, but if his mother's interference was to be avoided, she could see why Henry would want things to be kept quiet.

After breakfast, but before she left on her morning walk, Julia was surprised by the sound of a carriage. Barrington was so quiet in the mornings, the sound seemed almost foreign. She heard the carriage stop and was even more surprised. Martha's visitors didn't typically come in carriages. Julia had plenty of time before she was to meet Henry for their riding lesson, so she waited in the sitting room to satisfy her curiosity about Martha's visitor.

Julia could not have been more surprised when her own mother was shown into Martha's sitting room! She couldn't hide her surprise or the distaste in her voice as she asked, "Mother, what are you doing here?" Not the friendliest welcome, but her mother was too preoccupied to notice.

"Harriet wants to end her engagement to Lord Blakely!" her mother exclaimed. She didn't look happy to see Julia after their weeks of separation or happy at all to be there; she merely shot a disapproving look over her shoulder as Harriet entered the room behind her.

Julia took a few moments to try to take in the situation and while she was silent, her mother continued, "She has been flirting constantly since her engagement was announced and Lady Eldridge warned me two days ago that she had seen her in the park with the same man *three* times. Harriet even admitted that she wants Lord Blakely to find out and cancel their engagement! She *wants* to create a scandal!"

Julia swallowed. At first, she thought her mother was overreacting, but she remembered that Harriet had wanted to end her engagement and hadn't seemed to grasp how unacceptable that was. Glancing over at Harriet now, she saw her sister roll her eyes.

"How will being here help?" Julia asked. She was pretty sure she understood the situation, but was still trying to make sense of their presence in Barrington.

"Harriet has to be kept far away from that rake who is trying to ruin her. Our only hope was leaving London until the wedding."

"You're not staying here, are you?" Julia asked, fearing the answer.

"Of course we've got to stay here. We'll return to London the day before Harriet's wedding," she said, looking annoyed with Julia now that she was forcing her to repeat herself. "I am convinced she'll embroil herself in scandal just to end her engagement if we are there for even a day longer than necessary."

Julia's heart sank. The rest of her time in Barrington would include her mother and sister. She could already feel the difference in the room. There would be no more quiet evenings with Martha, no more dinners at Barrington Court without her mother looking on, and no more friendly chats when Henry dropped in. Her mother's presence would suppress it all.

The peace she had felt in Barrington was gone, and Julia realized it wasn't London she had been trying to escape. It wasn't even having to get married, although that was certainly part of it. Primarily, it was her mother she had needed to escape from. Having her here felt stifling. Barrington lost much of its appeal with her mother in it.

While the realization washed over her, her mother said, "Julia, if you can impress Mr. Jenks—which I don't think will be difficult to do, even for you—then your wedding can follow soon after." It took a moment before Julia could remember who Mr. Jenks was, but then the recollection came and she felt as though a sack of flour had been dropped on her. He was the man in London her mother wanted her to marry.

Julia had been feeling uneasy about the idea of a secret courtship with Henry, but now with her mother here, it would be so much better to court openly. She wanted to tell her mother so she would never mention the dreaded Mr. Jenks waiting for her in London again.

Julia would talk to Henry about it today. In the meantime, she decided a complete change of subject would be best. "I'll find Martha. I'm sure she'll be happy to see you both."

"Have her tell the housekeeper to get rooms ready for us. Although, from the size of this house, I don't think she has enough spare rooms. You should mention to her that she can put Harriet in with you."

"Mother, the room I'm using is Martha's only spare room. You'll both have to stay there with me."

"You cannot be serious!" Julia was worried her mother was angry with her, but instead she turned to Harriet and said, "This is your fault. We could have stayed comfortably home in London if not for your scandalous behavior."

"We could have stayed comfortably home in London anyway," was Harriet's unrepentant reply.

Her mother looked very much like she was grinding her teeth in frustration. She turned back to Julia and said, "Fine, ask Martha if she can accommodate all of us in the one room."

Julia supposed it didn't matter; it was just one more thing she had loved about Barrington that felt ruined now. But it would be fine. If she needed solitude, she still had her morning walks. And if she needed solace, she had Henry. With that comforting thought, she smiled at her mother and sister and said, "Of course, Mother," then set off to do her bidding.

Julia found Martha in her room and informed her of the morning's events. She offered to oversee all the preparations herself. Martha agreed and with a reluctant look made her way to the drawing room to greet her new guests. Julia found the housekeeper and informed her of the work to be done to ready the room for her mother and sister—it looked like she would be sleeping on a cot on the floor from now on—before returning to the drawing room. When she walked in the room, Martha was in her usual chair embroidering. "Everything all sorted?" she asked Julia.

"Yes, the housekeeper is taking care of everything," Julia replied.

Turning to Julia's mother, Martha said, "I hope it's all to your satisfaction, Marianne."

"Thank you, Martha," her mother replied. "I'll look over my room after we've had a chance for some refreshment."

Julia sank down low on the sofa, wishing her mother would be gracious for a change. She glanced over at Martha and saw she was setting her embroidery down again so she could go interrupt her housekeeper to request a snack for their new guests. Julia jumped up, feeling that the weight of responsibility should be hers, and said, "Let me go find the housekeeper and let her know refreshments are needed."

"I'll find her," she said. "I'll have to find Anne too and send her to Barrington Court with the message that we won't be able to dine with them today."

"What's this?" asked Julia's mother.

"We usually dine at Barrington Court on Saturdays," Martha replied. "But they won't mind at all if we can't attend. It's just a dinner among friends."

"Oh no, don't cancel," protested Julia's mother. "Harriet and I don't want to sit around here, bored all day. Barrington Court will certainly be more interesting. I love to visit fine country homes."

Martha shrugged and said, "Then I'll send a note instead, letting them know we have two extra guests with us today. I'm sure they'll be delighted to have you come."

Julia didn't know if she should be relieved or anxious that her mother and sister would be at Barrington Court today. She wanted to spend time with Henry; just thinking his name made her heart flutter. And she always enjoyed her cousin's company. But the rest of the party she could do without. Her mother was very controlling over how Julia behaved in company, her sister seemed more petulant than usual, and Lady Chamberlain would ask too many questions. It would not be a restful afternoon.

Realizing it was time to leave for her riding lesson, Julia left the room after Martha and slipped out of the house. She set off down the lane that led to the pasture where she would soon be meeting Henry.

Chapter 15

Julia waited for Henry to arrive with a pounding heart. She wished it was pounding merely in anticipation of seeing him again for the first time since they had kissed, but the arrival of her family had caused her a significant amount of agitation. She felt that being with Henry and riding Pegasus again would be a relief, an escape even, from her strained state since her mother arrived. A month ago, she would never have dreamed that she would look forward to riding a horse as a relaxing activity, but it was so.

This was the first time Julia had arrived before Henry for their lesson. She had left at the same time as usual, at least according to the clock by the kitchen when she had slipped away, unless it hadn't been wound properly. But still she couldn't be more than fifteen minutes early. Julia hadn't announced to her family that she was leaving. Martha could tell them—if they bothered asking—that she was out for a walk, but she wouldn't risk missing her lesson today.

Julia felt too worked up to stand and wait patiently so she began to pace. She was so worried that her mother and sister's presence would ruin her visit to Barrington. She longed to talk it over with Henry, hoping that reassurances from him would calm her. She had never relied on previous suitors for anything before, but it seemed the most natural thing to want Henry by her side as she dealt with this new ordeal. He was so calm and reassuring during their riding lessons, but she hadn't realized how important that characteristic was to her until now. It wasn't just that that drew her to him. She loved his confident smile, but even more, when he laughed in surprise. And perhaps her very favorite thing was his selflessness when he had played the pianoforte before her performance. She had been the one to laugh in surprise then.

Julia hoped that he wouldn't mind being so selfless once more and allow their courtship to be out in the open. If she could tell her mother of Henry's interest in her, the most significant of the pressure from her would be dispersed. But even if he still wanted their courtship to remain just between them, at least she could look forward to a knowing look when they were in company with others. Her mother's intimidation wouldn't feel so horrible if Julia at least knew Henry was there supporting her, even silently. Julia also needed a chance to warn Henry about Mr. Jenks. If her mother mentioned him at dinner today, Julia would be mortified. She had never even met the man, but her mother would be sure to imply a flirtatious history between them as she hinted at Julia's future wedding.

Julia wished for a watch. What time was it? Surely Henry was quite late by now. She continued to pace and noticed the grasses in her path were flattened. Hopefully he would arrive soon with a simple explanation of meeting with his mother or his steward and losing track of time. Julia paced for several more minutes, casting her eyes often in the direction Henry should be coming from, but Henry, Felix, and Pegasus didn't arrive. She decided she couldn't wait anymore and began walking toward Barrington Court, thinking she could meet Henry halfway. Around the first corner she saw the groom who usually accompanied them walking toward her. She pulled back and stopped, waiting for him to approach, wondering how much he knew of what had happened yesterday and what reason he brought her for Henry's absence today.

He pulled a note from his pocket as he reached her and said merely, "Mr. Chamberlain asked me to give you this." He waited while she read the short missive and when she looked up he asked, "Would you like me to escort you back, Miss?"

Julia could see the pity in his eyes and wanted desperately to erase it, but couldn't shake off the hurt fast enough to fool him. She still tried though by responding in a bright voice, "No, thank you, I'll just continue on my walk." She smiled at him and his returned smile, laced with sympathy, told her he knew exactly what her hopes and expectations had been and that they had all just been dashed.

Julia turned and walked back the way she had come. It was the opposite direction she needed to go, but she needed a long walk now more than ever. She pulled the crumpled note from her fist and read it again, feeling the distance he had intended with his words.

Miss North, I'm sorry I cannot attend to you today. I will contact you sometime if I have the opportunity to give another short lesson. My apologies. H. Chamberlain

The brevity of the note itself was insulting, but the condescending language of it made Julia feel pitiful. Everything Julia had feared about getting close to him had been confirmed. He could not *attend* to her today? As though she were some small child who needed minding! And him offering to contact her if he could accommodate her for another lesson? As if she had begged him to teach her rather than him insisting she learn to ride!

His purpose all along must have been to reduce her to a simpering admirer of his. He must not be able to stand having even one lady unwilling to fall at his feet. She couldn't deny that she had surpassed even Miss Clifton: she was the pathetic one now. She had been completely taken in. All his good qualities that she had been admiring before receiving his note, now struck her as devious manipulations. The only thing she could take comfort in was that she had been more of a challenge for him than most of his admirers. He'd had to give her private horse riding lessons before she had succumbed to his charms. But succumb she had, just like everyone else. Julia thought about the pitying look the groom had given her as he handed her Henry's note. He had probably delivered dozens of notes just like it on Henry's behalf.

It wasn't the first time Henry had disappointed a young lady, she felt sure of it, but little did he know that it wasn't Julia's first time being disappointed. She was just being abandoned by another suitor. Nothing more. Henry was nothing more. She was so experienced at this that she wouldn't even let it bother her at all. At least her mother and sister didn't know about it or they would reprimand her for it like they always did. In fact, it was quite good luck that no one even knew he had intended to court her.

She suddenly stopped in her tracks as she remembered their kiss. Their private, beautiful, life-changing kiss. Was that how he treated all the young ladies who threw themselves at him? Julia felt repulsed at the thought and her anxiety grew, as did her anger. Yesterday, during their riding lesson, she had told him about the promise she had made to let her mother choose her husband. Perhaps Henry had felt he could kiss her without any repercussions because she was practically betrothed to another man. Regardless of his reason for kissing her, she was appalled that she had almost given Henry Chamberlain the power to break her heart. *Almost.* But it was clear to her now just how right Martha had been from the beginning. Henry Chamberlain didn't have a heart open for love and marriage. She had been fooling herself, thinking that somehow she was different from all the others who had tried before her.

The hurt, angry thoughts continued to come and Julia realized she had walked quite a ways. She would have to turn back soon for home. She still didn't know the time, but she would need to get ready to dine with her family at Barrington Court. She would have to face Henry again and she hated the thought, but the only thing worse would be what Henry would assume if she didn't go. She had experience putting on a brave face in front of former suitors. Today would be no different.

When she finally arrived back home, she went to find her mother first thing. Dining at Barrington Court today would be difficult enough without her mother mentioning certain things.

Her mother and Harriet were in the sitting room; strangely Martha was not, even though that's usually where she was. "Mother and Harriet," she said, "can I ask a favor of both of you today?" Julia's mother wasn't completely unreasonable and Julia hoped she would agree to her request.

"Why aren't you dressed for Barrington Court, Julia?" she asked. "I hope you haven't developed country habits, like dining casually."

"No, Mother," she replied. "I'm about to get ready; I just wanted to ask this favor first."

"What is it?"

Julia didn't feel that her mother would be receptive to her request, but she didn't have time to wait for her to be in a more cheerful mood. "Will you please not mention Mr. Jenks today at dinner?" Her mother arched an eyebrow and Julia hurried on, "Or any of my courting history. It's common knowledge in London how many suitors I've had, and I cope with the reputation I have there. But here in Barrington . . . ," Julia paused a moment, wondering how she could make her mother understand. "It's nice that no one knows," she finished flatly.

Her mother looked at her suspiciously, almost definitely knowing that Julia wasn't telling her everything, but she relented, saying, "Have it your way, dear. We won't mention Mr. Jenks or your past suitors."

Next, Julia performed a most difficult task by telling her mother and Harriet about Henry, emphasizing strongly that although he was an unattached bachelor, he was *not* open to be pursued. She had to include his sad history, but it was imperative for her mother to understand that he was not a potential suitor. After the explanation, her mother said, "Very well, Julia. I see that you don't want this Mr. Chamberlain for a suitor. Honestly, I'm surprised you think I'd pressure you into trying for him. You know I already found you a perfectly willing suitor in London."

Julia just hoped that her mother would keep her word after she met Henry and saw Barrington Court. But with nothing left to say, she went to get ready. Dining with Henry today would be bad enough without her mother embarrassing her. She already felt pathetic for falling for Henry Chamberlain's charms, but hopefully her mother wouldn't make less-than-subtle comments suggesting she try to impress him. And if her mother mentioned her three disastrous London seasons, then Henry would know how pathetic she truly was. She wished she could never be in his presence again and the dread built within her as she imagined how his gaze would avoid hers. The only thing to do now was to save her pride, so Julia took extra care with her appearance as she prepared for the dinner that she didn't want to happen.

Chapter 16

Henry watched from the window for the guests to arrive. His parents invited two or three families to dine at Barrington Court most Saturdays. Miss Abbot had a standing invitation of course. She didn't come every week, but she'd only missed one Saturday dinner since Julia had come to stay with her. He expected them both today and hoped to speak to Julia before the entire party was gathered together. He had forgotten about their riding lesson this morning until it was almost too late and had scrawled off a quick note for the groom to deliver as he and Jonathan had been on their way out hunting. But he needed a chance to explain why he couldn't court her after all.

Luck was with him—although he felt anything but lucky—because Miss Abbot's carriage was the first to arrive. He moved back from the window and waited in the shadows in the corner for the guests to be shown into the drawing room. It turned out to be the perfect maneuver because Miss Abbot and two other women he didn't recognize followed the butler into the drawing room, but Julia was several steps behind them, walking slower.

"Miss North," he called her name quietly before she could join them in the drawing room. She looked up and as she saw him she took an immediate step back, almost in recoil. Henry felt terrible that her reaction to him was such, but relieved that this conversation might not be as difficult as he had supposed. "May I have a word with you?"

She closed her eyes and let out a small sigh before answering simply, "Yes."

Henry held the door open for the library just across the hall and Julia preceded him into the room, but she seemed so uncomfortable and almost cringed away from him. He stayed just inside the room, knowing this would need to be a brief conversation so the others wouldn't take notice of Julia's absence.

"Miss North," he began, "I need to apologize for my behavior toward you yesterday." He watched her for a reaction, and she gave a succinct nod, giving him permission to continue, although he wished he didn't have to. "I took liberties that I should not have taken, and perhaps gave you reason to believe I had intentions toward you that I do not have. It was an impulsive thing to do and I apologize." It sounded so stiff and formal to talk to her this way, but Henry reminded himself that it was necessary and pushed himself to finish his prepared words. "I hope you will forgive me and we can continue to be . . .," Henry paused briefly, but made himself say, "friends."

She gave another brief nod and asked, "Is that all?"

Henry paused for a long moment, surprised at her calm demeanor and wondering if that really was all—the end of all private interactions between them. She looked more beautiful than ever today. But he made himself look away. He really wished the strange attraction he felt for her would go away, because the guilt he felt since Jonathan Corey arrived and the memories of Miss Corey so fresh again had made up his mind for him. "Yes, thank you for your time," he said formally. Julia immediately left the room, and Henry stood at the doorway and watched her cross the hall and enter the drawing room, but Henry needed a few moments alone before he could be in the company of others.

Once, when he was younger, before even Miss Corey, he had accidentally raised the expectations of a young lady. When he had set her straight, she had cried and begged him to reconsider. That had been excruciating. That one experience had taught him that when dealing with young ladies, it was important to never raise false hopes. He didn't often repeat past mistakes, but in his defense, when he had kissed Julia, he thought his feelings were sincere. Still, he had expected that when he told her he couldn't court her, she would cry and beg. But Julia never did what he expected, even in this. Perhaps she understood from the missed riding lesson and the short note he sent that his feelings weren't as strong as he had implied yesterday. Or perhaps she didn't care for him and was relieved to be rid of his attentions. It just didn't matter. Having Jonathan Corey here made it feel like Miss Corey had died last week, not three and a half years ago. He and Jonathan had talked last night about her, how sweet and kind she had been, how she would always volunteer to play the pianoforte because she hated dancing, and how she loved to read. He felt like scolding himself for almost forgetting her.

Henry tried to shake off the melancholy before he crossed the hall to join the group gathering in the drawing room, but he didn't succeed.

His mother didn't notice as she claimed his attention by cheerfully saying, "Henry, come meet Miss North's mother and sister. They just arrived in Barrington this morning. Isn't it wonderful?"

He glanced at Julia, knowing this wasn't wonderful for her, but she was looking at her feet. He dropped his gaze to her feet too, but then quickly glanced away, not letting his thoughts dwell on her slender ankles. He felt more guilt now for how he had treated her. He knew having her mother here would be distressing for her.

In response to his mother's question, he turned to Miss Abbot and asked, "Will you introduce me to your guests?"

Henry could tell that Miss Abbot was trying to act pleased with her new visitors as she said, "My late cousin's wife, Marianne North, is here to join Julia as my guest. And this is her other daughter, Miss Harriet North."

"So nice to meet you, Mr. Chamberlain," she said.

"How do you do?" he asked their new guests as he took them in. Julia's mother, Mrs. North, was a lovely woman, but he was predisposed to find fault with her so he admitted it to himself grudgingly. She looked too dressed up for a dinner at a country house. Her jewelry and dress looked more fit for the theatre in London. She was pretty for her age, he supposed, and he could see that Julia's chin and nose were similar to her mother's. While he was observing her, he realized she was doing the same to him. She was looking him over with the admiration he was too used to. Her smile broadened and a calculating look entered her eye. She glanced at Julia, who didn't look up from her feet, and back at him.

"It is so interesting to meet you, Mr. Chamberlain. I had no idea you would be so handsome." Turning to her elder daughter, she said, "When you told us about Mr. Chamberlain earlier, you failed to mention that detail." Then, returning her attention to him, "Such a glaring omission seems telling, I'd say." Again she shot a look at her daughter, this time with one eyebrow raised. Julia did look up from her feet then, her cheeks pink and her expression anxious.

Henry didn't know what to think of that. Julia had spoken to her family about him. What kind of report had she given? If it had been after the missed riding lesson, it might have been a less favorable description. Regardless, he could tell that Julia was distressed, and he knew enough about the relationship she had with her mother to know Mrs. North was the reason for Julia's discomfort. Henry could think of nothing more to help the situation than to remove his attention, so he turned to the younger sister and bowed while she curtsied.

Henry's mother was oblivious to what Mrs. North implied and said, "It's lovely to have guests, but I'm a bit disappointed that Miss Harriet North is engaged." Then, turning to Mrs. North, his mother explained, "I'm always hoping for eligible young ladies to visit. Henry has been suffering from a broken heart for ever so long, but I'm convinced that he'll soon meet a young lady who will make him fall in love again."

Henry had never been quite so frustrated with his mother's interference as he was at that moment, but before he could either contradict her or just change the subject, a voice from the doorway said, "Your mother is quite right, Henry. Falling in love again would be just the thing to cheer you up."

Henry looked over as Jonathan Corey entered the room and wondered what he could possibly be speaking of. Miss Corey's own brother would surely not want him to forget her. While Henry stood there feeling bewildered at his pronouncement, his mother exclaimed, "Exactly! I'm so glad you agree with me, Mr. Corey. Perhaps you can convince Henry to go to London with you one of these days. I'm sure if he meets more young ladies, he will find one he wants to marry."

Jonathan hesitated for a moment, and while he did Henry glanced again at Julia, who continued to look anywhere but at him. Jonathan finally replied, "I can hardly think of returning to London when I've just escaped it. And I must admit, there are many fair prospects here in Barrington, more than I expected, I assure you." He smiled and nodded politely at Julia and her sister. Then, turning to Henry, he asked, "Haven't any of the local girls caught your attention?"

Henry had been asked similar questions scores of times, but he could hardly believe it was Jonathan asking him now. It was an offhand comment and Jonathan didn't expect or even wait for a reply, so Henry managed to avoid answering as Jonathan and their other dinner guests were introduced, but his mind didn't leave it. Even as they sat down to dinner he wondered how Jonathan could be so offhand about the matter. Jonathan had seemed so sad when they had talked about his sister.

Henry's thoughts kept him separate from the conversation around him. As he thought about Jonathan's question, he knew there was one girl who had most definitely caught his attention. If he was honest with himself, she had caught his attention as easily as she had caught that ridiculous fly. But he had just told her he had no intentions toward her. That was probably the right decision. His heart was still broken; he couldn't move on.

After escorting Mrs. North into the dining room, Henry sat and watched as Jonathan escorted Julia to her seat. He held her chair for her, but then leaned in and said something in a low voice. Julia looked at him with a quick smile and whispered a reply. He had seen them introduced not ten minutes ago! What was Jonathan thinking, being so forward with her?

"Jonathan, what was that you said to Miss North?"

He had hoped his blunt question would embarrass him, but his friend just gave a rakish smile and said, "I just told her that I was leading her to the chair where I would have the best view of her beauty." He announced it without any shame, but Julia blushed. Jonathan moved around the table and took his seat directly across from her. "This is the best view I've ever had. I plan to converse with you through the whole meal," he boldly declared to Julia and then added, "I'm sure I won't even notice what I'm eating." Henry knew his mother wouldn't care about the breach in etiquette—their dinners were almost always informal—but Henry was completely annoyed by Jonathan's intention to talk across the table.

Julia didn't seem to mind though. She just shook her head with a good-natured smile at his exaggeration. "Well, Mr. Corey, I'll have to save you from such a fate by describing every dish in detail for you."

"Your very descriptions will enhance the taste; I'm looking forward to the meal even more."

Henry really hoped that Julia would give him some sort of set down, but she was still smiling as she exclaimed, "I won't hold your interest long if all I speak of is food!"

"You could speak of grass growing and I would be enthralled."

Henry didn't think he could take another moment of Mr. Corey flirting with Julia. He interrupted them by saying, "How has your father been, Jonathan?"

Amazingly, Jonathan was able to withdraw his attention from Julia's beauty and he turned to Henry and answered, "He's better now, but he had bronchitis this winter. He and his wife didn't come to town this season because of it."

Again, Henry couldn't believe what he was hearing. He tried not to show how much that news affected him as he asked, "Your father is remarried?"

"Oh, yes. I didn't realize you wouldn't know. He married a spinster from Bath about two years ago."

It took him a moment to reply, "No, I hadn't heard that."

"She's a nice enough lady. She takes very good care of Father; fusses over him too much if you ask me, but he seems quite happy with the arrangement."

"I'm glad to hear he's happy." What else was there to say? Of course Henry wanted him to be happy. He had lost his wife and daughter in one day, but Mr. Corey was still among the living. He could hear an echo in his mind of his mother's voice making a similar argument. She only ever wanted his happiness. Why had he not wanted the same thing? For some reason, he could never believe the same argument for himself, but now he realized how he felt about Miss Corey's father remarrying and he was happy for him.

The soup was brought in and the meal began, but he hardly noticed. Henry hadn't been constantly miserable over the last three and a half years. On the contrary, after he had returned from travelling, he had enjoyed a small amount of society, but never enough to form lasting attachments—really just enough to maintain the friendships he had. More recently, he had been working hard, trying to be useful to his father, who hadn't pressured him with any responsibilities since Miss Corey's death.

Henry had made up his mind to never move on, but through it all, Henry's heart had been slowly letting go of Miss Corey, until there was really nothing holding him back from forming a new relationship. He had almost grasped that with Julia, but Jonathan's arrival had stopped him in his tracks. It had been a last flare of guilt for living when she couldn't, a last surge of sadness for the loss of someone he had loved. All these thoughts continued to consume him all through the meal. He had taken a few bites of each course, but couldn't remember anything he had eaten.

Jonathan's father had experienced even more loss than he had—his wife and daughter both gone—yet he had been able to carry on. Hearing that his almost father-in-law was remarried made him realize that the flame of guilt that had burned bright and hot at Jonathan's arrival had just as quickly burnt out and was gone. Henry knew in that moment that his life could go on too. Not only that, but he could be happy.

The digestives had been finished and his mother was standing to lead the ladies from the room. Henry stood automatically with the other gentlemen as the women withdrew and he stared longingly at the person he wanted in his life more than any other. Julia wasn't looking at him, but was smiling at Jonathan over her shoulder as she left the room. Henry felt a surge of jealousy again, but at least he admitted it to himself this time. He didn't want Jonathan to flirt with Julia; he wanted her for himself.

He felt like hitting his head against a wall for being so stupid. He wished he'd come to this realization before Julia had arrived. He could have made everything right so much easier if he hadn't told her he had no intentions toward her. Only an hour or so had passed since then, but his whole perspective had changed. He wouldn't be able to repair the damage he had done in the course of the evening, but he'd at least try to begin.

When the gentlemen joined the ladies in the drawing room, the first thing he did was let his eyes look at her, something he had been avoiding, even when they had spoken alone. She was wearing a blue gown with white lace at her neck and wrists. Julia was always beautiful, but this evening she was also elegant, with curls framing her face. But it turned out to be an error on his part to just look, as Jonathan took the opportunity to claim her attention first. As she spoke with Jonathan, her cheeks flushed slightly at his repeatedly flirtatious comments.

Henry approached then, and he couldn't help the annoyance he felt as he had to wait for Jonathan to stop speaking before he could address Julia.

"Miss North," he said when he was finally able to get a word in, "have you had an opportunity to show your mother and sister around Barrington?"

Henry watched Julia, who had been leaning forward in her discussion with Jonathan, pull back as she shifted her attention to him. She sat up straighter and her smile—which hadn't seemed completely genuine before—became forced. It pained Henry to see her reaction to him, but he knew he deserved it. He felt terrible for disappointing her. She cleared her throat before responding, "As they just arrived this morning, we haven't had time to show them the town."

Henry cleared his own throat. He wasn't sure how to proceed. Julia's reaction to him was most definitely cold, and he didn't have practice diffusing resentment. "Perhaps I could be of service and help you show them the sights, and include some of the history of Barrington," he offered.

He watched Julia's face, hoping for even the slightest softening of her features, but she turned from him and looked at her sister, then back at him with what he thought was a suspicious glare. "Perhaps," she finally replied and then turned away from him and joined her sister on the short sofa so that it was impossible to address her once more.

Henry tried talking to her several more times, with only the shortest replies in return. He realized he would need to apologize before proceeding further. He'd have to find a private moment with her once more, which shouldn't be too difficult, but there was no hope of saving this evening. Instead, he decided to engage Jonathan in conversation to at least stop him from flirting with Julia any more, and he was successful in that. But once Julia knew he had changed his mind, they could pick up where they left off.

Chapter 17

As Julia walked along the path a week later, she wished she had someone to confide in. Her mother and sister had never inspired her to share her feelings, and their recent arrival in Barrington certainly hadn't changed that.

After meeting Henry last week, her mother had said to her later that night as they climbed the stairs to their shared room, "I'm amused that you thought I would try to pressure you to snare Mr. Chamberlain. Considering all the suitors you've let slip through your fingers these past few seasons, I obviously know you'd be out of your depth with that one." Her mother's words hurt, but since they were true she had kept her mouth shut.

As for Harriet, Julia had worried that she would disregard her engagement and flirt with Henry, and maybe she would have, except that she had seemed in a bad mood that night, hardly talking to anyone. But her bad mood hadn't lasted and Julia had been surprised over the last week to observe that her sister seemed to love Barrington. Julia would often return from a walk to find that Harriet was out on one herself. But since Harriet seemed to prefer solitary walks, she hadn't confided in her either. Julia would have loved to tell Martha about the hope she had briefly cherished for Henry and the frustration she now felt—mostly frustration at her own actions. But she could never tell Martha about it, since she was the very person who had warned her that if she got close to Henry, he would break her heart.

It had been several days since she had seen him, which helped, actually. It was the reason she was walking along her favorite path this morning that would take her past the back pastures where their riding lessons had been. He was obviously avoiding her, so there was no reason for her to do the same.

There was another dinner this evening, just as always on a Saturday, but at breakfast this morning, Martha had said, "I think my sore throat is worse this morning. I'll send a note to Lady Chamberlain that I won't be dining there today. What about the rest of you?" she had asked Julia, Harriet, and their mother. "Would you like me to send your excuses as well, or do you plan to attend?"

Harriet immediately replied, "I plan to attend. There is so little to do here, it will be almost a novelty to dine out."

"I thought you were loving it here," said Julia, surprised. "You've been out for walks exploring every day."

Harriet froze for a brief moment as she was setting her cup down. She glanced at their mother and then back at Julia and said, "Solitary walks aren't the same as being out in company."

Her mother, without noticing Harriet's suspicious reaction, had also voiced her intention to go, saying, "Yes, I'll attend too. It seems we have to take every opportunity we get while in the country."

Julia had been annoyed at their criticism of Barrington, but slightly torn as to what she should do. She didn't want to leave her mother and sister alone with the Chamberlains, but her desire to avoid Henry had been the greater incentive and she replied, "I'll stay at home with you, Martha. Perhaps I've been often enough that the novelty of dining at Barrington Court has worn off."

The novelty of solitary walks hadn't worn off for her though, and Julia hoped it never would. These morning walks had saved her sanity this week. For that one brief day, she had cherished the hope that Henry would be her future. It was taking much longer than a day to brush off the hurt of his rejection. Every other suitor that had rejected her had left her with hurt pride, but Henry's dismissal had been more than that. Her pride was certainly a factor, but the humiliation was different. No one else even knew that Henry had briefly wanted to court her, so there wasn't the embarrassment of others knowing she had been rejected again. This time it was just the humiliation of realizing she had thought she would be enough for him and she wasn't.

The thought had barely formed when Julia heard a sound behind her and looked over her shoulder to see Henry himself riding Felix. Much to her surprise, she saw Pegasus behind him and realized that Henry was leading him. Julia had the horrible thought that he was giving riding lessons to some other young lady. He could be on his way to meet her now, and he would convince the unsuspecting girl to keep it all a secret. They were coming toward her on the path, but still a ways off. Julia knew he had already seen her and there wasn't time to avoid a meeting by changing course, but she had time to prepare herself for a civil "hello" as he passed. The last time they had spoken privately, she had barely been able to get two words out without losing her composure. This time would be different.

In less time than she expected, Felix was standing next to her and Henry was dismounting. She was surprised by that. She was always a little in awe when she saw him. After the way he had treated her she thought it was unfair that his handsome features hadn't diminished somehow. With what she hoped was a casual tone she greeted him, "Hello, Mr. Chamberlain."

"Hello, Miss North." His tone sounded easy, but his manner looked as though he was uncomfortable. Julia hoped that he was. "I was hoping to find you this morning."

Julia didn't know if she should feel upset that he was seeking her out—why would he do that?—or relieved that he wasn't meeting someone else for riding lessons. "Was there something particular you wanted to talk about?" she asked.

Henry held her gaze for a moment as if trying to gauge her mood before he responded, "I thought perhaps you would like another riding lesson or two."

After their last conversation, Julia had resolved to avoid Henry; she had been certain he would do the same. All the others who had rejected her had certainly never sought her out afterwards. "I think I've learned all I need to know about riding for my purposes," she answered.

He was about to launch into a persuasive argument, she could tell, but he stopped as he realized her response and asked, "Your purposes?" There was definitely curiosity in his voice. "What do you mean?"

Julia was silent a moment as she tried to think how to respond. She definitely didn't want to admit that she had only learned to ride so future suitors wouldn't find her inadequate. She wanted to kick herself for not just saying "No, thank you," and walking on. Finally she lifted one shoulder in a shrug and said, "Nothing, really . . . Just that I've learned all I wanted to know, and I'm not frightened of horses anymore." It was true, just not all the truth. "It was more than I ever expected to accomplish."

"But I haven't taught you to gallop," he said, gesturing to the horse she thought of as her own. "It's why I brought Pegasus today. You wouldn't want to stop now that you've come so far."

Julia contradicted him, "I do want to stop now. I've no reason to learn more."

"What was your reason for letting me teach you in the first place?" He was looking at her suspiciously.

Julia shouldn't have even implied there was another reason. Did he think it was so she could be alone with him? She wanted to set him straight, but Julia couldn't lie, and the truth was not an option either. Feeling flustered, she said, "I don't know. Or rather, I know, but I don't want to say."

A knowing smile spread across Henry's face and Julia realized he would think from her refusal to admit her reason that it must have been to get close to him that she had learned to ride. Ridding him of such a notion was worth giving up the truth. "Fine, I'll admit that my reason for learning to ride was so I could use the skill to ride with other gentlemen when I return to London."

His smile faltered at her reason and he looked slightly deflated by her words, his green eyes taking on an innocent but wounded look. Yet he was not defeated. "You better learn to gallop then so you can impress all your friends as you tear through Hyde Park." He put his hands on her waist and lifted her up on Pegasus. It felt so natural she didn't think to resist until she was already looking down at him from the saddle.

"I don't need to . . . ," she began, but realized she didn't have the will to argue. With a sigh she said, "Very well. If you think Pegasus will actually gallop, then by all means teach me how to make him." She didn't say the words "so we can get this over with," but they were implied in her tone.

"Let's get to the pasture first."

The horses both walked along at a slow, steady pace. Pegasus went to his natural place next to Felix as a silence descended between them, which Julia found uneasy. The path was a familiar one now for Julia, but in studiously avoiding Henry's gaze she was noticing things she hadn't before, like dead branches in distant trees and old, decaying leaves trapped at the base of the hedges.

She was more than a little surprised to find herself in this position. After the last lesson that Henry had missed, she thought that nothing could induce her to ever agree to another lesson. Henry would probably again imply that he was doing her some sort of favor, when he was the one pressuring her to have another lesson. Julia had been avoiding looking at Henry, but now as she looked over at him, she thought his expression was pleased and comfortable.

She ground her teeth in frustration and decided she shouldn't be the only one feeling distressed in the other's presence. "Mr. Chamberlain," she began formally, "I am surprised you want to give another riding lesson. Your note when you missed our last lesson certainly implied this was a burden to you."

Julia felt a little better as Henry's smile turned to a look of consternation. "I don't remember exactly what I wrote, but I don't think I would ever have implied such."

"You said you couldn't *attend* to me," she emphasized. "And that if you had time, you would give me another *short lesson*. I suppose you are just fulfilling that obligation today?"

"That note was written in a great hurry," he explained. "I'm afraid I don't remember how my words were phrased, but if I was rude in any way, I apologize."

She hadn't been expecting an apology. She thought he was much more likely to brush it aside as her being oversensitive. She didn't bother responding, but instead asked, "Your insistence to teach me riding today is even more surprising given our conversation before dinner last week."

Julia had achieved her purpose; he looked decidedly uncomfortable now. He cleared his throat and surprised Julia again by looking up directly into her eyes and saying, "For my words to you then, I most sincerely apologize. I can hardly explain my reasoning, as I don't even understand it myself now, but I thought at the time that I couldn't court you. I hope you'll forgive me and allow me another chance to prove myself."

Julia was at first more shocked than ever by Henry's apology and his desire to renew their courtship, but she realized quickly that she should have been expecting this rather than being surprised by it. She had been avoiding him; he must be suffering from the lack of attention. He had worked so hard to have her fall at his feet; of course he would want to keep her there. Henry Chamberlain would have to realize for himself that she would not be constantly waiting for crumbs of attention from him. Narrowing her eyes, she said, "How do I gallop?"

Henry looked a little confused at her abrupt change of subject. "Miss North . . . Julia," he began again, reverting to her first name once more. "I knew almost immediately last week that I had made a mistake. When Jonathan flirted with you so shamelessly at dinner, I realized that I couldn't stand to see you with another. I know I'm asking a lot of you, but I hope you'll allow me the chance again to court you."

It was exactly as she suspected! He had never seemed as arrogant to her as he did in that moment. He was so sure she would give him another chance, and only wanting it because of his need to feel superior or acquire her attention as a possession he felt he deserved. Well, Julia couldn't quite put his arrogance into words, but it was obvious his feelings had more to do with his feelings for himself rather than her.

She had very little trouble replying, "No, thank you, Mr. Chamberlain. I am not interested in being pulled about by your whims again. Now, if you intend to teach me to gallop, I suggest you begin, before I figure out how to do it myself and gallop home."

Henry visibly swallowed, and Julia felt a tiny bit of remorse at her harsh words, but not enough to recall any of them. He looked worried as he pulled his reins to the side to move around in front of her to begin the lesson.

Julia watched as Henry showed her how to spur her horse to action and then took off with speed across the pasture. She had seen riders gallop before and hoped she'd never have to try it. Her fear of horses wasn't completely obliterated and Julia wondered if she was wise to be pressured into this last lesson when it included galloping. Henry pulled Felix in a loop and was soon back facing her once more. "Do you think you can do it?"

Julia's competitive nature wouldn't let her do anything other than try and her biggest reassurance was the lazy horse beneath her. Pegasus had barely glanced up as Felix raced around the pasture. She knew that the horse Henry had chosen for her would prefer standing still to anything else.

Following Henry's example, Julia spurred Pegasus forward. At first he trotted and, just like the two or three other times she had been at a trot, the jarring sensation of riding a horse was worse than ever. But Henry called out, "Kick again; he'll realize you want to go faster."

Julia cringed inwardly at the thought of going faster. It was already a bruising ride as she bounced up and down in the saddle. This would be her last lesson though. She would master galloping so Henry wouldn't have another excuse to pressure her into yet another lesson.

Julia urged Pegasus forward with another kick to his flanks and for the first time in her experience Pegasus lived up to his name: she felt like she was flying! The jarring up and down motion of trotting was gone; all the movement for both her and Pegasus was forward. The speed made her feel frantic for a moment, but she held on tight and felt a smile spread over her face. This was why riding was something people enjoyed, not just a way to get from here to there. Julia felt that the gallop was worth every moment it had taken to overcome her fear of horses and learn to ride.

Julia rode without worrying where she was going. At some point, Henry and Felix had galloped in front of her and Pegasus. As always, Pegasus followed Felix, so Julia let herself enjoy the freedom of galloping. She let every bit of herself enjoy the amazing sensation. When Henry had stopped her on the path, their conversation had consumed all her thoughts, but galloping consumed all her senses. It was exhilarating.

Pegasus slowed to a walk before she was ready to be done, but Henry and Felix had stopped up ahead of her, a clear signal to Pegasus to end his exertions.

"That was amazing!" Julia exclaimed. "Can we keep going?" She recalled herself almost immediately. This was Henry Chamberlain she was speaking to.

"Oh, never mind," she said at the same time that Henry said, "Yes, let's go on."

She looked at him. He was smiling at her hopefully and Julia felt worse than before. Spending time with Henry alone like this was a mistake. He didn't even have a groom with him today, although it felt less necessary than ever for them to have a chaperone. "No, I shouldn't. I . . ." Julia tried to quickly think of a reason and she could hear the relief in her own voice when she said, "Martha isn't feeling well today. I want to get back to see how she's doing."

It was a weak reason, and she could tell Henry knew it, but he didn't try to persuade her. They just turned their horses back. "Would you like to try galloping again?" he asked.

Julia nodded and tried to hold back a smile as she nudged Pegasus up to speed again. The smooth rush of galloping thrilled her for a few minutes before they reached the lane and let the horses walk. Her smile faded as she remembered that she wouldn't be doing this again. Henry had helped her overcome her fear of horses, but really Pegasus was the only horse she would feel comfortable riding. She felt that she could rely on Pegasus to be idle whenever she would let him, but all other horses, even Felix, were unpredictable. She had told Henry she had overcome her fear of horses, but it might only be true with Pegasus.

Whatever reason Henry had for retreating away from the closeness they had briefly shared was still there. Today he was being so kind and solicitous, seeking her out like he had. But what would he do tomorrow? Or the following week? Julia knew she couldn't trust him just to be disappointed again. He didn't mean half of what he said or did.

Julia realized that Henry was coming back with her to Martha's. Except for the day he had kissed her, she had always walked back from the pasture alone after their lessons, but now they were nearing Barrington proper, together. This was just what she didn't need. She had to convince Martha to let her stay and soon. She had wanted to stay with Martha so much, but since Henry's rapid desertion, Julia's desire to stay had cooled. She still wanted to stay much more than she wanted her mother to choose her husband, but it wasn't as ideal of a solution to her problem as it had been before. But she didn't have a better plan, so she couldn't be seen with Henry.

Feeling resolved, she said, "You go on. I think I'll finish my walk."

With disbelief in his voice he replied, "I thought you wanted to see how your cousin was doing."

"Yes, I did. But you're here, and you can check on her now, then I'll come back later and check on her." Julia knew that there was no good reason she could share with Henry as to why she wasn't going back to see Martha with him, but to try to convince him she added, "She'll probably appreciate that more; two visits instead of one."

"What if she's indisposed in her rooms? You'll need to see to her then. I won't be any help," he protested.

There was no way he was going to change her mind. She couldn't show up to see Martha with him. "She was reading in the sitting room when I left," she reassured him. "I'm sure that's where you'll find her." Julia dismounted when they reached the footpath leading off the lane that wound past the village then looped back again. She intended to walk the full length of it.

Henry's expression became solemn and he was quiet for a moment before saying, "You really don't want to spend time with me, do you?"

A polite reply sprang from her lips, "It's not that . . . ," but it was definitely part of it. Julia had engaged her heart too much where Henry was concerned. She needed time away from him to steel her heart to care about him less, and although it hurt her pride to admit that she was avoiding him, Julia decided it would be better than admitting anything else. She patted Pegasus and avoided Henry's gaze as she said, "If given the choice, I would prefer not to be in your company."

When he didn't reply, Julia looked up at him. Henry held her gaze briefly then looked down at the reins in his hand. The deep *V* between his brows conveyed disappointment, but it seemed to Julia that it was directed at himself, not at her. Julia didn't try to explain. She couldn't let Martha see them together, and her feelings needed time to change. She handed Pegasus's lead rope to him, but before she could bid him farewell he said, "Please let me just explain what happened before."

Julia shook her head definitively and said, "Goodbye, Mr. Chamberlain."

Julia walked away quickly and didn't look back. Hopefully someday she could comfortably be Henry's friend. She'd need to in order to achieve her goal of living in Barrington. He was a good friend of Martha's after all.

Martha was an easy person for Julia to get along with. The *only* thing Martha had ever asked her to do was not to set her sights on Henry. Thinking back on that conversation during her first week in Barrington, Julia remembered her cousin's words sounding like she was trying to protect Julia, but there was an undertone of wanting to protect Henry. If Martha thought she was like every other girl, pestering Henry endlessly, she would send her back to London with her mother.

As Julia walked along the path she glanced up to see a couple walking toward her. She moved off the center of the path and kept walking, with her head down, thinking. She glanced up again at the couple approaching her and let out an audible gasp. Harriet was coming toward her with her arm linked with Mr. Corey's.

Her gasp caused the pair to notice her for the first time. Harriet quickly pulled away from Mr. Corey, looking frightened at being caught.

Julia quickly recovered from her shock, folded her arms, and glared, particularly at Mr. Corey. Julia had noticed the adoring look on Harriet's face before her presence was noticed. It reminded her of how Mr. Corey had acted with her when they first met. This sudden revelation of a romance between her sister and Mr. Corey brought the immediate question to her mind: was Mr. Corey a shameless flirt without honor? As Julia watched, she grew more worried as he placed a hand on her sister's arm and whispered something in her ear. Harriet nodded and Mr. Corey turned to Julia and with a bow and a brief, "Good day, Miss North," he departed abruptly back the way they had come.

Julia rushed up to Harriet and pulled her in the opposite direction. "Harriet! What are you doing?" Julia asked, feeling appalled at the implications of what she had just seen. "You've known this man a week and you're . . . what *are* you doing?" she asked again, this time waiting for a reply.

Harriet looked for a moment like she would try to convince Julia there was nothing untoward going on, but Julia gave a stern look. In response, Harriet sighed and said, "We were just walking, Julia."

If Harriet hadn't been engaged to Lord Blakely, it wouldn't matter at all. It did matter, though. Julia had expected her sister's flirtatious behavior to end once she became engaged. "Has anyone else seen you? You realize you could ruin everything."

"I don't want to marry Lord Blakely!" she declared. "He doesn't love me and Mother just pushed me into accepting the first man who offered without even considering love."

Julia couldn't believe what she was hearing. While that was all true, Harriet had never seemed opposed to the idea leading up to her engagement. She glanced back over her shoulder to where Mr. Corey had disappeared, making sure he wasn't listening. Looking back at Harriet, she asked, "Do you think what you have with Mr. Corey is love?" When Harriet just looked sullen and didn't answer, Julia continued, "You two have only known each other for a week. You aren't in love. And what about the trouble you were causing in London? Isn't that the reason Mother brought you here, to get you away from some other rake you were trying to cause a scandal with?"

"He's not a rake," Harriet immediately defended. Looking hesitant once again, Harriet bit her lip then reluctantly admitted, "Mr. Corey was the same man I was seen out with in London. But you and Mother are wrong about him. He's not a rake," she repeated.

Julia was starting to realize that this was much more serious than she had thought. And it wouldn't be fixed by a stern lecture to her flighty sister. She didn't know Mr. Corey well at all, but she hadn't thought of him as a rake. In fact, she was fairly certain he wasn't, otherwise he wouldn't be a good friend of Henry's. Although, perhaps Henry didn't know all his friend was up to.

"But Harriet, he is spending time alone with you while you're engaged to someone else. And if he is the same man you were seeing in London, does that mean he followed you here?"

"Yes, when Mother decided to bring me to Barrington until the wedding, Jonathan left London at the same time to pay a surprise visit to the Chamberlains." Julia remembered again how Mr. Corey had flirted with her when they first met. Perhaps he wasn't a shameless flirt, but he had only been trying to disguise his true feelings for her sister. "Luckily Mother hasn't discovered his identity yet. We've managed to meet in private much more successfully here than in London."

The implication was clear. She was asking Julia to keep their secret, but Harriet didn't leave it at that. She grabbed Julia's arm and begged, "Please don't tell Mother. She won't let me cancel the wedding and if she knew about Jonathan she wouldn't let me see him again."

"Harriet," Julia replied, exasperated. "She's right. You can't let another man court you while you're engaged!"

Harriet's voice turned from pleading to frustrated as she said, "I would think that you, of all people, would be on my side with this. You know how Mother is, how she has always been, but especially since Lord Montague proposed to her. All she wants is to marry us off so she can happily live her life without us."

"Harriet, I don't agree with Mother trying to get us married as fast as possible," Julia said with reproach in her voice, "but you have agreed to marry Lord Blakely. Cancelling the engagement would be quite scandalous." Seeing the dismay on her sister's face, Julia couldn't help but add, "But if you were willing to weather the scandal and immediately form an engagement to Mr. Corey instead, perhaps Mother would let you. I don't think she

cares precisely *whom* we marry as long as we *are* married."
Julia wasn't really certain about that. Mother would be upset about Harriet giving up the title. She wondered too, if Lord Montague would be annoyed with the scandal and possibly even cancel his own private engagement to their mother.

"I'm not certain if I would immediately become engaged to Jonathan." Julia's heart sank at Harriet's admission, and her sister added, "He likes me I'm sure. I think he might even love me, but he can't talk to me about marriage while I'm still engaged to Lord Blakely."

"And you can't cancel the engagement because Mother won't let you," Julia concluded.

"Precisely!" she exclaimed. "It's so unfair."

Julia couldn't think of a good conclusion to this mess. And despite Harriet's defense of him, she was seriously doubting Mr. Corey's good character. Clandestine meetings with an engaged young lady? What gentleman would behave in such a way? "Does Hen— er, Mr. Chamberlain know about your secret?" Julia asked Harriet.

"I'm almost certain he doesn't. We haven't told anybody, although in London, we weren't as cautious as we should have been. I suppose we weren't being cautious enough today, since you discovered us. At least it was you and not Mother or Martha."

Julia wished she didn't know. She couldn't fail to realize that now that she knew, any resulting scandal would be partly her fault if she didn't do something to stop the pair of them.

After thinking the matter over for a few moments, Julia suggested, "What if you write a letter to Lord Blakely and ask him to cancel the engagement?"

"I thought of that, but it would be much more scandalous if he cancelled it than if I did, so I don't think he'll agree."

"But it's still your best option. Besides, maybe you're wrong. Once he realizes you want out of the engagement he very well might be willing to end it. Perhaps he won't want to marry an unwilling young lady."

Harriet's eyes brightened at the tone in Julia's voice. "Maybe you're right. It's worth a try anyway. The wedding is only a few weeks away now, and every day I'm more worried I won't be able to stop it."

"Mother would be furious if she knew any of this," Julia stated the obvious.

"Mother has her own secrets which would cause just as much scandal if they were known," Harriet replied with a return of her saucy attitude. "Both Mother and Lord Montague's despicable characters would be revealed if their secret ever got out."

Julia felt the truth of it, but Harriet had never been upset about it before. When their mother had told them of her secret engagement almost a year ago, it had meant an early come-out for Harriet, and she had loved flirting and mastering the art of catching a gentleman husband. Harriet's current sentiments must have been influenced greatly by the predicament with Mr. Corey, and if Julia was honest with herself, she didn't think that was a bad thing. She hadn't thought her sister capable of forming a deep enough attachment that would ever be worth sacrificing anything for. She just worried about Mr. Corey staying constant. Would he really offer for her if she was embroiled in the scandal of a cancelled engagement?

All these secrets brought her own recent heartache to mind and she finally replied, "Secrets aren't anything but trouble."

"Hopefully mine won't be a secret much longer," Harriet said, sounding more cheerful now. "I'll send Lord Blakely a letter right away, and once my engagement is cancelled, Jonathan can court me openly."

Julia supposed that was the most reasonable thing to do. She wondered how Lord Blakely would respond. Even if he was amenable, their mother could probably cause the wedding to happen by her will alone. Julia sighed. Her own wedding would follow shortly thereafter to an unwanted husband if she didn't find a way to stay in Barrington with Martha.

Brushing the self-concerned thought aside, she smiled a little at Harriet and said, "So your solitary walks haven't actually been solitary."

Harriet's answering smile was tinged with relief as she said, "I've never enjoyed walking alone, and the countryside is pretty, but boring in about a minute. Barrington's only saving grace has been Jonathan's presence."

Julia heard her sister's words with unease. She wondered again if Mr. Corey was honorable and what his intentions were. When they had met, he had been overtly flirtatious with her in a way that denoted his experience. Julia observed as much to Harriet. "You know, Mr. Corey was perhaps a little too friendly toward me when we met last week."

"He didn't want to mislead you," Harriet defended, "but we couldn't let Mother suspect anything."

"He didn't mislead me," she reassured. "I didn't ever think his interest went beyond the superficial. I do wonder if it will hurt your cause in the end. People might think his feelings for you aren't sincere."

"Perhaps you are right, but I don't doubt him and no one else matters."

Julia wondered if there was any way—besides asking Henry—that she could find out more about Mr. Corey.

Julia and Harriet returned to the house mostly in silence now, each lost in her own thoughts. Julia felt frustrated that there was nothing she could do. But it was a problem of Harriet's own making. Harriet had always been impulsive and emotional and it appeared that her come-out hadn't changed that; her emotions still directed her actions.

Despite having had many suitors, Julia had never been in love with any of them. Harriet was now in love with a second man in as many months. Julia was grateful again that she had escaped Henry's presence earlier. She couldn't handle the highs and lows of romance that Harriet seemed to thrive on.

Chapter 18

$\mathcal{H}$enry sat astride his horse and checked his pocket watch. Another difficult week had gone by since he had taught Julia to gallop, and he'd hardly seen her since. Well that wasn't precisely true. He'd seen her at church. He'd seen her at Barrington Court. He'd even stopped by Miss Abbot's twice and seen her there. But in all those several meetings, he hadn't had a single moment to speak with her privately.

He had finally admitted to himself that he was ready to court her, and he was growing impatient. Having her within reach, yet being unable to have a relationship with her was frustrating. It was the reason he was out with both horses again today, hoping to intercept Julia on her walk and convince her to ride with him instead. Once she heard him out, she was sure to forgive him for his inconsistent behavior and they could begin their courtship in earnest. His only obstacle was finding Miss Julia North on her own. He didn't blame her entirely for avoiding him. But if she just knew what he had to say, she wouldn't be preventing a private meeting; she would be encouraging it.

Glancing at his watch again, Henry knew that if Julia had been out walking this morning, she was most likely home by now. He was near the path where he had watched her walk away last time. He had been a little frustrated, even then, that he hadn't been easily able to fix his mistake. When he had asked her if he could court her again, he had seen a look of anger in her eyes. But she would forgive him eventually. She would see that he was sorry for hurting her and that he sincerely wanted to be with her forever. In fact, when they finally resolved this, it would be that much sweeter for working for it rather than just having her give in so easily.

Thinking of that moment in the hopefully not-too-distant future, Henry decided not to give up quite so easily today. He rode Felix toward Miss Abbot's house, leading Pegasus behind him. Henry arrived at Miss Abbot's home and tied both horses to the front gate before knocking.

He called unexpectedly often enough that it wasn't unexpected at all and he was shown right into the drawing room, where Miss Abbot was the only occupant.

With all the visitors she had had lately, he was surprised to find her alone. "I thought I'd find you with some of your guests," he said as he sat down.

"Julia and Harriet are out walking and Marianne hasn't emerged from her room yet today."

"Julia *is* out walking?" he asked. At Miss Abbot's sharp look, he realized he had used her Christian name. He wasn't too worried about that. He was more concerned with finding a way to explain his feelings to Julia. It seemed she wasn't going to give him the chance. He noticed Miss Abbot still watching him closely. "I didn't see her on my way here and I thought if she was out walking that I would have . . ." Henry trailed off. "Never mind," he muttered.

"Henry what's going on?" Miss Abbot set her needlework down on a table near her and turned her full attention on him. "This is the third time you've called on me in a week. I could flatter myself that it's my company you enjoy so much, but I'm beginning to think you are seeking out Julia."

"I've hurt her feelings, I believe, and I need a chance to speak with her," Henry explained, brushing imaginary lint from his trousers.

"You hurt her feelings?" Henry nodded and waited for her to question him about it. Instead she heaved a big sigh and said, "I see. Julia's become attached to you, just like all the others." She rubbed at her temples as if trying to dispel a headache. "I hope you'll believe me Henry that I did warn her right from the beginning not to bother you. I know how you try to avoid these awkward situations with young ladies and I'm sorry that a guest of mine is making things uncomfortable for you."

"You warned her?" he asked with disbelief. "What do you mean you warned her?"

"When she first arrived, I told her what happened with Miss Corey and how low you have been ever since. I told her how every girl thinks she'll be the one to 'fix' you or some such nonsense. I have caught her staring at you in admiration from time to time, but I truly thought she had been convinced."

She seemed stern, but Henry couldn't help but feel relieved enough to see the humorous side to it all. "I'm actually quite surprised to hear all this Miss Abbot. I had no idea you were trying to protect me from ambitious young women." He was smiling now, but Miss Abbot didn't look any less annoyed.

"Not all young women, just Julia. I'm sure you don't need my help, but I thought I could prevent at least one young lady from pestering you." Shaking her head, Miss Abbot turned to pick her embroidery back up.

"Actually, I wouldn't mind if Julia pestered me," he admitted.

Miss Abbot dropped her embroidery and looked up sharply at him. "What are you saying?" she asked.

Henry made his decision then. Miss Abbot might as well know, and then maybe she could help his cause. "I'm saying, I wouldn't mind if she admired me."

"Henry!" she said his name in a tone full of reproach. "I never thought you would toy with someone's feelings. I know you've done so before unintentionally, but you can't go about giving false hope. If you encourage Julia, she'll fall in love with you in an instant. You'll break her heart."

Henry hadn't interrupted her, but now he felt he'd better explain himself completely. "I have no intention of breaking her heart. I want to court her."

Miss Abbot was searching his gaze, trying to determine if he meant what he said. So he added, "Julia captured my attention from the first moment I saw her. I've felt . . . different since I met her. Happier, I think."

"I haven't noticed any difference. You always seem happy enough, Henry, but it's just putting on a good show."

Henry realized he would have to explain himself further. "I think it's been more than that for a while now. I've been living my life and acting happy and at some point—probably when I met Julia—I stopped acting. Julia's had my attention since she arrived, but each time we meet she captures more of my . . . interest."

"Are you certain, Henry? Have you really turned that corner?" Miss Abbot asked with hopeful concern.

"I've been telling myself I was miserable for so long, but I'm just not anymore. I hope you don't think I'm terribly inconsistent."

Miss Abbot wasn't looking annoyed anymore; more than anything she just seemed surprised. Henry was relieved when she said, "Not at all, Henry, I'm so pleased you realized it before this opportunity passed you by."

Henry did want Miss Abbot's approval, but he also wanted his feelings validated if possible. It was a risk to ask, but he wanted her true opinion. "But your situation was the same as mine and you've never entertained the thought of moving on. Do you think I'm being unfaithful to Miss Corey's memory?"

"Our situations weren't precisely the same, Henry. My Charles claimed me as his when we were quite young. When I lost him, I lost more than my heart; it was practically my whole identity. I wasn't able to figure out who I was without him until it was much too late for me to think of courting again. I know you truly loved Miss Corey, but you only knew her for two months. I've never even heard you use her Christian name. Except for her brother's visit now, you haven't seen her family. I don't mean to say you weren't as devastated as I at the death of your fiancée, just that the shorter duration of your love perhaps means a shorter time for your heart to heal."

It had been some time since he and Miss Abbot had had a discussion this serious. Henry wondered if she was just trying to make him feel better about loving again, or if she truly believed what she said. It made sense to him and he felt the truth of his situation, not just in comparison to hers but in how his heart felt now. Henry let out a breath and felt some tension slip away. "So you think it would be suitable then? My courting Julia?"

"It's not my permission you need, but I'll give it just the same. I'm so pleased that it is my sweet cousin you've set your heart on. I can see her good qualities that put her above all the other girls, I just didn't think you could or would."

It was more encouragement than he had expected from Miss Abbot, who was usually so stoic. But it didn't necessarily make his path any easier. "As I said, her feelings are hurt at the moment and I think she's avoiding me, so it might take a little time."

Miss Abbot narrowed her eyes now and looked at him curiously, "How did you hurt her feelings?"

"I'd rather not say . . ." Henry hesitated a moment debating what he should admit to Miss Abbot. "Well, I've had some trouble making my mind up about what I really want." He knew now what he really wanted though, and he continued, "But now I know for certain I want to court Julia and hopefully convince her to marry me." As soon as he said the words he felt his heart pick up speed. He had thought about courting her, hopefully being engaged to her, and of course he had thought about kissing her, but the thought of Julia as his wife made him catch his breath.

Miss Abbot looked very much like she was holding back a smile. It was enough for Henry to know she was pleased by his interest in Julia, but all she said was, "Why are you telling me all this? Shouldn't you be telling Julia?"

"I should, but I can't find an opportunity," Henry said, with a return of his earlier frustration. "Every time we are in each other's company, there are too many people around. I need to speak to her privately, which, I suppose, is my reason for telling you my intentions. Would you help me? I'm sure as soon as I can explain all this to Julia, I can convince her to stop avoiding me."

Miss Abbot gave Henry a thoughtful look. "Very well, let me see . . . Perhaps something out of the ordinary would be best." It was silent for a few moments as they both tried to think of any unusual activity they could do in Barrington. Finally Miss Abbot's face lightened as she said, "A picnic to Blackdown Hills might be the very thing. It's a bit of a distance, but if we have a fine day, that won't matter. I believe my London guests have lacked amusements during their stay here and I should have thought of this before. I'm not sure they've been content with our small village life."

"Has Julia seemed unhappy here?" Henry hadn't thought to pay close attention. She had mentioned to him before that she didn't miss London, but that seemed to do more with her mother than the actual place. Perhaps she had been bored here as well. He hadn't thought to ask.

"I didn't think so before her family arrived; she always occupies herself so well that we get along famously." Henry smiled a little at that. He knew Miss Abbot enjoyed a fair amount of solitude. "But she has seemed less content lately. I had just assumed that she wasn't pleased with her mother and sister here, but perhaps she's been moping over you."

Henry certainly hoped so. He didn't like the idea that she had been sad because of him, but he'd love to be the one to cheer her up. "Blackdown Hills sounds perfect. In fact," he said as he remembered picnics in the past, "if I remember correctly, there are quite a few easy paths that could lead away to privacy."

Miss Abbot gave him a knowing look, but he didn't mind that she knew what he was up to; it had been her idea in the first place.

They finished planning out the excursion, agreeing that Miss Abbot should be the one to sponsor it. Henry's only dissatisfaction with the plan was that they would wait a week to go. He understood that it would take some planning and Miss Abbot intended to invite another neighbor or two, but Henry wanted Julia to forgive him already. It would be another long week.

Chapter 19

*D*ays before the planned picnic, Henry found himself in Julia's company again at the home of his neighbors, the Trevons. In his hopes of spending time alone with her, he found himself in gatherings like this more often. Over the last few weeks he had shown up wherever he thought she might be, accepting every invitation. Of course, as was usual, she was barely civil, just speaking to him enough to avoid any awkward scenes or questions, which made Henry more impatient for Tuesday's excursion to Blackdown Hills.

Perhaps he could find an opportunity to speak to her this evening. He let himself imagine briefly how he would behave tonight if Julia had already forgiven him. Instead of casting tentative glances her way and being ignored, he would catch her eye and share a secret smile. The thought of his mother intercepting such a look still made him wince, but even if she did discover his feelings for Julia, he would be better off than in his current state.

When the gentlemen joined the ladies again in the drawing room after dinner, Henry watched to see how his evening would go. Henry knew that Mr. Trevon strongly preferred an evening of cards to anything else, but his wife detested cards and almost never lost an argument. He hoped that the decision could be made without a disagreement. He felt enough tension in the air from Julia without having to witness an argument. Mr. and Mrs. Trevon surprised him, however. Mrs. Trevon called for the attention of the group and said, "Mr. Trevon and

I couldn't decide what our evening entertainment should be. So we have decided to let you, our guests, help us decide. We are going to put it to a vote." There was a ripple of murmurs through their small group at the announcement.

Mr. Trevon cleared his throat. "Your choices are: dancing," he said the word with utter disdain, leaving no doubt about his opinion of that activity; then his expression lightened and his tone became persuasive as he said, "or a wonderful evening filled with the intrigue of exciting card play." The guests were all amused at his tactic, but paid him no more attention as they talked among themselves about which they would choose. Mrs. Trevon, who had rolled her eyes at her husband's attempt at wit, called for the vote. When she said, "Those in favor of dancing raise your hand," Henry's hand went up with several others. He would love the opportunity to dance with Julia and was already anticipating the unexpected closeness. He wasn't sure he would get the chance, as he noticed that Julia did not raise her hand for dancing. But when Mrs. Trevon asked who was in favor of cards, her hand still stayed down, and he wondered what she was thinking. Henry was pleased when dancing instead of cards won the vote.

Henry helped push aside furniture as a maid went to fetch the Trevons' daughter from the nursery to come and play for them. Mr. Trevon refused to let his fifteen-year-old daughter come out for another year at least, but she would be allowed to join the adults in the useful capacity of providing the music.

Henry was startled when a voice at his shoulder said, "Hello, Mr. Chamberlain."

He turned and saw Miss Trevon, who had come into the room behind him. She was getting quite tall and

Henry thought that Mr. Trevon's efforts to keep her a little girl weren't working. "Hello, Miss Trevon," he replied with a smile. "It seems we are dependent on you for our entertainment this evening."

"Yes, you need me." She seemed to love the idea and her smile got bigger as she said, "And for my payment, I only expect your undying devotion."

Henry hesitated with a reply. Was young Miss Trevon trying to flirt with him? His discomfort increased as he looked down at her wide eyes staring up at him. Yes, her father's efforts to keep her from growing up were decidedly not working. He took a step back in reflex and muttered, "I'm sure we all appreciate your playing very much."

Her face fell a little, but she continued to smile up at him until her mother called her to come take her seat at the pianoforte. Henry could only feel relieved.

Mr. and Mrs. Trevon had the perfect group gathered for dancing. Once his mother and Miss Abbot said their intentions were not to dance, they had equal numbers of men and women. It couldn't have been more ideal, except that while Henry had been distracted with Miss Trevon's arrival, he had missed his opportunity to ask Julia to dance. In fact, Miss Clifton was the only woman still free. He approached her and offered his hand, and they joined the other pairs in the center of the room.

They began to move up the dance with the other couples and Henry saw that Julia was dancing with Jonathan. It reminded him of the flirting he had witnessed between the two of them and he resolved to dance with Julia next. He wondered why Julia gave Jonathan as much attention as she did. When he listened to their conversations, everything she said sounded so uninspired, as if she were responding to him from a script. It was obvious that she was pretending to enjoy flirting with him. He wondered if it was obvious to everyone else. Jonathan seemed to think their flirting might mean something. His mother had even remarked in the carriage today that Jonathan might be forming an attachment. He sincerely hoped his mother was wrong about that, just like she was with so many other things.

His preoccupation made him miss what Miss Clifton was saying, so he asked, "I beg your pardon. What did you say?"

She should have been annoyed that he ignored her, but she just smiled brightly. "I said, this dance is so fast, I'm already feeling warm. I'll probably want to step outside to cool off after this."

Henry knew she wanted him to offer to accompany her, and normally he would, but he planned to dance with Julia next. "Perhaps you have a fan . . . ," he began to say, but something about dancing with Miss Clifton reminded him that he had never danced with Julia, because she had promised not to. In fact, it might have even been Miss Clifton she had made her promise to. He looked up at Julia again, his hope of dancing with her this evening fading.

"No, I didn't bring a fan this evening. I think it will have to be fresh air to revive me."

Even though he knew his mother would take note of it, Henry didn't see a way around it, and so, suppressing a sigh, he offered, "I would be happy to escort you to the garden, Miss Clifton."

"Oh, thank you for thinking of that, Mr. Chamberlain. You are too kind."

Henry wasn't feeling "too kind." This evening wasn't any different than so many other evening parties he had attended, but the attention he received from young ladies had never bothered him before. Tonight though, the attention from Miss Trevon and Miss Clifton had been frustrating. He felt ready to be done with this ridiculous game of careful avoidance he had been playing. Being with Julia would be just the thing to protect him. With her by his side, ambitious young women would leave him alone. Henry was more determined than ever to speak to her this evening. Maybe after he convinced her to forgive him, she would break that promise she had made so many weeks ago and they could have their first dance. The anticipation of it brought a smile back to his face.

Julia watched Henry leave with Miss Clifton and berated herself for ever falling for his charms, but in the next moment she congratulated herself for not tagging foolishly after him once again.

It was so ridiculous to watch Miss Trevon, a mere girl from the nursery, as taken with him as anyone. And he responded to her just the same as to every devoted female—a smile, kind words, a touch of humor—just enough to let her spin a fantasy that she was different somehow and had captured his heart. Then Miss Clifton had showed how truly pathetic she was by refusing to dance with Mr. Hibbert and Mr. Trevon, keeping her gaze fastened on Henry across the room. Because of Miss Clifton's scheming, Henry didn't have any choice whether or not he danced with her. So it was Miss Clifton's turn now to receive Henry's momentary affection and Julia was glad she wasn't in line for a turn anymore.

Julia had danced with Mr. Corey for the first set and she was asked to dance now by Mr. Hibbert. They stood at the end of the line of couples and Miss Trevon began to play. Julia couldn't stop her gaze from darting to the door where Henry and Miss Pathetic had disappeared, but they didn't return.

His disappearance with Miss Pathetic reminded her of the conversation earlier this evening. When the gentlemen had withdrawn after dinner, Martha and Lady Chamberlain had led the conversation in the drawing room. The discussion had begun with Shakespeare. Mrs. Trevon had brought it up saying, "My favorite of Shakespeare's plays is *Much Ado About Nothing*. I do enjoy the comedies so much more than the tragedies."

Martha agreed wholeheartedly with her and said, "Especially all the misunderstandings in love. Those divert me the most." She chuckled and, turning to Lady Chamberlain, said, "Do you remember when Henry was young and fell in love with his friend's governess?"

"It was his cousin's governess," Lady Chamberlain corrected. She went on to recount the story with enthusiasm for the subject. "Henry was only ten when he fell in love with Miss Simpson, and she, in turn, was in love with the cook's son, who probably had never thought of her before. Henry decided to declare his love in a letter. After writing it out once, he recopied it in his nicest writing and left it under her door." She paused a moment with a fond look of remembrance on her face. "The note wasn't signed, so Miss Simpson came to her own conclusion that it was the cook's son who had sent it. Poor Henry was the one who spotted them in the garden sharing a kiss and his little heart was broken."

"It probably improved his character," Martha had replied. "It must have been the first time in his life things didn't go his way and he had to decide whether to accept defeat or try harder to pursue what he wanted." Julia had looked up to see Martha's eyes on her.

Lady Chamberlain had looked a bit confused by this. "He didn't pursue her; he was dejected for a few days, but then he became interested in archery."

"It must not have been true love then, if he decided not to pursue her," Martha had replied.

Thinking about that conversation, Julia was more convinced than ever that Henry had only ever fallen in love once, and that was with Miss Corey. Every other passing infatuation was just a distraction for him.

Julia realized that she had spent almost her entire dance with Mr. Hibbert in silence. She looked at him now and realized his attention was not on her, but on the young Miss Trevon at the pianoforte. Perhaps their group was more like Shakespeare's comedy than she had realized.

Henry returned by the time the dance ended and Julia's eyes followed him as he bowed to Miss Clifton in farewell, then turned around and made his way directly to her.

When he was standing in front of her he asked, "Miss North, will you *not* dance with me?"

Julia noticed his emphasis and was confused by the question. Was he asking her to dance? "You want to dance this set with me?" she clarified.

Henry looked out at the couples arranging themselves for the next dance. "I remember from the last time I asked you to dance, you refused because of a promise. I assume you still want to keep your promise, so I am asking that if you will not dance with me, perhaps we could again observe the dance together?"

"I suppose." Julia knew her reply was less than enthusiastic, but she actually was relieved that she wouldn't have to dance with Henry. It had been many weeks since that dance at Martock Priory when she had refused to dance with him because of the ridiculous promise she had made to Miss Clifton and her friends. She couldn't remember if she had promised to *never* dance with Henry or if it had just been for that night. Either way, she was glad Henry assumed she would refuse to dance with him.

They moved to the far side of the room, beyond the last pillar, and leaned their backs against the wall. Julia took a deep breath to fortify herself for a conversation with Henry. She felt stronger than she had when he'd taught her to gallop; her heart was not susceptible to him now. With the story his mother told and then watching him interact with the other young ladies here this evening, she felt herself building a case against falling for him that was stronger all the time.

As soon as the music began, Henry said, "I've been hoping for some time alone with you." He paused and took a deep breath of his own. "I know I hurt you before, but I want to explain why and ask for your forgiveness."

Julia might be stronger than before, but she would still prefer to avoid the subject altogether. "Please don't trouble yourself. I understand you just fine and would prefer to avoid the topic altogether." Henry looked like he wanted to convince her otherwise, so Julia continued quickly, "I've actually been wanting to ask you about Mr. Corey." It was a subject that she hadn't thought she would ever have the chance to ask him about, but she had been curious about Mr. Corey's character and *anything* was better than another excruciating apology for kissing her.

"What do you want to know about him?" Henry asked and Julia noticed his voice had turned hard. That couldn't be a good sign; perhaps they weren't such good friends after all.

"I was just wondering about his character. I don't know him well and you do. Do you think he is an honorable man?"

Again Henry hesitated and Julia wondered what that meant. "As far as I know he's honorable, but I don't know him well. Until a few weeks ago, I hadn't seen or heard from him in more than three years." Julia felt disappointed by his answer. He couldn't tell her if Harriet was truly safe in Mr. Corey's hands or not. Her thoughts were interrupted when Henry continued, "That is actually what I wanted to talk to you about. Mr. Corey showed up the day that I kissed you and—"

"Stop!" Julia's whisper was insistent. "I want to forget that ever happened."

Henry looked half surprised and half hurt by that. "You only want to forget it because there is still a misunderstanding between us. Please just let me explain."

Julia tried, but there was no excuse she could think of to avoid the conversation. He was so determined and she finally resolved to let him say what he wanted to and be done with it. He waited another moment before taking Julia's silence as consent. He looked around, as if to ensure no one was close enough to hear. "When I . . . when I kissed you, I wanted to court you. I would never have been so bold if my intentions weren't serious."

Julia didn't believe a word. She lowered her chin and reminded him, "And yet, you asked me to keep it a secret."

He was facing her now, with just one shoulder leaning against the wall. He raised his hands, palms forward, probably trying to look blameless as he said, "That had nothing to do with my intentions." His voice was entreating as he continued, "I just wanted to court you in my own timing, without my mother pushing us too fast. The very idea of courting again was too new for me and I needed time to get used to it."

Despite the fact that Lady Chamberlain thought Henry could do no wrong, Julia quite admired her, so she said, "I doubt your mother would understand or agree with all you hold her accountable for."

"You're right. It's not her fault; it's mine." Henry's voice was quiet, but sounded a little frustrated. "But my intentions to you were sincere. Just remember that when I left you that day, I was called back to the house to meet a visitor and it turned out to be Jonathan. I wasn't prepared to see Miss Corey's brother again and it brought back all the painful memories of losing her. That was why I told you my intentions had changed, because of Jonathan's arrival. But once the shock wore off, I realized that I was fine."

Julia hadn't expected that and she knew the surprise was evident in her tone when she said, "You're fine? Just like that, you're fine now, so your intentions have changed again?" Julia was momentarily bewildered. Did he really think that he could change his mind *again*, and she would be at his side in an instant?

"Yes, that's it exactly. My heart has truly healed now and it's all thanks to you, and this time, I'm quite certain." With that declaration Henry took a step closer and, behind the cover of the pillar, reached for her hand. Julia took a step back, but Henry didn't release her hand. Henry's tender words didn't reassure her; rather, they caused a spike of fear in her heart. She tugged at her hand and he instantly released it. She turned back to face the room so he couldn't look into her eyes anymore. She *couldn't* hear a tender declaration and get her hopes up, just to have them dashed again. Julia wondered how many other girls had heard a similar speech. How many thought that they were different somehow from all the others throwing themselves at him?

Maybe Jonathan's arrival had something to do with the timing, but Julia had no doubt that Henry would have ended their relationship anyway. It had hurt more than when any other suitor had deserted her. She would never give Henry another chance. If he changed his mind again—which seemed a sure thing—she wouldn't recover.

"When you kissed me, I got my hopes up, but I won't do that again. I'm not going to be your next Miss Pathetic."

"What are you talking about?" Henry asked her, looking confused.

She really needed to be more careful about that, but "pathetic" and "Clifton" were interchangeable in her mind. "Miss Clifton, and all the rest," she explained in a hushed voice. "They adore you and wait their turn for your attention. You give them five minutes of your time and they pathetically build dreams around those little scraps of attention. I won't do that. I won't dream of a future that will never be real!"

Julia felt her heart beating faster as she laid out her fears in front of Henry. He was looking at her with disbelief and responded, "I don't want to give you 'scraps of my attention.' I want to court you in earnest."

"No one wants to court me in earnest. No one ever has before. Every suitor I've ever had has changed his mind about courting me." Julia hadn't meant to admit that and now she kept her gaze on the dance floor. This must be the longest song Miss Trevon knew; it felt like the dance would never end. She could tell Henry was watching her, but he didn't say anything for a long moment.

"I assumed you must have had plenty of proposals and turned them all down."

Julia gave a mirthless huff of laughter, "As if my mother would ever let me turn down a proposal." Another thing she shouldn't have admitted.

Henry didn't seem to know quite how to respond, but finally he said, "I never thought to wonder why you aren't already taken, but I'm relieved you aren't. I can only be grateful that those other men changed their minds; otherwise I would never have met you."

Julia pointedly reminded him, "You changed your mind about courting me, just like they did."

"Yes, but I've realized I made a mistake and changed my mind again." Henry's voice was still quiet, but it was very evident that he was exasperated.

"And what's to stop you from changing your mind the next time? Forgive me for not putting my trust in you completely," she replied with an arch look.

The dance was *finally* winding down and Julia knew she would soon need to look unaffected by their intense conversation. "Henry—" she began, then corrected herself and tried again, "Mr. Chamberlain, I think it would be best if, when we find ourselves in each other's company, we interact as little as possible. In fact, I insist upon it."

The last notes played, the dancers clapped their hands, Julia could hear Mrs. Trevon tell her daughter she could take a short break, and through it all Henry stared at her with a stony expression. His frustration must have turned to anger. Julia hadn't meant for that to happen, but she didn't see an alternative. If she let him have his way now, her heart would be crushed later.

"You are resolved then?" he finally asked.

Julia hesitated for just a moment, sensing the finality in his tone. But she knew what her heart could handle and what it couldn't. "Yes, completely resolved," she said, not meeting his eyes.

Without another word he turned and walked out to the garden once again and Julia breathed deeply to try to stop tears from forming. She had thought she was so much stronger than before, but she felt as fragile as an autumn leaf.

Chapter 20

$\mathcal{T}$he next day, Henry was spending a quiet morning at home. He wished he had some activity to distract himself, but nothing tempted him. He was currently staring morosely at a stack of papers that represented his entire complicated deal with Mr. Dunn. He had planned to look over them one last time for errors this morning, but hadn't made any progress yet. He tried once again to focus, when there was a knock at the door.

Henry was not in the mood for company.

Last evening at the Trevons' had left Henry feeling incredibly disappointed. He hadn't entertained the idea that Julia wouldn't give him another chance. He had thought all along that it was just a matter of time before they would be together. But he now had to accept the possibility that Julia would never give him another chance. He had explained everything to her, but still she didn't trust him, or maybe she just didn't care for him. The thought brought the sting of rejection sharply back.

When Jonathan was shown into his library he felt his mood darken further.

"Hello, Henry. Why are the curtains all drawn?" Jonathan asked as he made his way to the window to move the curtains aside. Henry hadn't noticed the dimness, but the bright sun coming in made him squint.

His feelings toward Jonathan were less than cordial at the moment and he didn't respond to his question, instead asking one of his own. "Have you already been out for a walk this morning?" Jonathan had taken frequent walks since his arrival. Henry had just assumed that was his habit, but now he wondered if Jonathan had been intercepting Julia on her walks.

"Ah . . ." He hesitated and Henry ascribed it to guilt. "No, I'm just about to go on a walk, but thought I'd stop and say hello first."

"Are you meeting someone?" Henry asked suspiciously.

Jonathan narrowed his eyes a bit and Henry could see him trying to decide what to admit. Finally he shook his head and said hesitantly, "No. That is to say, I'm not sure if I might meet someone or perhaps several people while I'm out. But I don't plan to meet anyone . . . in particular."

Ha! If Julia asked him now if Jonathan were honorable, he'd definitely tell her not to trust the man. He was obviously lying.

Jonathan was speaking of something else and Henry had to recall himself to answer a question about the book on his desk that Jonathan had picked up. Julia's questions last evening made him wonder if Jonathan was the reason Julia wouldn't give him another chance.

If they would make a good match, it might be possible to see Julia happy with someone else, but she and Jonathan were so different. His only sincere moments were in emotionally charged moments. At all other times he spoke only of trivial things. Henry had watched Julia interact with Jonathan on several occasions now and he could see how she adopted his insincere manner. Henry couldn't stand to see her with someone that, in order for them to be together, caused her to adopt a different character.

If Henry understood the situation correctly, Julia would be on her way to London soon to marry a man far beneath her that her mother chose for her. Surely she would choose him over that terrible option. But now with Jonathan here, maybe she thought he was the most likely to offer for her. It was a terrible realization for Henry's confidence, to think he could be so easily replaced. He had thought, for that one brief moment in time, that Julia's feelings for him were as sincere as his own, but perhaps she was just trying for anyone in order to get away from the fate her mother had in store for her. Could Julia truly not see or perhaps not even care that she was choosing a man who didn't understand her at all? The thought of watching Jonathan court Julia was unbearable.

Henry's thoughts finally led him to the only reasonable conclusion and disregarding whatever Jonathan had been saying, he said, "You know Jonathan, your stay in Barrington has caused me . . . a bit of difficulty. I think it might be best if you leave."

Jonathan looked up, surprised, and smiled a little as if waiting for the other end of the joke. Henry kept his expression serious and finally Jonathan asked, "Er, what are you talking about? What difficulty?"

"Having you here, well, it's brought back to mind those darker times for me." Henry cleared his throat. He'd just been internally criticizing Jonathan for his dishonesty, and his conscience pierced him. He wasn't lying, but he wasn't telling Jonathan his primary reason for wishing him away.

After a long pause, he replied, "I understand. I'm sorry, Henry, that my presence has made things worse for you." He set the book back on Henry's desk and stood to leave. "I was surprised, when I saw you again, that you haven't moved on. I hope that my leaving will make everything easier for you. Perhaps you won't mind very much if I delay just a day or two? I've sent away for a special l—" he paused briefly then continued, "a special letter, and it should be arriving soon."

Henry wasn't interested enough to ask what Jonathan's business was so he just replied, "No, that's fine. Of course wait for your letter before you go." His guilt increased, but he couldn't bring himself to invite Jonathan back. He could just enjoy a guilty conscience along with the sting of Julia's rejection.

On the morning of the picnic, Julia rode in Martha's carriage as they made their way to Blackdown Hills. Her day was not off to a good start, and riding with her mother and Harriet wasn't improving her mood. Her mother had been disparaging of the idea of a picnic from the first time it was mentioned, and Julia wondered why she had decided to join them at all. The early hour had been her most persistent grievance this morning and Julia was thankful that at least her mother had now fallen asleep across from her, her chin resting on her chest as her head bobbed to the gentle swaying of the carriage. Julia had been looking forward to the excursion since Martha had told her about it last week, but they hadn't even arrived and already she was disappointed.

Henry wasn't coming. When her carriage arrived to pick them up, Lady Chamberlain had said that both Henry and Mr. Corey wouldn't be joining them.

She shouldn't be disappointed. Julia hadn't seen Henry since they had not danced together at the Trevons', not even at church. She assumed he would be one of their party today, but he wasn't. She had been avoiding him for weeks, so she should be grateful, but it felt awful to know he was now avoiding her just as persistently as she had ever avoided him. He was following her wishes after all; they were interacting as little as possible. Julia had heard Martha say that she and Henry had come up with the idea for the picnic. Now he wouldn't even join them and she knew it was her fault. The angry look she had last seen on his face came to mind. Henry Chamberlain never wanted to see her again; she was certain of it. Besides his anger, he must also think she was pitiful. She couldn't believe she had admitted her appalling history with suitors. He must be so relieved by now that he hadn't allowed him to coax her into courting again.

She wondered, for the thousandth time, what about her had made him decide to stop their brief courtship in the first place. Maybe it was that she was too level-headed. All those other girls were fine fantasizing about Henry choosing them. Those fantasies were nothing more than lies they told themselves and too often believed.

Even Harriet fantasized about impossibilities. Harriet might be ruled by every passing emotion, but Julia wouldn't be. In fact, Harriet seemed to be bouncing in her seat this morning, more than just the usual rocking of the carriage. Just yesterday she had been so down when returning from her "solitary" walk. Julia had followed her to their room for a private moment with just the two of them and asked, "What is the matter, Harriet? Have you had a letter back from Lord Blakely?"

"No," she had answered. "That's just the problem. Lord Blakely hasn't replied to my letter requesting we cancel the engagement. A reply should have arrived by now." Harriet seemed devastated.

"Well, don't be too discouraged. Maybe it will arrive in the post today," Julia reassured her. Julia wondered if the awaited letter would help. Lord Blakely would not want the scandal associated with a cancelled engagement but he also wouldn't want to marry Harriet against her will. Julia wasn't sure what reply Harriet should expect, but at least once his letter arrived, Harriet would know one way or the other.

Harriet had fidgeted nervously with her bonnet strings before admitting, "When I was walking with Jonathan this morning, I told him about Mother and Lord Montague's agreement."

"You shouldn't have done that," Julia had responded sharply. "If word of that got out, it would be just as bad for us as it would be for Mother."

"I know, but Jonathan was talking about leaving. My heart would break without him! I was hoping that if he knew about Mother's scheme, he would offer for me so that I could break the engagement to Lord Blakely."

"But that didn't happen?"

"No, he just seemed frustrated that I hadn't told him sooner," Harriet admitted. "I wish he would just take me away. It would solve all our problems." A dreamy look entered Harriet's eye as she continued, "Wouldn't it be so romantic if we eloped?"

"Harriet, that's the most scandalous idea you've had yet!" With a shake of her head at her sister's ridiculous idea she added sensibly, "Just wait for Lord Blakely's letter and even if he's not agreeable, we can reason with Mother. If we really think it through, perhaps we could present it in a light that will make Mr. Corey's courtship seem favorable to her." Julia knew that was the only incentive that would work on their mother, but truly she didn't know how they would ever convince her that Harriet should end her engagement.

Harriet had let out another sigh of frustration. "But what if Jonathan won't wait that long? Oh Julia, if he leaves me, I would die!"

Julia had managed not to roll her eyes as she comforted Harriet and assured her that Mr. Corey was just upset, and that he would come around.

But Harriet had been excited this morning with a smile of anticipation for their outing, and even finding out that Mr. Corey wouldn't be coming on their picnic today hadn't seemed to dampen her excitement. The thoughts that had weighed so heavily on Harriet's mind yesterday seemed to be forgotten.

Watching her sister try to hold back a smile across the carriage from her, Julia wondered how long it would be until she was in tears once more. Days, hours . . . maybe even minutes from now Harriet would be devastated again.

Julia had felt pulled about by Henry in just the same way, with her heart jumping from one excessive emotion to another like that. It wasn't pleasant and she wouldn't ever become accustomed to it. If she ever felt like Harriet, that she was so miserable she would *die,* there would be no quick recovery for her.

The carriages arrived at their destination and as Julia's mother straightened her bonnet, she said, "We drove all this way for this?" But despite her mother's comment to no one in particular, their group quickly set off with energy and made their way up a gentle hill.

Their group spread out, some hurrying to the top to see the view and others stopping frequently to look back at the changing perspective. Julia couldn't feel enthusiasm for the view. To her it was just various shades of green, with houses and farms that looked small in the distance.

Julia found herself walking by Martha. She'd had very few opportunities to monopolize her cousin's attention since her mother and sister had arrived in Barrington. Their return trip to London was only days away now and Julia decided this might be the best opportunity she had to ask Martha about staying.

Before she could begin, however, Martha said, "You know, Julia, I've been thinking about something we talked about when you first arrived. You mentioned your poor luck with keeping a suitor through the last three seasons and I distinctly remember you mentioned that it was some flaw of yours that drove the men away."

"Yes," Julia answered a little hesitantly. "I remember when we talked about it. You were certain I was mistaken and said there must be some other explanation."

"That's right, that is what I said, but now I think you may have been right after all."

Julia felt her heart drop. Martha had discovered what was wrong with her? Maybe it was a small thing that could be corrected. Maybe she would let her stay despite it. What was the horrible thing she did that drove suitors away? Actually, maybe it wasn't just suitors. Maybe Martha was annoyed with one of Julia's bad habits and would be happy to see her return to London. Julia braced herself for the worst. "What is it?"

"I have noticed that since your mother arrived, your manners have been different, more . . . contrived. When you are in company with your mother, it's like you are pretending to be someone you are not. But when you are not yourself, there is no sincerity. Perhaps this flaw you are so concerned about is only present in the person you pretend to be for others."

Julia tried to think through Martha's insight to see if it felt true. *She* knew she kept her true self hidden, but had all those suitors realized that? "Do you really think that's it?"

"Not to offend you dear, but when I have watched you in company since your mother arrived, you seem to always say just the right thing, but you are so detached. You are conscientious in what you do and say, but it's become obvious—at least to me—that your emotions aren't involved."

Well, of course her emotions weren't involved; she had been careful to make sure of that. Her emotions had certainly never been involved with Mr. Bedford or any of her suitors in London that her mother insisted she try for. There had never been any sincere attachment. In her very first season, after the first suitor had left her behind, she had realized that her detachment was a good strategy. If she didn't care, then it didn't hurt anything other than her pride when they left.

Julia thought about her annoyance with Harriet, not just now with Mr. Corey, but always. The ups and downs of her emotions seemed an exhausting exercise to Julia. Harriet invested herself fully into everything she did. But Julia didn't want to put her heart into something that she thought might fail. What was the point? She had approached her London seasons with the same attitude. She had tried to do just what her mother said to catch a husband, but she had never included her feelings in her efforts.

"You are right. I do that." Julia felt like the obvious answer had been in front of her all along. "I've been thinking there must be some outward flaw of mine that men just couldn't stand, but each suitor must have come to realize that I didn't care for them. Not a bit."

But with Henry—against her better judgment and Martha's warning—she had cared. She had cared too much and was having an extremely difficult time convincing herself not to care anymore. It had been easy with other suitors, but with Henry, she just couldn't do it.

With Henry she had never been anything but herself. Their very first meeting had caught her off guard and it had never changed. She had caught a fly, fallen off a horse, and beaten him at cards, and after all that he had kissed her. For once, a suitor really knew her, but he had ended their courtship of one day just the same.

They had almost reached the top of the hill when Martha interrupted her thoughts, saying, "Men's egos are fragile things, I believe. I'm no expert, but I think most would not like the idea of a wife who just pretended regard for them."

Julia's first thought wasn't for those suitors in London who had discarded her, but for Henry. She hadn't pretended to care for him; it had all been real. But she had assumed that *he* was the one who was insincere. She thought of all Henry had said to her at the Trevons' when they had not danced together. Her feelings had still been too hurt to trust him, but Julia suddenly wondered if his words had been sincere. Julia's heart dropped and she stopped walking when she realized Henry might have truly cared for her. She had rejected him, more than once. And the last time, his anger had been obvious and final. He would probably never even speak to her again.

"Julia, what's the matter dear?"

Julia looked up to see Martha watching her with a concerned expression. "Nothing. It's nothing; I just remembered something." Shaking off the horrible idea, she brought her thoughts back to their conversation. "You are right, I'm sure of it. I'm not certain knowing this flaw of mine will do me any good now, but at least I don't have to wonder anymore."

Julia continued walking next to Martha, who pointed out sights that she was familiar with, but which couldn't interest Julia. Eventually, blankets were spread and hampers of food were opened. Julia went through the motions, but couldn't focus on anything but this new idea in her mind of her insincerity. She remembered every detail she could think of from courting through three London seasons. Except when she had honestly asked Mr. Bedford why he had ended their courtship, she couldn't think of any time when she *had* been sincere.

After their picnic, most of the group reluctantly prepared to leave, but Julia had been longing for privacy for some time. She felt that she had come to know herself better during these short hours wandering over these hills. But mostly she was wondering if understanding her past mistakes sooner would have made any difference with Henry.

As they packed up the remains of the picnic, there was some confusion as they prepared to depart. Several of the younger members of their party wanted to explore one more path that could possibly afford a better view of the little village to the south, that they had merely had a glimpse of. There was debate whether to wait around and let them or just insist that it was time to go. Harriet, who seemed to be the one most wanting to stay longer, suggested instead that the carriages be rearranged for the return trip and offered to leave later. Her mother made certain her desire to leave immediately was known and Julia quickly offered to depart with her, securing her place in the first carriage to leave. After that, she didn't pay any attention to the other arrangements.

Julia felt that the walk back down was longer than the walk up had been; her mother leaned on her arm a good part of the way. As they climbed into Lady Chamberlain's carriage, her mother said to her in a whisper, "Just one more week and we can finally return to London, permanently." It wasn't until that moment that Julia remembered she hadn't asked Martha if she could stay. Well, there was still one more week for her to find an opportunity so she could stay in Barrington, permanently.

The carriage ride was long, and made longer by the fact that they returned Lady Chamberlain to Barrington Court before returning to Martha's house. When they passed through the gates of Barrington Court, Julia looked toward the Dower house. Pressed against the window as she was, there wasn't much choice. How had Henry spent his day, and what must he think of her now? She didn't catch a glimpse of him and felt it was just as well. His angry glare would only make her feel worse.

Chapter 21

On the morning of the picnic to Blackdown Hills, Henry waited until he saw the carriage leave before he went for a ride. There was no way he would join the group. It had been two days since he had asked Jonathan to leave, and although he still felt guilty over it, he was mostly annoyed that Jonathan was still here. He couldn't stand the thought of Jonathan flirting with Julia on the outing that he had planned. So he stayed behind, realizing that Julia's rejection had shaken his confidence more than he had first thought. Just like when he lost Miss Corey, all his plans had been frustrated. This time though, he felt anger along with the grief.

Miss Abbot had stopped by to see him just yesterday to finalize their plans for the picnic, but he had told her he wouldn't go after all.

"What's wrong, Henry?" she had asked. "You wanted a chance to talk to Julia. Have you changed your mind?"

"I don't change my mind as easily as some people imply," he had snapped at her. He reproached himself immediately before she could, saying, "I'm sorry, Miss Abbot. I'm just frustrated, but not with you. I had an opportunity to speak with Julia at the Trevons' the other night and she was unwilling to give me another chance."

Her reaction showed surprised disappointment. "That is not what I expected. Did you bungle the whole thing and offend her?"

"I don't know. Perhaps. She just seemed so sure that if I courted her, it wouldn't last and I would change my mind again."

Miss Abbot's expression had become knowing and she had said, "Oh, I think I understand. She probably wouldn't want you to know this Henry, but Julia hasn't had much luck with suitors. They seem to tire of her after a few weeks or so. Just shows what idiots there are in London if you ask me."

"She admitted as much to me, although reluctantly. How am I supposed to convince her that I won't be like them when I already have proven that I am?" he had asked without hope of a solution.

"Would you like me to talk to her for you?" Miss Abbot had asked him. "Perhaps I could convince her where you could not."

"No!" he had exclaimed, and then more politely added, "I'd rather you didn't. I think I know her character enough to rightly assume that she would think me a coward and be more annoyed with me than ever if I sent someone else to plead my case." Miss Abbot had nodded her agreement, looking rueful. "Besides, she was completely resolved when we spoke. If I'd thought I had a chance of convincing her, I would go with you tomorrow on the picnic and try again."

"So what are you going to do?" Miss Abbot had asked.

Henry honestly didn't know. He couldn't bring himself to say he was giving up, but he didn't think Julia would change her mind. "Perhaps give her a little more time and then speak to her again?"

Miss Abbot had shrugged her shoulders, clearly realizing the futility of the situation.

Henry was brought out of his thoughts and back to the present as he heard his stomach growl. A quick check of his pocket watch told him this was a much longer ride than usual. He turned Felix back for home after realizing he was several hours late for lunch, and he was starving.

Henry didn't keep a cook for just himself at the Dower house, but always had his afternoon and evening meals at Barrington Court. He wasn't sure how long the outing at Blackdown Hills would take, but he hoped his mother and Jonathan wouldn't arrive back too soon. He wanted to eat quickly and be gone before they arrived back. He still wasn't in the mood for conversation with anyone.

It was after three when he returned to the stable and he noticed that both of Jonathan's horses were gone. Jonathan hadn't used his carriage once since he arrived. Henry was sure the horses had been there when he left on his ride several hours ago. That was strange. Had Jonathan not ridden with his mother? Had he taken his own carriage to Blackdown Hills? Or had he actually left Barrington?

When he arrived at the main house, he went to find Martin first thing to get his questions answered. "Martin," he began when he found him in the hall, "has Jonathan Corey left?"

"Yes, sir. He left this morning." Martin reached into his coat pocket as he spoke. "And when Ellen was making up his rooms after he left, she came across this letter addressed to you, sir."

Henry reached to take the envelope from Martin and as he pulled the note from the envelope he asked, "Did he leave Barrington completely then, or just leave for the picnic with my mother and the others?"

"He didn't say he was leaving permanently, but Ellen said all his things are gone and it appears that he has. Perhaps his letter will tell you more than I can."

"Thank you, Martin," Henry said to the butler's retreating back. He shook his head slightly as he unfolded the note, realizing Martin had dismissed him rather than the other way around.

Henry quickly scanned the page written in Jonathan's hand. Hardly believing what he had read, he went over it once more, not the first paragraph with its boring gratitude for hospitality, but the last few lines. Certain phrases stood out because of the alarm Henry felt as he read them. *Sorry to have kept a secret from such gracious hosts . . .* and *My bride and I will return for a visit . . .* and *Please put in a good word for me with Mrs. North . . .* and *Assurance that I will take good care of her daughter . . .*

No. No, it couldn't be. Henry didn't know how long he stood there staring at the paper in front of him, trying not to feel devastated. He thought he had lost hope to gain Julia's affection, but never until this moment had hope truly been gone. He had lost her completely.

Henry moved into his father's library without much thought and sat down hard in a chair just inside the door. He dropped Jonathan's letter and ran his hands through his hair. It took some effort, but he tried to reason with himself. At least this wasn't the worst thing that could happen. Julia would never be his, but she wasn't dead. He could be grateful for that, but it did nothing to improve his frame of mind and several more long minutes passed as he tried to become accustomed to despair.

He wished he had thought to elope. They could have easily left for Scotland some night and no one would have been the wiser until they were too far away to stop. Julia hadn't trusted him to court her again because she thought he would change his mind. An elopement would have proven that he had no intention of ever changing his mind again. But would even that have worked? When he had told her his intentions had changed after Jonathan arrived, it was the last time she had even really listened to him. It seemed that Julia North only ever gave one opportunity to have her good opinion. If he had known he would never get a second chance to prove himself with Julia, perhaps he wouldn't have messed up so badly in the first place.

Gradually Henry became aware of the sound of an approaching carriage. For Henry, the sound of the carriage wheels seemed to wake up his mind to a new idea. Perhaps they could chase down Jonathan and Julia and prevent the marriage. If there was any chance of stopping the pair, he would have to hurry.

Henry ran to the front window and saw his mother about to ascend the steps to the house and the carriage driving away. Without waiting to greet his mother, he turned and ran to the back of the house and out the door by the kitchen to reach the stables as quickly as possible. It was a few minutes later that he had Felix saddled and was riding toward Miss Abbot's home. Perhaps Julia had left a note giving her family a clue as to where they were headed. Tracking her down and stopping her before a wedding could take place was his only goal now. The thought of failure was truly painful for him.

How would he cope now, knowing he had lost her for good? Henry could hardly determine how he'd get through the next ten minutes. How would he survive for years? He tried to contemplate three or four years from now. Would his heart recover without him realizing like it had with Miss Corey? No, it would not. He would never move on knowing Julia was alive and well but out of his reach.

He could see their party exiting the carriage as he arrived at Miss Abbot's home. While he quickly tied

Felix to the gate, Mrs. North nodded her head in his direction as a brief greeting and continued into the house. Miss Abbot emerged next and he hurried over to her and asked, "When did they leave, do you know? Did Julia leave you a letter?"

Suddenly, before he received an answer, Julia herself was standing beside Miss Abbot. "What letter? What are you talking about?" Julia asked.

He was so surprised to see her, that for a moment he just took her in. Her hair had loose strands around her face the way it often was after their riding lessons. Her dress was pale green and her brown eyes looked light in the sunshine. She looked beautiful in an effortless way, just like always. Not at all like someone who was planning a devious elopement. He was not sure his senses were serving him well, and he grabbed both her arms and exclaimed, "Julia, you're here?"

Julia's eyes widened and her expression became one of alarm. Seeing her reaction, he recalled himself and quickly stepped back, releasing her arms. There were other matters to attend to.

"Where's that miscreant? Where's Jonathan?" Henry demanded. He stepped around Julia to look in the carriage. It was empty, though. He turned back to Julia and demanded, "Where is he? Are you meeting him somewhere?" He wanted nothing more than to find the man just so he could run him out of town.

"Mr. Corey? No. Isn't he at Barrington Court?" Julia didn't look as though her plot to elope had just been discovered. In fact, she just looked confused as she added, "He didn't come on our excursion today."

Miss Abbot drew his attention again, saying, "Henry, you seem upset. What's happened?"

Henry shook his head, now feeling quite confused himself. "I'm not sure exactly. I received a note . . ." He patted at his pockets and then remembered he had dropped it in the library. "I don't have it with me, but Jonathan left a note saying he had eloped. I assumed it was with Julia. In fact, I think he mentioned her in his letter." Henry shook his head in confusion still, wondering what piece of the puzzle he was missing. "And he is certainly gone. He left this morning." Henry turned to stare again at Julia, so relieved that it wasn't true. At the same time he noticed that she looked upset and maybe even a little guilty. Still not understanding, he said with a question in his voice, "But you are here."

Miss Abbot, looking as though she had been betrayed, turned to Julia and asked, "Were you going to elope with Mr. Corey? Without even telling me?"

Julia shook her head no. Looking worriedly at Martha, she said, "It's Harriet." Henry watched her eyes leave Miss Abbot's to briefly glance at him, but his expression must have looked just as confused as Miss Abbot's because she finally clarified, "Mr. Corey is in love with Harriet, not me." Henry's lungs drew in a deep breath. In the last half hour he had felt as though he could hardly breathe, but finding out that Julia was in no danger of running off with his friend left him finally able to draw a real breath again.

"But Harriet was with us at Blackdown Hills and Mr. Corey was not. Surely they could not have eloped," said Miss Abbot.

"But she didn't return home with you?" Henry asked, beginning to realize what the two had planned. It was quite clever, really; by the time anyone noticed they were missing, they would already have a fifteen-mile head start. It was interesting to discover how logically he could think now that he was no longer devastated and panicked.

"No, she wanted to stay longer and asked to ride home in the Clifton's carriage," said Miss Abbot. "I heard her mother agree to it."

There were several seconds of silence as the three of them thought how the scheme had been done. Finally Henry turned to Julia and asked, "Should we try to track them down, do you think? Did your sister leave a note, perhaps with a clue as to where they were going?" He was so much less concerned now that he knew Julia was in no danger. But he felt a heavy responsibility for the behavior of his guest.

"I'll go check," Julia said quietly, the mood having changed from alarmed to somber.

Henry followed Miss Abbot into the house, but his thoughts followed Julia. She seemed to have known something about her sister and Jonathan. Which meant, when she had asked questions about Jonathan's character, she had been asking on her sister's behalf. The relief he felt was again almost overwhelming, as he cast aside the worry that had plagued him for days.

Henry sat down in the drawing room while Miss Abbot went to find Mrs. North to tell her what was happening. Henry watched her leave with a look of worry on her face and realized that despite his relief, there were still worrisome repercussions to consider. But the most important repercussion in Henry's mind was that Julia didn't love Jonathan and she never had.

But if Julia had never been interested in Jonathan, then why had she not given him another chance? Henry was beginning to think that everything he had assumed about Julia since the day he kissed her had been wrong. He had convinced himself that it was just a matter of time before he talked her into giving him another chance, but that wasn't the case at all. Even though she hadn't left with Jonathan, he still had no idea how to convince her to trust him again. Henry knew there was nothing he wanted more than Julia, but he had explained everything to her and she had still refused to give him another chance.

Henry pulled himself out of his musings at a slight noise, and saw Julia herself standing uncertainly in the doorway.

"Oh, um. Where are the others?" she asked uncertainly.

He had no idea how to make her his. He knew he had to do something different than what he had tried already, but he didn't know what. His uncertainty made his mind freeze and he felt almost afraid to say anything, lest it make his situation worse. But a reply was necessary.

"Coming, I think," he finally replied. "You found something?"

"Ah, yes. Not a note from Harriet, but a letter from Lord Blakely, which I think must have arrived yesterday."

Henry had heard Mrs. North mention Lord Blakely, but just to clarify he asked, "Your sister's fiancé in London?"

"Yes. You see, my sister had sent him a letter asking to end the engagement. His reply came yesterday and it isn't favorable," said Julia.

"Wait a moment. For how long have your sister and Jonathan been planning this?" Henry thought that Jonathan had met the Norths when they arrived here in Barrington. Even then, Jonathan's preference for Julia had been obvious. Had he already known Harriet?

"They met and quite liked each other the night her engagement was announced. He left London when she and my mother did. He basically followed Harriet here. I caught them together once out walking, but I had no idea they were contemplating an elopement." Julia actually looked worried about admitting as much, as though it were her fault.

"So that was Jonathan's real reason for coming to Barrington," Henry thought out loud. It had had nothing to do with him at all. "And Lord Blakely?" he asked, gesturing to the letter still in her hand. "He said 'no' then to ending the engagement?"

Lifting the paper she held in her hands, she searched it and said, "Well, more precisely he said he 'couldn't deal with the nuisance of a cancelled engagement' and then he said, 'Your affections, which have so easily turned to another, will surely change just as easily back to me when we next are together at our wedding.'"

"I'm less surprised your sister eloped."

Julia let out a startled chuckle, and then nodded in agreement.

Henry tried to think of something else he could say. Something that would end the silence, but he couldn't help but think of what he wanted to say to her, what he had already said to her, and the rejection that would come if he tried to say it again. He didn't know how to proceed with Julia anymore. Nothing like this had ever happened to him. She felt as unattainable as if she really were halfway to Scotland with another man.

The long silence ended when Miss Abbot and Miss North entered the drawing room mid-conversation. "I can't believe Harriet would do this to me. She's so headstrong, always acting without thinking first." Mrs. North gestured angrily with her hands as she spoke. Once in the room, Mrs. North looked directly at Henry and asked, "Is this true? Has Harriet eloped with Mr. Corey?"

"It appears to be quite true, ma'am," he replied.

"Well, she's made her choice; I suppose there is nothing we can do about it now," said Mrs. North.

Henry watched Julia give her mother a disbelieving look. "Don't you think we should have someone go after them?" she asked. "They can't have set off more than two or three hours ago; they could still be stopped."

"There would be no point in that, Julia. Harriet has made her choice, and while I think it's quite the stupidest choice she ever made, it's her problem now. Or rather, she is Mr. Corey's problem now."

Henry could sense that Julia was angry with the turn her mother's thoughts had taken, and he spoke up, saying, "I feel partly responsible, as Mr. Corey was my guest when this happened. Let me at least see if I can track them down."

"It's not necessary," retorted Mrs. North. "By the time you find a trace of them, it will be too late. Besides, Julia and I need to return to London right away."

Julia looked up at her mother with surprise. "But, Mother, I'm supposed to stay here with Martha until the twenty-fifth. It's what we agreed on."

"I think we agreed you would stay until Harriet's wedding. Since your sister has gone off to be married, it's time for us to return to London."

Julia had that look of her mind racing to think of a strategy. Despite the new panic he was feeling that she might be leaving so soon, Henry was proud of her. After only a few seconds' pause, she said, "I agree with Mr. Chamberlain that we should try to find them. Let's be as certain as we can that they are *actually* to be married."

Henry heard the emphasis in Julia's voice and turned to Mrs. North to see if the strategy worked. For the first time Mrs. North looked worried. "Didn't the letter say they were to be married? Let me see it."

"I'm sorry," said Henry. "But in the confusion and hurry, I left the note from Jonathan behind. He implied they were to be married. But . . ." Henry trailed off and shrugged his shoulders.

Mrs. North looked frustrated. "Well, yes then. I suppose you'd better track them down. Be sure they are at least en route to Scotland. I suppose it's too late for us to leave for London today anyway."

Henry had already thought about the best possibility of tracking them down and said, "Their most likely path would be through Taunton. Would you agree, Miss Abbot?"

"Whether they go by boat or carriage, they would almost certainly pass through Taunton," she replied. "Why don't you take Julia and her maid with you in the carriage to search for them."

Mrs. North objected, saying, "Julia and her maid need to stay here to pack their things for our journey back to London."

Miss Abbot quickly replied, "If they find the pair in Taunton it won't take long. Besides, Julia and Harriet look alike, so someone might remember seeing Harriet if Julia goes along too. You wouldn't want to return to London without knowing that Harriet at least intends to marry Mr. Corey, would you?"

Mrs. North looked like she wanted to do just that, but with a long-suffering sigh, she turned to her daughter and said, "Julia, you go with Mr. Chamberlain and make sure you find evidence that they are heading to Scotland and then we'll know Harriet means to marry Mr. Corey. We'll leave for London first thing in the morning."

Miss Abbot spoke up then, "If you really are leaving in the morning, perhaps you could squeeze in a farewell visit to Lady Chamberlain before you go. I'm sure she would be so sad to have you leave the neighborhood without a word of goodbye." Henry appreciated the thoughtful gesture even amidst the returning feeling of panic he was feeling that Julia was leaving tomorrow.

Mrs. North just gave a frustrated grunt and left the room. Hopefully that was her agreement.

Chapter 22

$\mathcal{A}$fter Henry held her hand to help her into the carriage, Julia gazed out the window in an effort not to make eye contact with him as he climbed in after her. The touch through both their gloved hands affected her while she wished it had not. She should be getting stronger at resisting the pull of attraction she felt by now, but a little touch seemed to weaken her instead.

They made their way toward Taunton, as they would begin their search there and see if anyone locally had noticed Mr. Corey's carriage pass by. Julia should have realized what Harriet's plans were. If she hadn't been so wrapped up in her own thoughts, she would have asked Harriet about her strange behavior today.

Just before she had climbed back in the carriage, her mother had pulled her aside and said, "Make certain Harriet is married or on her way to Scotland and then come straight back. We need to get back to London before word of this does."

"What? Why should that even matter?" Julia had asked.

"Mr. Jenks wants to marry you because he wants his name associated with ours. If word of this scandal reaches him before he has committed himself, he'll back out," her mother explained.

"Mother, I agreed to stay here with Martha until the end of June. Surely you won't have me go back on my word? I must stay until her new companion arrives." She had used the same persuasive tone with her mother many times and Julia dreamt of the time when she wouldn't need her mother's permission for every decision she made.

Her mother said, "When Lord Blakely hears about the elopement, he certainly won't take the blame. The disgrace from this will be insurmountable. We are returning to London in the morning, and I'll expect you to agree to everything I arrange, just like you promised."

With these thoughts heavy on her mind, Julia knew she would have to ask Martha tonight if she could stay in Barrington with her forever. But all those thoughts couldn't quite distract her from sitting across the carriage from Henry. Her maid, who had had much more to do since her mother had arrived in Barrington, had scooted across the carriage and rested her head against the soft, satin wall. Her eyes closed with a contented look on her face at the unexpected opportunity of an afternoon nap in the Chamberlains' luxurious carriage.

Julia had thought that her last private conversation with Henry at the Trevons' would have been their last one ever, but now she found herself enclosed in a carriage with him for the next three hours at least.

"Are you comfortable, Miss North?" Henry asked.

Julia looked at him then, only to find that his gaze was as studiously focused at the passing scenery as hers had been. "Yes, thank you," she replied.

Still looking out the carriage window, he said, "You must be tired of being in a carriage all day."

Without thinking about whether or not she was, she politely answered, "No, I'm fine. Thank you."

Their conversation continued in short, hesitant bursts with long, silent stretches interspersed. Julia wished that Henry would put them back on even footing, but he still seemed angry with her. For a few moments when she had first seen him this afternoon, he had looked like he was concerned for her and even relieved to see her, but it hadn't lasted. He had quickly become silent and sullen. She felt incapable of removing the tension between them. Even if he had completely given up on her because of her stubborn lack of trust, at least he could use his practiced charm to put her at ease. She'd gladly take his careful allotment of attention over this grudging conversation.

When they arrived in Taunton, Henry directed the driver toward an inn and they were soon exiting the carriage and making their way inside. Henry asked the first person he saw for the proprietor and they sat at a table while they waited for him.

Again an uncomfortable silence settled between them and Julia wished she had not joined him on this errand. Especially as she looked around and noticed that the other patrons of the place were eyeing her and Henry speculatively. "Well," she observed quietly to Henry. "If Mr. Corey and Harriet came here, I'm sure they would have been noticed as everyone seems to be noticing us right now."

Henry glanced around and nodded his head in agreement. He looked like he was about to comment, but the door to the back room opened and a man dressed a little finer than most of his clientele emerged. He strode over to their table and at Henry's invitation joined them.

Julia had already decided not to leave all the difficult questioning to Henry and was about to ask Mr. Cummings—as he had introduced himself—if he had seen her sister, when he asked, "Are you come to get married today too? If you can believe it, you'd be the second couple to ask for directions to the parsonage today."

Henry looked at Julia with an expression of startled surprise. Neither of them responded for a few moments as they took in Mr. Cummings's meaning. "No, *we* don't want to be married," Henry asserted. "But we are looking for our friends who might be the couple you mentioned." Julia let herself lose track of the conversation for a few moments as Henry's words settled distastefully. *'We don't want to be married.'* It confirmed what she had suspected; he would not ask to court her again. Well, what did she expect? She had already told him no three times. And besides, she didn't even want him to ask her again. Despite what she'd learned about herself, Henry was still the same. He would never recover from his broken heart. He just wanted attention because he was so used to it and thought that it belonged to him. Somehow that same excuse she had clung to through the weeks since he had ended their brief courtship fell flat.

Julia gave her own attention back to the conversation as Mr. Cummings finished describing a couple that was almost certainly her sister and Mr. Corey. "Could you tell us where the parsonage is?" Henry asked. "We would like to know for sure whether our friends were married today." Mr. Cummings gave the easy directions and they stood to go. Henry handed the man some money with a word of thanks and they departed.

As they climbed in the carriage for the short drive, Henry remarked, "The couple he described can only be Jonathan and your sister. I can't believe they got married."

Julia was less certain and asked, "How would that even be possible? The banns have to be read for three weeks before the ceremony."

"Not if Jonathan had a special license."

Julia suddenly realized that perhaps this whole elopement had been far better planned than she had ever given Mr. Corey credit for. "If he did have a special license, they could have been already married before we even realized they were missing."

Henry had the driver take them to the parsonage. In a short conversation with the vicar, he was able to verify that the man had married Jonathan Corey and Harriet North earlier that day by special license.

Instead of a long search for evidence of a journey to Scotland, in no time at all they were back in the carriage and were making their way back to Barrington at a good pace. Julia's head was spinning. She had known only a tiny portion of what her sister had been up to, but if Julia had at least told someone what she did know, all this could have been prevented. Her sister was very likely better off with Mr. Corey than she would have been with Lord Blakely, but there would still be the scandal to weather. And through it all, Julia would feel guilt for her role.

Henry interrupted her thoughts by saying, "I fear I am to blame for this fiasco."

"How so?" It was strange that he would think that when it was really her fault.

"I asked Jonathan to leave," he admitted guiltily.

Henry looked like he was about to say more, but Julia couldn't let him feel responsible. "I'm afraid most of the blame lies with me," Julia quickly said, "as I knew that Harriet had been meeting up with Mr. Corey in private every chance she got."

"But I hurried them along. Jonathan had to leave because I asked him to go. I just never thought he'd take your sister with him."

Hearing Henry trying to take accountability for his friend's actions made her frustrated with both Mr. Corey and Harriet. The fault was theirs. Pushing aside her own guilt, she said, "The special license indicates that this was planned before either of us got involved. Let's try not to assign blame to ourselves. Perhaps another subject altogether."

But her suggestion was met with silence. She couldn't think of anything to say and quiet reigned once more as there weren't any subjects that felt safe to talk about, and Henry once again turned and looked out the window.

Julia didn't like being ignored, but the stilted conversation hadn't been pleasant either. Finally, Henry turned to her and said as he pointed out the window, "Do you see that windmill? That is near the corner of the property I'll soon be acquiring."

Julia leaned forward and looked where Henry indicated. Not sure what response to give, she nodded and acknowledged, "You must be pleased." He turned and looked out the window again. But as she thought about it, she remembered something, and asked, "Is this the business you've been arranging with Mr. Dunn? I think I've heard you speak of it before."

"Yes that's right," he said turning back to her and looking for the first time today like he actually wanted to speak to her. "It's been the most complicated business arrangement imaginable. Now that the deal is completed, I'm excessively proud of it."

Julia felt a small hint of a smile on her face to see his countenance change as he talked about it. In order to get him to speak more she asked, "What was so difficult about it that makes you feel that way?"

"Unfortunately, for some time, I've been a bit useless to my family. My father—at my mother's insistence, I'm sure—has required nothing of me for the last three and a half years. I've had a few token responsibilities given to me around the estate, but nobody has pushed me to do anything."

Julia wondered about Lord Chamberlain. What was Henry's father like? She would probably never meet him, but she wondered if Henry resembled him. She didn't expect such a trivial thing to make her feel sad. Henry had mentioned his younger brother a few times too, on a tour of the continent if she remembered correctly. She would probably never meet him either. Henry kept speaking as these musings went through her mind.

"Mr. Dunn has the land bordering ours to the west and Father has always wanted to expand that direction, but no negotiation could bring Mr. Dunn to an agreement. I've been working for months on a plan that is full of layers that will finally see the expansion to the west. The tenants we already have and the new ones that will come will greatly benefit from the deal. The key was to focus less on money and more on what could be done for the people. There are stipulations in the contract that include long-term positions and each one was painfully negotiated. It's like a carefully constructed tower and I've been a bit nervous that one wrong move would bring the whole thing tumbling down."

"It sounds complicated," Julia responded. She hadn't given much thought to what Henry's responsibilities were before now, but of course she knew he had met with Mr. Dunn several times over the course of her stay in Barrington.

"It is. I'm quite looking forward to my father's return so I can show him what I've done. If it had been another easy chore, it wouldn't have been worth mentioning."

Julia could see the satisfaction on his face. Then suddenly, she saw his gaze turn speculative. Julia didn't know for sure, but he looked as though he was thinking up a difficult strategy. He probably didn't even realize he was looking at her as he thought out plans for his next difficult negotiation.

Their conversation fell silent and the noise of the horses and the wheels of the carriage sounded louder without their voices. Suddenly a fly flew in the window of the carriage. It buzzed around for a few moments before landing on the back of the seat between Julia and her maid. She stared at it in surprise, although having a fly join you on a carriage ride was almost as common as the carriage ride itself. This fly was smaller than the one she had caught two months before. And it was just an ordinary black fly, no jeweled colors on it that she could see. She looked up to see Henry's green eyes watching her closely, rather than staring out the window. Julia watched his gaze move pointedly to the fly then back to her, eyebrows raised in expectation. Did he really think she would try to catch a fly again?

Her maid, not noticing any underlying tension with the arrival of the fly, reached a hand over and shooed the thing away, and it quickly found its way out the window once more. Julia turned back to Henry, trying to ready her wits, knowing he would tease her about catching flies, but he just gave her a perfunctory smile and turned his gaze away once more.

When they arrived back at Martha's, Henry very quickly hopped down from the carriage, helped Julia and her maid down, then climbed back in again and bid her farewell as he tapped for the driver to depart.

Julia was left once again with her head spinning. For a few moments there, when he had told her about his land purchase, she had felt that Henry didn't hate her. He had shown a side of himself that she had never seen before: a hardworking, persistent side that earned her admiration. But he had only started that conversation to ease the awkward carriage ride. His discomfort in her presence had proven that. From the first moment she had met him it had never been that way. Their conversations had been dynamic. Why had she not seen that he was merely polite to other girls? She hadn't seen it until now, when he was treating her just the same, with a cold politeness that showed how clearly he was merely tolerating her company. He had deposited her on the doorstep and driven off as quickly as he could. Why did her own feelings have to be so contrary? Now she wanted him to ask for another chance? Now she wanted him, when he couldn't wait to get away from her?

Julia felt her eyes well with tears as she thought about what she had lost. She had won Henry's affection, but hadn't reached out to claim her prize. She had shooed him away just as her maid had shooed away that fly in the carriage and he would never let her get close enough to have another chance.

Suddenly Julia was completely annoyed with herself. She stomped her foot and said out loud, "Comparing men to flies is ridiculous!" She quickly wiped any moisture out of her eyes and went into the house to tell her mother and Martha what they had found out about the missing couple.

Chapter 23

 *J*ulia approached Barrington Court for what she was sure would be the last time ever.

Last night, she had finally spoken to Martha privately. They had discussed the elopement first and Martha had assured Julia that Harriet's elopement with Mr. Corey would soon be forgotten. It would cause only a small amount of interest in Barrington, which was reasonable considering Harriet and Mr. Corey had both just been visiting a few short weeks when they eloped. Julia knew it would affect her much longer. Along with the guilt she felt for not sharing her knowledge of their courtship was the sadness that she and her sister hadn't been close enough to confide in one another. She truly was sorry not to be present at her sister's wedding and wish her happiness and joy with her new husband. It felt too late to try to make it right now, but she was determined to write to her sister and at least try.

Following that discussion, Julia had finally asked Martha if she could live with her permanently. It hadn't gone well.

"Martha," she had begun tentatively. "I've wanted to ask you for some time if you would allow me to stay here with you in Barrington to live with you permanently. I know you've already arranged for another young lady as a companion, but perhaps you could send her away and keep me instead." Martha had a rueful look on her face and Julia knew already that her answer would be no. Julia hurried to add, "I know my family arriving uninvited was quite inconvenient for you, but Harriet is married now and my mother won't travel so far from London again. Please, Cousin. I won't be any trouble."

"I would love to have you stay Julia, but I've arranged for Miss Dunn to live with me and her family very much needs the help, and I don't have the room or means to keep you both." Martha really did look regretful. Julia could tell she had already thought about having her stay, but had decided against it.

"Oh, I didn't think about Miss Dunn's situation." Julia said.

"I'm sorry I can't keep you instead of Miss Dunn; it's just that Henry helped me arrange this. It was one of the conditions Mr. Dunn insisted on in order for Henry to buy his land. Their family is really in a desperate way since Mrs. Dunn died and Mr. Dunn needs the money from the sale of the land and a place for his girl to go. Although he was insistent that she not come until the 25th when the contract will be final. I think it's been a difficult negotiation for Henry, and Miss Dunn coming to me has to happen for the contract to be fulfilled."

There was a huge temptation for Julia to adopt a persuasive tone and try to convince Martha, just as she always did with her mother. But Julia wouldn't do that. Henry's entire deal that he had worked so hard on would fall apart without the arrangement that Martha had with Miss Dunn. Julia thought about what Henry had said in the carriage earlier, and she knew she wouldn't ask again.

She had protected her heart by not letting Henry pull her along at his whim, but now here she was, feeling hurt again anyway. And it was Henry himself who was preventing her from staying in Barrington. It was unintentional of course, but if he ever found out he would congratulate himself on his ingenuity.

Realizing that Martha couldn't change the arrangements, she had said, "I understand. I just wish I had a way out of my mother's control. It's going to be worse without Harriet there."

"Perhaps you could stay another month, maybe even two. Would that help?"

Julia had shaken her head no. Nothing less than a permanent change would help. "Thank you anyway, Martha."

After that conversation, she had been surprised that she hadn't felt more disappointment. Staying in Barrington with Henry hating her just wasn't that appealing, although it still would have been preferable to returning to London with her mother.

Julia had never met Mr. Jenks, of course, but she had asked Harriet a few weeks ago about the man her mother wanted her to marry.

"He's not a catch, certainly," Harriet had said. "But he's so concerned about not making mistakes in society that he's mostly just quiet. If you go along with Mother's plan for you, he won't be the worst husband." Her argument was less than convincing.

"That doesn't really make me feel better," Julia had replied. "I want out of this scheme of Mother's more than anything."

Harriet hadn't known that Julia's plan was to stay in Barrington so she had thought of another strategy. "If you can find someone quickly she won't make you marry him." Harriet had looked at her almost triumphantly as she said, "I know! You can try for Mr. Bedford again. Lizzie Tomlinson threw him over when Lord Vaughn arrived in town."

Julia had hated the idea and responded, "Not likely, Harriet."

"Oh, you should just try," she had tried persuading. "A little groveling on your part just might do the trick."

Julia had cringed at the very idea and Harriet, noticing her expression, had said, "Well, I think you should try. Mr. Bedford is a far sight better than Mr. Jenks."

Now, as Julia thought back on the conversation, she knew she might have to swallow her pride and try. At the time she had been fairly certain that Martha would let her stay in Barrington. Without that option, Mr. Bedford probably was her best choice, or more accurately, her last resort.

Of course her mother couldn't be bothered to pay a farewell visit this morning. Instead she had slept late, leaving the task to Julia. More than anything she wished this last morning call to bid farewell to Lady Chamberlain was already behind her. But, perversely, there was a small part of her that wanted to savor every moment of her last time in Henry's home.

She still didn't know what to think about Henry. He obviously wanted nothing to do with her now, but she wondered about before. She was fairly certain that he hadn't really meant it when he told her that she was the one he wanted. But there was that small bit of uncertainty that was constantly nagging her. Perhaps it had been true. But when so many other young ladies thought the same thing, doubting him was inevitable. Her thoughts always came to the same final conclusion: it didn't matter either way. Even if he had cared for her, he didn't now.

Julia tried to shake off the depressing thoughts. There was a positive in all this: at least she had learned to stop doubting herself. It was just too bad her realization had come too late to do her any good. She had wasted three London seasons pretending to admire the men who courted her. She could have been herself and who knows how things would have gone for her instead? Now she would return to get a husband of her mother's choosing.

Hmm, Julia thought to herself, *shaking off depressing thoughts is proving difficult*. These were the same thoughts that had kept her awake late into the night. But Julia wasn't giving in to her mother's will quite yet. Besides trying to hunt down Mr. Bedford again, she had already come up with several desperate schemes to get out of marrying Mr. Jenks. She had invented several new flaws for herself that would be sure to scare the man away. But Julia couldn't think about that now; she knew she needed careful conversation skills with Lady Chamberlain, so she tried to focus her thoughts once more as she and Martha were let into the house. Even though she was the one bidding farewell, she hoped Martha would do most of the talking.

Lady Chamberlain was waiting for them in the hall when they entered and most surprisingly walked up to Julia with a grin on her face and embraced her. Julia's arms returned the gesture more out of surprise than anything. Truthfully, she hadn't expected so much affection from Lady Chamberlain. And shouldn't a farewell embrace come at the end of a visit? Lady Chamberlain pulled away and held Julia by the shoulders. She was smiling a wide smile and looked more genuinely happy than Julia had ever seen her as she said, "I'm so glad you've come this morning; I've been aching to see you." She wrapped an arm around Julia and turned and walked to the drawing room. "I wanted to rush over and see you last night, but it was so late that the entire household had already retired. And I knew you were coming this morning for a visit, but I assure you I could hardly sleep with anticipation."

Julia lifted a hand to brush away a curl that had fallen forward so she could see Lady Chamberlain's face. She stared at her curiously for a moment, but they were in the drawing room now and she turned away to find a seat.

Before she sat, however, she saw Henry standing there. Lady Chamberlain's strange behavior was temporarily forgotten as Julia tried to think how to react to his presence. He had been clearly frustrated and angry with her stubborn refusal at the Trevons' and had hardly spoken to her as they looked for Harriet and Jonathan yesterday. Julia had not thought he would be here at all this morning and she wondered what had induced him to be in her presence now. Was he still frustrated with her? Or was he perhaps just indifferent now? She'd probably never know; he surely wouldn't show any genuine emotion in front of his mother. Julia decided she would try her best to do the same.

Henry was still standing, and Julia finally realized he was waiting for her to sit so he could as well. Julia knew that her slow reaction to seeing him again must have looked strange to the others as she and Henry just stood a few feet apart, staring at one another while Martha and Lady Chamberlain sat and watched them. Julia quickly sat and wished for the ability to pretend with Henry. Why could she do it with every other man, but not with him?

Julia watched Henry take his seat across from her. His green eyes never left hers and his expression remained serious.

Julia was startled out of her observation of him when Lady Chamberlain said, "Miss North—actually, may I call you Julia?" Without waiting for an answer, Lady Chamberlain continued, "I'm curious what your plans are. Now that there has been this new, ah . . . development, are you still planning to return to London? Of course, we'll join you there if you choose to return with your mother, but I hope you'll be my guest here instead when Miss Dunn arrives to be Miss Abbot's companion."

It was such a curious statement that Julia couldn't make sense of it. The only new development she could think of was Harriet and Mr. Corey's wedding. Why would Lady Chamberlain think that Julia should be her guest? She stared at Lady Chamberlain for a few moments in expectation of her saying something that made sense. "What exactly are you speaking of?" Julia finally asked.

"Oh, I know better than to say. These things are always kept quiet until there is an official announcement. I won't say a word until you and Henry give me leave, but I can tell you, it won't be easy." Lady Chamberlain pulled out a handkerchief and dabbed at her eyes. "Forgive me for being emotional; I've just waited so long for this."

Julia was trying her best to figure out what Lady Chamberlain meant. Feeling bewildered, but trying to hide it, she glanced at Martha. She was smiling too, a smile of clear understanding. What had she missed? She turned her gaze to Henry and found his expression serious. No, not serious, it was intent. He was watching her closely, searching her gaze. Julia only felt confusion and was sure that must be written clearly across her face.

Julia knew that somehow the other three knew something she did not, and she couldn't pretend that she understood. Turning back to Lady Chamberlain, she asked, "I'm sorry, Lady Chamberlain, but I'm confused. You seem to be discussing some wonderful event that I haven't heard about yet. I'd love to congratulate you on your happy news, only I don't know what it is." She gave an apologetic smile for her ignorance.

Lady Chamberlain's face fell a little. "Oh, it's your news I'm so happy about, but perhaps—" she broke off and looked at Henry. "Have I said too much?"

Julia noticed that Henry hadn't spoken since she entered the room. Even now there was a long pause before he said, "No, Mother, you haven't said too much." He looked back at Julia and she felt her heart leap when his green eyes met hers. Was there a chance that her stubborn refusal to trust him hadn't completely driven him away?

Julia's thoughts were interrupted by Martha saying, "Lady Chamberlain, won't you show me your rose garden?"

"Yes!" she exclaimed, far too enthusiastically. "Let's go look at the roses." Then to Henry she said, "Will you keep Julia company while we are in the garden? We'll return shortly—" she began, but then correcting herself, said, "or rather, as long as it takes to see *all* the roses."

Before Lady Chamberlain left the room she turned back in the doorway and said, "Julia, I must say again how glad I am you've come. It was so generous of you to leave London and stay with your cousin during these months she needed you. Such a selfless, kind young woman was exactly what I had been hoping for. I couldn't be happier that you've noticed the same qualities in my Henry."

Julia couldn't possibly reply to that. She was suddenly overcome by embarrassment and couldn't look anywhere but at her feet. She had been trying so hard for the last two months to make sure that Martha and Lady Chamberlain didn't know how she felt about Henry. Their behavior this morning, especially Lady Chamberlain's, indicated that they already knew. Had her feelings for Henry been so obvious that Lady Chamberlain had jumped to a wrong conclusion? If that was the case, Henry would be more annoyed with her than ever. He had worn a serious expression on his face since she had entered the room. Julia looked up from the corner of her eye and glanced at Henry to try to gauge his mood. From their previous experience, she was sure that the reprimand for giving his mother the wrong impression would be kind and he would try to hide his annoyance. Henry stood and looked down at her. Julia was surprised to see that his expression wasn't annoyed at all; instead, he looked rather nervous.

But he couldn't be feeling that way any more than she was. The longer he waited to speak, the more certain she became that a reprimand for misleading his mother again was imminent. "I'm sorry," she said, jumping up. "I don't know why your mother thinks there is something between us. If I gave her that impression, it was a mistake. I . . . I didn't mean to. I'll explain when she comes back and . . . and hopefully she'll understand. I promise I didn't say anything."

Julia still stared at the carpet as she paced, embarrassed of her stammering. But at the sound of Henry's voice, she looked up. "I know you didn't say anything to my mother." He paused and Julia saw him nervously swallow. "I did."

Julia couldn't comprehend for a moment. It seemed the last thing Henry would ever do and she felt betrayed that he would have so little regard for her feelings. "Why would you do that? Why would you ever tell your mother that I have feelings for you?"

"I didn't. I told her *I* have feelings for *you*." He paused and Julia noticed again his nervousness as he rubbed his hand along his jaw, then once through his hair, and finally folded his arms as if to keep his hands still. "I'm afraid she just assumed that you would feel the same way.

She's my mother, after all, and she thinks everyone loves me as much as she does."

Julia just watched him warily for a few moments. His mother wasn't wrong. If Henry declared his feelings for any young lady, it was inevitable that she would be in love with him too. But did Henry truly feel that way toward her? Julia felt hope within her, which caused her stomach to drop and then swoop up into her chest so that she couldn't speak. Henry had told his mother! Did that mean what she thought it meant? She just wished she could open her mouth to ask him.

Henry was the one pacing now and Julia followed him with her eyes as he explained, "I wanted my mother to know. I want everyone to know. My mother said she would be discreet, but she'll announce it to everyone, of course. I would be surprised if the entire household hasn't already been told."

Julia was trying to swallow back the lump in her throat, worried that if Henry really had feelings for her, she wouldn't be able to hold back the tears of joy. She had to clear her throat twice before she could ask, "Why would you want everyone to know?"

Henry stopped pacing and met her gaze as he said, "Because I want you to finally believe me when I say I want to court you, and I will never change my mind. No more secrets." With his arms crossed in front of him, Henry looked at her and Julia almost thought his expression was fearful. When he spoke again, his words sounded less rehearsed. "Give me one more chance, Julia. I know I don't deserve it. I don't deserve you, but I want you to trust me. I've explained what happened to me when Jonathan arrived. I panicked and hurt you. But I swear it will never happen again. Please believe me."

And finally Julia did believe him. Completely, and with her whole heart, she believed that she could trust Henry. Julia again couldn't respond without crying. She sat down again and turned her face away from Henry. She just needed a moment to compose herself before she could answer just as eloquently, without her voice cracking.

Before she realized it, Henry was kneeling in front of her. Even though she was sitting and he on his knees, she still had to look up slightly to meet his gaze. He picked up her hand and implored, "You cannot doubt my true intentions now. You know my mother; she'll begin planning our wedding today," he warned her. He was looking at her like he expected her to refuse. He began speaking again, more quickly. "I want her to plan the wedding. In fact, I won't rest until you've agreed. I love you and I want to marry you. I'll follow you to London and court you there if I have to. You are my match in every way and I—"

Julia finally stopped him by putting her fingertips over his mouth. She cleared her throat to find her voice and said, "And you are mine." Her voice did crack, but only a little.

Henry gently took her hand away and held it in his own. She could see he was breathing faster and he lowered his head a little to look directly into her eyes, searching them. He looked so nervous and unsure of her answer, as if he was expecting her to say no. "Julia," he whispered her name. "Are you saying yes? We can be together?"

Julia nodded and although she had felt like tears of joy were imminent just moments before, when she finally gave up on holding her emotions back she found herself smiling broadly instead with all the relief she felt that Henry truly wanted her. She tentatively lifted her free hand to his chest and tried not to let herself be overwhelmed that his heart was hers. After a deep breath she was able to say, "I was so scared you hated me now."

"Hate you? Impossible," he declared.

"But you hardly spoke to me yesterday at all. Even when the fly flew in the carriage, you didn't even tease me!"

Henry smiled at her strange logic and said, "Yesterday I was too afraid that if I started talking, I would say too much and you would refuse me again. And as for the teasing . . . If I promise to tease you every day, will that convince you that I don't hate you?"

"There must be a better way than that to convince me," Julia challenged him.

Henry placed his hand over hers and leaned in even closer to her. Julia felt certain that he was going to kiss her, which indeed would help convince her. Just before Henry's lips touched hers he stopped and said, "I love you with my whole heart, Julia."

She had relived their only kiss so many times in her mind, but this was the feeling she could never recreate. The anticipation of his lips on hers had her heart racing and rational thought was no longer possible. Julia quickly licked her lips between shallow breaths and her eyes began to drift shut. And then he finally pressed his lips to hers, and if possible, it was better than the first kiss they had shared. His lips moved over hers with purpose and desire, but more with tenderness than anything else. At some point, Henry had joined her on the sofa and she found herself pushed against the corner. She didn't feel trapped in the least, but took the opportunity to push back, and as their kiss deepened, Julia realized she was quickly gaining a new skill.

It was several moments or minutes later that words were possible between them again. With hands clasped together Henry said, "I can't quite describe how devastated I would have been if you had turned me down again." But there was no nervousness in his words now, just relief.

Julia smiled, "Not as devastated as I would have been if you had never asked again." Her voice was a bit more serious as she admitted, "I didn't think you would. I thought I had lost my chance after I told you we couldn't court at the Trevons' dance."

His look was mockingly stern as he replied, "Good point. After what you've put me through, it's amazing I still want to marry you."

Julia just smiled and said, "I want to marry you too."

"Are you certain?" he asked. And Julia thought there was a slight hint of nervousness on his part once more. "Because I do have a whole plan in place to convince you if you're not."

"What plan?"

Henry tucked a stray hair back behind her ear in a gesture that would have felt too familiar just ten minutes ago, but was now effortlessly natural. "It came to me yesterday that I was never going to win you over without a brilliant strategy, so I came up with one." He raised a finger as he said, "Telling my mother was just the first part. Next, I was going to follow you to London and court you there, as my mother implied earlier. Then, I was going to ask you to ride through Hyde Park with me every day." Henry lifted her hand in his and brought his other hand up to hold hers between both of his. He gazed into her eyes and Julia felt entranced by him and loved the new feeling of not fighting it. "I was going to give you Pegasus—well, I still am. He's yours. And, of course, Pegasus is too lazy of a horse for London, so I would have tried to convince you to bring him back to Barrington. And as a very last resort, I was also going to ask your mother to pick me as your intended husband so you would be forced to marry me because of your promise to her. And finally, I would just hope that sometime in our years of marriage you would forgive me."

Julia laughed at that, fairly sure that most of his "plan" was not real, but certainly not the last part about her mother. Henry smiled with her but didn't laugh, and Julia looked at him in askance. "You wouldn't really have plotted with my mother, would you?"

Henry paused a moment, and before he could come up with an answer Lady Chamberlain and Martha came back into the room. Their close proximity on the sofa seemed to be all the confirmation Lady Chamberlain needed and she said, "The two of you have been so sly, I never suspected a thing. But that has always been Henry's way. When he told me last night what has been going on, right under my nose, I was so happy I didn't even mind being the last to know."

"You weren't quite the last to know . . . ," Julia said. Despite the fact that Henry had tried to tell her, she hadn't believed he really cared for her. Now she finally knew, and with the absence of doubt had come overwhelming happiness that was making her restless.

"Can I assume that you are going to be my guest for a few more days after all, Julia?" asked Martha.

Julia had pretty much forgotten that she was supposed to be departing for London soon. She nodded her head in response to her cousin, whose reassuring smile let her know that she wasn't upset about a match between her and Henry. "Yes, I'd like to stay if you don't mind."

"And then she can come stay here with me until the wedding," pronounced Lady Chamberlain. Then, turning to Martha, she said, "How soon do you think we can hold the wedding? Lord Chamberlain will be back in three weeks when Parliament ends. Do you think the wedding could be four weeks from now?"

Julia hoped it could, but didn't listen to Lady Chamberlain and Martha's plans; they continued talking while she turned her attention back to Henry. The reminder that she must go tell her mother had her saying in a quieter voice, "I don't want to hear what my mother has to say when she hears about this." Julia could predict that her mother would be happy to have Julia engaged, but mystified that Henry would want her. It wouldn't be flattering. "If she wasn't trying to take me back to London today to marry someone else, I'm not sure I'd bother telling her."

Henry lifted the back of his finger to gently caress her cheek as he said, "Not a chance. I've learned my lesson. Secret courtships cause all kinds of problems." Suddenly the stroke of his finger stopped and Julia realized the room had gone quiet. They both turned to see Lady Chamberlain smiling down at them in rapture, and Martha looking on with fondness. Henry dropped his hand away from her face, stood up, and pulled her up too as he said, "I'll come with you. Let's go tell your mother."

Before they could leave the room, Lady Chamberlain asked, "Do I have your leave then, to spread the news that you are to be married?"

Henry glanced down at Julia with a question in his eyes once more. She quickly nodded in the affirmative and Henry turned back to his mother and said, "You have our leave to announce it. In fact, tell anyone who will listen that Julia and I are getting married."

Epilogue

$\mathcal{T}$hree days before her wedding, Julia finally received the letter she had been anxiously waiting for. Logically, she knew that she was lucky to receive the letter so soon, but after not hearing any word from her sister for almost a month, it was a relief to finally hold Harriet's letter in her hands.

She had written to Harriet the day after agreeing to Henry's proposal, hoping that at least her sister would be happy for her. Her mother had been almost indifferent at the news of her engagement, saying, "Yes, I suppose it's good news that you're getting married, Julia, but I wish I would have known that you would finally be able to catch a husband on your own. I didn't exactly promise Mr. Jenks your hand in marriage, but nearly. I don't think you have considered my position at all. Now it will be extremely embarrassing for me to go back and tell him he can't marry you." Her mother had still left that same day for London, with no daughters holding her back any longer.

Julia had sent her letter to Harriet to an address Henry had given her in Shepton Mallet, where Jonathan's father, Mr. Corey, lived. They didn't know where the couple had gone after their wedding in Taunton. Of course they hadn't gone on to Scotland since they were already married, but Henry and Julia couldn't guess where they would have gone instead. In the end Julia had addressed her letter to Jonathan's father's home in Shepton Mallet and hoped it would find Harriet there.

Henry walked into the room as Julia finished the letter. Since she had come to stay at Barrington Court, she usually saw him at breakfast every morning. But now that his father, Lord Chamberlain, had come home, he was busy showing his father all he had accomplished in his absence. Julia had been intimidated at first, but was coming to quite like her future father-in-law, so she didn't mind too much that Henry was busier now. Today, he and his father had gone to visit some of his new tenants and it was the first time today she had seen Henry even though it was late afternoon. Julia left her letter on the sofa and hurried over to wrap her arms around him in greeting. She gave him a quick kiss, which was barely a connection of their lips, then tried to pull away. "I've received a letter from Harri—" but she was interrupted as Henry brought his mouth down on hers once more for a much longer and more thorough greeting. Julia tried for a second to pull away, then quickly changed her mind, embracing the pleasure of the kiss and leaning into him. When Henry finally pulled away, it was a few moments before her eyes fluttered open. She cleared her throat and stepped away from him, but grabbed his hand and laced their fingers together to pull him over to the sofa.

When they sat down, she showed him Harriet's letter. "As I was saying," she began, with decorum that she didn't quite feel, "I've received a letter from Harriet finally, and actually she shared some surprising news. The best part of it is that she and Jonathan are coming to our wedding. They'll arrive tomorrow or the day after," Julia announced happily, remembering why she had wanted to tell Henry her news right away.

"Oh . . . well, that's good," Henry replied.

Julia narrowed her eyes suspiciously at her fiancé and stated, "You don't sound all that happy about it."

"Er, no, I am happy your sister will be here. It's just that I owe Jonathan an apology that I'm not looking forward to giving. But best to get it over with." He sighed and finished by saying, "And then it will be wonderful to have them here."

"You mean apologize for asking him to leave?" Henry nodded and Julia said, "Actually, you might not have to worry about that. Harriet's prone to exaggeration, but she mentioned in her letter that Jonathan laughed endlessly when he found out we were engaged and that if he had known you were interested in me, he would never have flirted with me." Julia smiled at him with as innocent a look as she could and said, "Surely you know that never meant anything. You weren't ever really jealous, were you?"

With an incredulous look he replied, "How can you ask that? Of course I was jealous. I thought you preferred him to me and it made me miserable for weeks!"

Julia tried to hide it, but she was pleased that Henry had been jealous and when she next saw her new brother-in-law, she would owe him a thank you. Who knows if Henry would have realized his feelings in time otherwise?

"Sorry," she said meekly. Then casting aside the pretended meekness, she said, "There is one other thing that Harriet mentions that I'm concerned about. You remember how my mother wrote that Lord Montague wouldn't honor their agreement because of the scandal of Harriet's elopement?" Henry nodded. Julia had confided to Henry about Lord Montague and her mother's strange agreement. It seemed unfair that because their engagement had been secret, Lord Montague had been able to end it with no repercussions whatsoever. Julia continued,

"Well, apparently Mother wrote to Harriet to tell her that it was all her fault. Mother ranted about what a horrible daughter she is and how her stupid, selfish ways ruined my mother's life."

"Like I said before, I can't feel sorry for your mother," Henry replied. "When I think what she put you and your sister through, I'm amazed that you have any sympathy for her." Then, as if he was already beginning to forgive her, he added, "But I'm sure she hopes as I do that Lord Montague marries a widow who doesn't tell him she has a dozen unwed daughters until after the wedding."

Julia smiled a little at the sentiment. She had never cared for Lord Montague, but as for her mother, she was sorry for her, but mostly because she had pushed Harriet away. Julia, Harriet, and their mother had been a trio for so long, but Julia had always felt like the outsider. Their mother and Harriet had always been close. Julia's temperament was quieter than theirs. Her mother and sister had always been united in their enthusiasm and despair, but this time, her mother's despair was Harriet's fault and her harsh words estranged her from her favorite daughter. "It seems that Mother vowed in her letter to Harriet to never to speak to her again. But I hope she'll soften up over time. Harriet says she doesn't care, but I think she does."

"For Harriet's sake then, I hope she comes around."

"For the sake of our wedding, I hope she comes around sometime in the next three days. My mother will be here too and I don't want our wedding day to be stained with their hostility." Julia's mind suddenly took a turn and she looked up at Henry with a smile as she said, "Perhaps we can devise a plan to get them to reconcile."

Henry smiled with fondness and said, "I should've known you'd have a plan. As long as your strategy doesn't interrupt the ceremony, I don't mind."

Julia squeezed his hand. "I promise." Then a new thought came and with a small shake of her head she raised her eyebrows and gave him an ironic smile. "If anything interrupts our ceremony, it will be the sobbing young ladies of all the surrounding areas who come to the wedding, probably all wearing black as though they are in mourning." Julia snorted a little at her own joke, but wondered how close to the truth that really was.

Henry grinned down at her and said, "I've been meaning to thank you for saving me from them, by the way."

"You're welcome," she said sweetly. "However, I doubt they will thank me anytime soon. You should have seen Miss Clifton's face when your mother told her we were getting married." It had been difficult for Julia to tell if the girl had been more angry or sad. But Miss Clifton hadn't been the only one. "The others were just as bad. Miss Dripple's reaction, and Miss Trevon's, and—"

"Not to worry," Henry interrupted her. "Charles is returning from his tour of the continent in time for our wedding. He can comfort the lot of them."

Julia didn't know how effective Henry's brother would be, but she didn't need Henry's advice not to worry about it; despite their reactions, she didn't care a bit that she was taking Henry away from every other young lady. She gazed up at Henry with all the affection she felt for him and saw the same love reflected back at her. She was amazed that she had never had to pretend to be anything other than herself with Henry; she had never hidden her imperfections from him and he had fallen in love with her anyway. In fact, he vowed he had fallen in love with her because of them.

About the Author

*P*aula Kremser began writing while living in England, so choosing to write about the Regency era was no coincidence. She is an avid reader, but decided to write because sometimes stories just didn't go the way she wanted. She obviously has control issues; just ask her four kids. She hopes to someday win an award for writing, in the meantime, she brags about once winning a bubble gum blowing competition. She continually practices that skill (along with writing) in her new hometown of Sandy, Utah.

Scan to visit

www.paulakremser.com